Praise for
Vanishing and Other Stories

"The emotional range and depth of these stories, their clarity and deftness is astonishing."
—Alice Munro

"The fourteen arresting stories in [Willis'] debut collection are about to hurtle her into the literary spotlight. . . . She elicits immediate curiosity about her characters. Right away we want to know: Who are these people? What are their stories? Yet her methods remain mysterious. If possible, Willis's prose is even less showy than Munro's: It is not merely down to earth, but of the earth. Her words feel essential and elemental. She is one of those writers who make fiction feel less of a genre than a language unto itself. The superb title story smoothly folds together the collection's seminal ideas. . . . Charming, warm, and humane."
—*Montreal Gazette*

"Short-listed for a Governor General's Award, the stories in *Vanishing* show the magic of fiction at its best: fully realized worlds inseparable from the uncanny fact that they exist as mere words, magnificently strung together. Willis's creative sleight-of-hand illuminates human intricacies as if tapping directly into your own."
—*Globe and Mail*

D0211631

"Even-tempered, sober and intimate, Willis's debut collection has a gravity that suggests both the conventionality and maturity of an author well into her career. But if echoes of Mavis Gallant and Alice Munro (and, in the hard-luck stories, Raymond Carver) reveal her as an astute apprentice, Willis also illustrates her talent for crafting stories that confidently reflect her distinctive techniques and voice. . . . Flecked with welcome humor. . . . Equally salty-sweet. . . . Her attentiveness to detail and her succession of insights about the small moments people share and the consequences of individual choices keep us turning pages, enthralled."
—*Vancouver Sun*

"If I were a betting man (sadly, my wife tells me otherwise), I'd put a sack of cash on Deborah Willis becoming a nationally renowned writer. . . . A remarkably accomplished collection. . . . The stories aren't linked, but many examine the arbitrary, sometimes brutal way in which people enter and exit the lives of others. . . . This story, like most of Willis's, concludes in a curious, unpredictable way that suggests the untidiness of real life. . . . Economical, artful description. With her stories, Willis boldly inhabits the skin of all sorts, of all genders. . . . Her talent and skill are nothing short of formidable. . . . Accomplished, edgy, dark stories."
—*Times Colonist*

"Spare, haunting and insightful, these stories are wonderfully wrought snapshots about human frailty and loss that will stay with you long after you've finished reading."   —*Calgary Herald*

About the Author

Deborah Willis was born and raised in Calgary, Alberta. Her fiction has appeared in *Grain*, *Event*, and the UK's *Bridport Prize Anthology*, and she was the winner of the 2005 Prism International Fiction Prize. *Vanishing and Other Stories* is her first book, and has been named one of *Globe and Mail*'s Best Books of the Year and was nominated for a Governor General's Award. She has worked as a horseback riding instructor and a reporter, and currently works as a bookseller in Victoria, British Columbia.

vanishing

and other stories

DEBORAH WILLIS

HARPER ● PERENNIAL

NEW YORK ● LONDON ● TORONTO ● SYDNEY ● NEW DELHI ● AUCKLAND

HARPER PERENNIAL

HarperCollins books may be purchased for educational, business, or sales promotional use. For information, please write: Special Markets Department, HarperCollins Publishers, 10 East 53rd Street, New York, NY 10022.

A paperback edition of this book was published in Canada in 2009 by the Penguin Group.

FIRST HARPER PERENNIAL EDITION PUBLISHED 2010.

Publisher's note: This book is a work of fiction. Names, characters, places and incidents either are the product of the author's imagination or are used fictitiously, and any resemblance to actual persons living or dead, events, or locales is entirely coincidental.

Library of Congress Cataloging-in-Publication data is available upon request.

ISBN 978-0-06-200752-0

10 11 12 13 14 OV/RRD 10 9 8 7 6 5 4 3 2 1

for my parents

CONTENTS

v a n i s h i n g

WEEKS PASS and the police give up their investigations. The newspapermen who wrote "Local Writer Vanishes" find other stories. Months go by, then a year.

Marlene and Bea drink afternoon coffee and their conversation slips back to the everyday: the price of potatoes at Loblaws, who's a good doctor and who's not, what kind of pictures are showing these days. Marlene goes to *shul* more often, and stands for the Mourners' Kaddish.

But Tabitha imagines that her father stepped onto a bus, then onto a boat, and soon they'll receive a postcard from India. She imagines him showing up in five years, his hair greyed or gone, with stories of living in Oregon, or Alaska, or the Alps. She imagines he simply moved into an apartment downtown. Sometimes—and this really puts ants in her stomach—she imagines he is hiding somewhere in the house, behind the couch or in the closets. She checks under her bed every night before she goes to sleep.

THE DAY NATHAN DISAPPEARED began like any other Saturday. Marlene put a long coat over her housedress and dragged Tabitha to Honest Ed's. They bought a pie plate on sale, six pairs of nylons, some patterned dishcloths, and—after Tabitha pleaded—a life-sized ceramic bust of Elvis Presley. "Where will we put that thing, Tabby?" Marlene said as they stood in line at the till. "What will your father say?"

But Tabitha knew her mother loved the Elvis too—the realistic folds in his collar, the glassy brown eyes, that smile. During the streetcar ride home, he sat on Tabitha's lap and she wrapped her arms around his smooth, painted shoulders. He made it all worthwhile—Marlene's housedress, the streetcar windows that steamed up from people's breath, and even Honest Ed's itself. The crowded aisles, high ceilings, and the sign outside that announced *Honest Ed's: Only the Floors Are Crooked!*

When they arrived home, Tabitha went in ahead to find the perfect place for the Elvis, and that's when she saw the attic's open hatch. She stared at the ceiling's gape. Never in her ten years had she known her father to treat his office carelessly. She thought of calling to Marlene, but Tabitha knew how slowly her mother moved—how her hips cracked when she bent to unbuckle her shoes, and how she hung each coat on its proper hanger. And Tabitha didn't want to speak her worst fear aloud, wasn't even sure if a nightmare thought like this could be spoken.

"Dad?" she called up into the dark place where he did his writing. No answer, and before she could help it, she imagined her father hanging from the ceiling. She pictured it like the movies: his crumpled face and a sinister, creaking rope. She imagined that his swinging body looked long—not tall, long. She climbed the ladder, feeling sick and dizzy as she put her foot on the final step. Then, weak-kneed with relief—initial, foolish relief—she found the attic empty.

HE SEEMED TO HAVE LEFT IN A RUSH. They know he walked out the front door and locked it behind him, bringing only his thick wool coat, his scarf and hat, his umbrella. He left his typewriter, his books.

They might have assumed he'd gone to the office for a couple of hours, or out for a walk, if he hadn't taken the time to tidy the attic before he left. The scripts of his finished plays were held together with paper clips, last-minute changes indicated in pencil in the margins. The more recent works were stacked on the floor. Marlene put these in a box and tied it closed with string, because he'd left a note that read, *Unfinished.*

THREE YEARS LATER, the plays Nathan completed are produced in Toronto and Halifax. Marlene gets a job as a bookkeeper and discovers that she's good at it. At Tabitha's bat mitzvah, the rabbi says he's rarely seen such a dramatic reading of the *parshah.*

Life is as uplifting as a musical, except that sometimes Tabitha wakes at night to find Marlene humming Paul Anka songs into her ear. "You had a bad dream," says her mother, and she touches Tabitha's forehead. "What was it? A monster? That falling feeling?"

No matter how hard she tries, Tabitha can't remember. All that lingers is sweat on her pyjamas and a bad feeling in her throat.

WHEN TABITHA SHOWED HER MOTHER the open hatch, the empty attic, Marlene stared at the floor and furniture, her hands hanging at her sides. She bent to look at some of the papers, then went to the window by Nathan's desk. "He's gone," she said, more to herself than to Tabitha. Then she descended to the kitchen, where afternoon light still brightened the room. She picked up the phone and Tabitha knew it was to call her sister, to ask Bea to come over, right away, please. But Marlene just held the receiver in her hand as though it were heavy, as though she were too tired to dial.

Tabitha touched Marlene's hip, where the housedress pleated. "I'll do it," she said. "I'll call her."

Half an hour later, Bea brought *mandel* bread and said things like, "Maybe he was murdered. Or kidnapped."

Marlene shook her head. "Kidnapped people don't bring umbrellas with them. Besides, everybody liked him. He was a gentle man. And a good lawyer."

Marlene didn't mention Lev, but Tabitha imagined her father leaving the house to see him, putting on a suit and brushing the lint from his hat. Nothing out of the ordinary, though maybe that day Nathan hesitated when he got halfway there. Anything could have happened. Maybe he turned into a shop and fell in love with the beautiful clerk. Maybe he stepped off the Bloor Viaduct. She imagined his body buried under snow. She imagined it would turn up in spring. But she didn't say any of this, because Bea was saying, "Maybe burglars broke in and attacked him," and Marlene was holding a cup of tea to her chest, shivering.

———

SIX YEARS AFTER NATHAN'S DISAPPEARANCE, one of his plays is performed off-Broadway, and an academic from Montreal writes about the influence of Yiddish theatre on his sense of structure. Marlene gets some royalties and moves in with Bea. They don't need to worry about coupons anymore, but they do.

At sixteen, Tabitha drops out of school and gets a job as a secretary. She buys a record player and collects LPs. She takes swimming lessons because she wants to be Esther Williams.

Nearly everybody's heard of the playwright who disappeared, and when people learn Tabitha's last name, three times out of five they ask if there's any relation. When she nods, they say things like, "He must have been such a fascinating man." Yes, she smiles. He was very clever. Vanishing, she thinks, was the smartest thing he ever did.

———

THE FIRST TIME Tabitha had gone into the attic, she was seven years old and forbidden.

"He's very busy," Marlene would say, never allowing Nathan's work to be disturbed. "He's writing."

But Tabitha needed to know what this word *writing* meant. Of course, she knew how to write. In Mrs. Hill's grade two class she was forced to spell out words in a notebook, and was learning how to form each letter: upper case, lower, cursive. But surely this wasn't connected to what her father did in the attic. *He's writing.* Marlene said it with such reverence that it was obvious she herself didn't know what, exactly, Nathan did up there.

So while Marlene weeded the small, patchy flower beds that lined the porch, Tabitha climbed the ladder. She knew her father was up there because she could hear the floorboards creak as he took a few steps or adjusted himself in his chair. She pressed against the hatch—it felt heavy to her then—and she was almost relieved when she couldn't lift it. But then it squeaked open and she saw into the cramped room. Even in the middle of the day, it was dark. She could smell the dust and the damp.

"Yes?" Her father sounded far away.

Tabitha knew she should gently ease the hatch down and run to the yard. She still wore her sun hat and she should be outside, helping Marlene water the marigolds.

"What is it?" Her father's voice sounded closer now, and he opened the hatch all the way. "Yes?"

It took a moment for her eyes to adjust to the dark. Then she saw his ironed pants, tucked shirt, slim and serious face.

"Does your mother want something?"

She shook her head. The sun hat, which was too big because Marlene wanted it to last, slipped over her eyes. He bent to fix it and she felt his hand on top of her head.

"I wanted to see the attic," she said. "I wanted to see what you do."

"I rarely do much." He nodded for her to climb into the dim room. The ceiling was so low it nearly grazed his thin hair. There were papers everywhere—organized, or perhaps not organized, on the floor, the desk, in boxes, and along the windowsill of the turret window. "Come on," he said. "You can help me with something."

She hated to hear these words from Marlene, as they meant Tabitha would be asked to put away dishes, or help pick rocks from the flower beds. But Nathan cleared some papers off an old wooden chair and nodded for her to take a seat. The chair had arms, a high back, and looked like his own. He handed her three sheets of paper that he had typewritten. "Well." He sat across from her. "You can read, can't you?"

The ink was smudged in some places, and there were pencil scratchings in the margins. It wasn't like the picture books she was used to, and she didn't know where to begin, so she said, "I'm an excellent reader." Her teacher had told her this after Tabitha read a passage aloud in class. "If only I'd spend less time daydreaming and more time concentrating on my studies." She imitated Mrs. Hill's stiff lips and intonation, her emphasis on less and more.

"Is that so?" Nathan smiled at her joke. For a second he looked at her the way he looked at Lev—as though she were a good show, one that captivated him. "What do they make you read in school?"

"Some poems. And the Lord's Prayer."

"Ah. Of course." He pointed to a sentence at the top of the page. "Start here and go to the bottom. It's a monologue."

So Tabitha sat across from her father and read what he told her to read. He closed his eyes, and she thought at first that he wasn't listening. But every once in a while he took the paper from her to slash out a word or add sentences in a hand she couldn't make out.

He didn't explain the plot and she couldn't understand it on her own; the person on the page seemed injured, but she didn't know how or why. Still, she read—with an even intonation, the way Mrs. Hill had taught. Occasionally her father said things like, "Can you repeat the last line?" or "Not so fast. Pay attention to the rhythm."

After this, going into the attic didn't scare her. If Nathan didn't want her help, she would sit in the chair—her chair—and watch him type. She was almost sure that he liked having her there, and once he said, "You are a good reader. Damn good." After three years, she got so she could decipher his handwriting.

Tabitha never told her mother of these visits, and she knew this was a betrayal. But she didn't want to share what she knew of his piles of paper and his slanted, chaotic notes. It was too precious, this secret.

—

BY THE 1970S, some critics claim him as a visionary of a socialist utopia, and the literary journals love him. A long-running production of his most popular work plays at the Eaton Auditorium.

Tabitha lives in New York, and she often sees her father. He'll be in brown polyester, or sometimes in cowboy boots. He'll be a man on a billboard, or a friendly, blurry face when she's smoked too much hash. The guy behind the counter at her local grocer's. Or a man in a dance bar, in a purple suit and fake eyelashes. She learns to ignore these visions so she can enjoy the city, her own success.

She is invited to every party worth attending and she is the life of them, sampling all New York offers her: the dancing, the three-somes, the various chemical highs. She has her mother's strong nose and dark eyes, mixed with a haunting kind of ingenuousness. This proves to be marketable. She gets cast in roles that involve crying and shrieking. As a lark, she keeps a running tally of how many times she gets to kill herself onstage.

———

LIKE EVERY OTHER FRIDAY, the night before he vanished, Nathan invited Lev for dinner. He liked to hear the law student's opinions, and Marlene liked to cook and fuss. Lev came over at six because he usually shared a Scotch with Nathan before dinner. They would go to the attic to avoid the noise of the radio that Marlene and Tabitha played in the kitchen. The smell of their cigarettes slipped through the attic's hatch and Tabitha imagined their hushed voices, the clink of ice cube to glass, and Lev in her chair. But that night, he didn't arrive alone. That night, Lev brought a woman.

Her name was Sofia, and she had brown hair that curled around her ears. She wore a pencil skirt, a wide red belt, and a small leather hat. She hadn't dressed up her outfit the way Marlene would have, with makeup and pearls. She didn't have to. Her skin had a natural blush and her navy sweater brought out her eyes. Tabitha had never seen anyone so graceful, so poised. Next to this woman, she felt ashamed of her mother, and ashamed of her own awkward body. She imitated Sofia's posture, stretched her neck and held her shoulders straight.

"This beautiful lady," said Lev as he stood in the doorway, "has agreed to be my wife."

Nathan curved the corners of his mouth into something that resembled a smile and nodded to the woman.

Marlene held out her hand. "How lovely to meet you." She took Sofia's coat and gloves. "How lovely."

Over dinner, the men spoke of books. Lev had recently published a first collection, and though Nathan never wrote a single line of verse, poetry was the only topic seriously broached at the Sabbath table. From nearly two years of these dinners, Tabitha learned that Nathan was forever grateful for Klein and Lev found him depressing. Lev deemed Pound "robust and brilliant"; Nathan thought him a fascist, and a victim of his own poetic rules. Nathan admired Elizabeth Bishop, but Lev didn't pay much attention to her. And they never agreed on Layton.

"I love him," Lev stated that Friday night. He was extremely handsome, which was maybe what gave him so much confidence in his own opinions. "I love him the way a son loves a father."

Nathan leaned back in his chair and shook his head, his cheeks reddened from wine. Their conversations sounded like arguments, but Nathan rarely appeared happier. He listened when Lev spoke and seemed to find everything about him—his youth, his ego—engaging. If Marlene noticed, she seemed to treat it as a necessary ill, like the arthritis in her fingers, the fluid that collected in her legs. "Now," she said. "Would anyone like more beans?"

"A tough, brutish father. That's the way I love the man."

"He's a drunk," said Sofia. She seemed older than Lev. Maybe it was her rich voice, or the way she so confidently helped Marlene in the kitchen before the meal.

"So he's picked his poison." Lev turned to her. "That's his right."

"Of course." Sofia placed her fork and knife on her plate with a click. "But I hardly find it charming."

"Sofia has little use for certain kinds of men." Lev smiled and showed his pleasantly crooked teeth. He picked up her hand and kissed the tips of her fingers. "Men who are wholeheartedly male."

"Then she's an astute young woman." Nathan looked Lev in the eye. He smiled the kind of smile people use to cover up anger, or simple heartache. The kind of smile that never quite succeeds. "She's a prize."

—

IN THE 1980S, someone publishes a biography that gets it all wrong, Marlene and Bea spend half of every year in Florida, and Tabitha has become brash, too loud, a lush.

She is well liked, though fat and poor, and she wakes one morning to find that her hair has become a brazen, phony blond. There is nothing of Sofia in her now. She has lost her grace, her ingenuousness, her youth. She treats it like a joke, a big joke, the way her old self has disappeared inside this other woman. But in private, she doesn't find it funny. She has nightmares—sweaty, waking nightmares—that her father will find her like this. In this body, in this hair, tipsy and hysterical.

—

TWO DAYS AFTER NATHAN VANISHED, Lev knocked on the door. He'd come from the office and said he didn't have much time, was just dropping by. He sat on the couch in a dark, pressed suit. Marlene took Nathan's leather chair and sat on the edge of it. Tabitha curled up on the couch, as far from Lev as possible.

Without Nathan in the house, he seemed less warm, less assured. He was interested in the legalities: what the police had said, how the search was proceeding. He interrogated Marlene and she repeated what had happened, exactly as it had happened. The streetcar trip, the shopping, the empty house. She answered Lev's questions but seemed worn by them. When she finished, he pointed to the corner of the room and said, "Is that Elvis Presley?"

Marlene refilled his coffee cup.

"There are only so many possibilities." He bit into a lemon cookie. "Either your husband's disappearance was planned or accidental. Either he's alive or dead." Lev seemed to find comfort in this kind of statement.

"He's probably just taking an extended day of rest," said Marlene. This was a joke, but even she didn't laugh.

"I'm sure this will all be cleared up," he said. "There's probably an explanation."

Marlene put her cup on the table. She hadn't touched her coffee.

"I can see him waltzing in here tomorrow like nothing happened." Lev smiled at Marlene, smiled at Tabitha, then laughed—a short, coughing laugh. "Wouldn't that be so like him?"

"Anyway, he'll be glad to know you dropped by." Marlene stood. "He cares so much about you."

Then Lev made a noise that was quieter than his laugh, and sounded even more like coughing. When he wiped his face, Tabitha realized he was crying.

"I'm sure there's no need for that," Marlene said, in the same voice she used to tell Tabitha to *Stop dawdling* or *Quit picking at your food.*

But when Lev turned away and choked out the word "Sorry," Marlene settled herself beside him on the couch and put her arm around him. Despite the suit, he looked like a child, helpless and shaky. He rested his head on her shoulder. "It's okay," Marlene said, and rocked him back and forth.

Tabitha heard Lev's strange sobbing and understood what her mother must have known. Marlene let him press his wet, closed eyes into her cotton shirt. "You poor thing," she said. "You poor boy."

———

IN THE EARLY 1990S, Tabitha checks into rehab, where she meets Charlie Sheen, then meets her future husband. His name is Stanley and he is shy. He admits that he wasted his life, and Tabitha finds this very honest, very brave. There is nothing like Betty Ford sex, and the first time they make love, he cries.

When they check out, he proposes. Two months later, they are married. One year after that, he is rebuilding his law practice and she is making a comeback, playing disturbed mothers and oversexed divorcees. They rent an apartment in Manhattan, and Tabitha learns him: his elaborate tea ritual, his fitful sleep, his splendid reading voice.

She eases away from friends and considers teaching theatre rather than acting. She takes up cooking and purchases things for their comfort—dishes and wineglasses and soft wool blankets. She feels a dedication as simple and big-hearted as Marlene's.

———

THE YEAR BEFORE HE LEFT, Nathan had begun to say things like, "Not now, Tabitha," or "I need to concentrate, please," when he heard her steps on the ladder. For a month before he disappeared, she hadn't ventured into the attic at all.

But that Friday evening, she silently climbed the steps after dinner. What drew her there was the look on his face when he'd stood and left the table in the middle of the meal. The defeated way he'd said, "I've got work to see to."

After Lev and Sofia went home, and while Marlene changed out of the blouse and green skirt she wore for company, Tabitha opened the hatch and pulled herself up, edging along the dusty floor until she slid into the office.

Nathan hadn't heard her come in—or if he had, he didn't find her presence important. He sat at his desk, facing away from her, and she stared at the back of his neck. He didn't turn to her or clear the stack of books from the chair. There was a blank sheet of paper rolled into the typewriter, so white it glowed under the lamp. He stared out the window, not even attempting to punch the keys.

BEA PASSES AWAY SUDDENLY, and Tabitha flies home to help Marlene with the details: obituary, casket, stone. Maybe it comes from age, or from living with a sister for decades, but Marlene has lost any sense of propriety. She rinses dishes instead of washing them with soap, and forgets to close the door when she pees.

After sitting shiva, they give Bea's clothes and her cribbage board to the Goodwill. Then they pack Marlene's dishes and the canned goods she stockpiles—*might as well buy lots when they're on sale*—so Marlene can move to a smaller place. As Tabitha fills a box with her mother's old records, she finds the Elvis. He's at the back of Marlene's closet, looking out like a ghost. He smells of mothballs, and his slim ceramic nose has broken off. Still, there's something about him. He's as strange and charming as ever.

———

TABITHA STRETCHED UP on the tips of her toes and her head nearly touched the attic's ceiling. She wanted, like her father, to see out the window. When she did this, the light must have changed, or the floorboards shifted, because he turned around. His wooden chair squeaked as it swivelled. "What are you doing here, Tabitha?" He was the only one, then, who called her by her full name.

"Nothing."

"Have they gone?"

She nodded. "I'm supposed to be helping with the dishes."

"I shouldn't have left the table like that. Tell your mother I'm sorry."

When she wasn't reading the lines he gave her, she didn't know how to talk to him, so she said the only thing that came into her head. "Wasn't Lev's fiancée pretty? Like a movie star?"

"Prettier," he said quietly. "Because it's real life."

Tabitha nodded and looked toward his desk. The typewriter, the blank sheet of paper.

"Did you know I haven't written anything in nearly a year?" He spoke as though it were a statistic, a fact that piqued his interest.

She shook her head. She understood exactly what this meant: that he wouldn't need her anymore, that there was no reason for her to be in the attic. That the chair was no longer hers.

"But that's a secret." He raised one eyebrow, an exaggerated expression that reminded her of when he would read bedtime stories. When he terrified her, doing all the voices. "Can you keep a secret?"

She heard Marlene in the kitchen, running water for the dishes. Tabitha had a few minutes before her mother needed her to dry. "Sometimes."

"That's a truthful answer." He leaned back in his chair. "Of course, I've written reviews and letters and things. But I haven't really written."

There was the sound of Marlene opening and closing a cupboard. "I should go down soon," said Tabitha. "She wouldn't want me here."

"Your mother is a very sweet person," he said. "I think that's why I married her. Because she seemed like the only honest person on earth." He laughed then, and it sounded hollow in the low-ceilinged attic. "Isn't that incredible? I married the only honest person on earth."

Tabitha stared at his shoes. They were brown leather and polished. "If it's just that you're not really writing," she said, imitating his emphasis on *really*, "then you should tell her the truth. It would probably make her happy, because then you could come downstairs more."

"The truth? It would break her heart," he said. "I don't suppose you're old enough yet. I don't suppose you've had your heart broken."

"Yes, I have." This was a lie. But Tabitha had seen enough romances to know how to cast her eyes down and pause, breathlessly, before adding, "Once."

"Then I'm sorry for you," he said, and turned back to the window. His voice had a harshness that told her she hadn't fooled him. He was the only audience, she would later realize, that she hadn't been able to fool.

WITHIN A YEAR OF BEA, Marlene dies. And after her mother's stroke, Tabitha can't think of a single thing to say to Stanley. He holds her, tries to give comfort, but everything about him seems foreign: his smell, his pilled sweaters. He is a stranger, a man she never knew. So Tabitha walks out of her own life.

She leaves her marriage and New York and moves to a more manageable city. One with glass-fronted buildings, and bridges that stretch over waterways. She doesn't know anyone there, though once she runs into Lev as she's buying groceries. "Tabby," he says. "Is that really you?"

He looks tired, less handsome, and he wears an expensive suit that doesn't fit his soft body. He says that Sofia left him long ago, after she too became a successful lawyer. He says he visits the kids every Hanukkah.

She wants to ask him questions. "Have you heard anything about my father?" Or, "Do you still miss him?" But it seems ridiculous to say those things under fluorescent lights, beside shelves of microwaveable popcorn and freeze-dried soups. And Lev is talking about how he'd seen her picture in a magazine years ago and couldn't believe it. "I said to myself, that can't be the same girl!"

Neither of them suggests staying in touch, and they never see each other again. Tabitha gets a job in a bookstore, where the owner finds it amusing that she was once well known on the stage. Eventually, she too finds it amusing. So she settles, for a while, into this role behind the counter. And cultivates—perfectly—the sad, knowledgeable smile that customers seem to like.

TABITHA STOOD IN THE ATTIC surrounded by Nathan's books and the dim light, faced with her father's back. She wanted to say something—apologize for her lie, or ask why he had left the table, who had broken his heart. But he stared out the turret window as though there was something out there. So she slipped down the ladder, closed the hatch, and ran to the living room. She looked out the big window, the one Marlene washed with vinegar every week. She wanted to see whatever he'd seen. But there was nothing outside. Just the usual street lamps and lawns. Houses with drawn curtains. The everyday, falling snow.

the weather

SHE CAME HOME with my daughter after school. The neighbour, Jerry, and the guys I hire for haying had left twenty minutes ago, half an hour. I was still in the field, and I saw the two of them walk along the highway: my daughter with her slouch and backpack, and the older girl with neither.

Edith hardly ever brought friends home, not since my wife lived here, so I stopped what I was doing—fixing a yard of fence—and went to meet them on the road. Edith's fifteen, a tough age, so this probably got on her nerves, probably embarrassed her. Her father with a loop of wire hooked on his arm and cutters in his dirty hand. This girl, her friend, obviously came from town. From a house with plastic siding and a lawn.

"Father," Edith said. "This is Rae."

The girl was tall, built like the spindly birch we use as windbreak. She reminded me of girls I knew when I was young, and I didn't like the arch of her back, her cut-off shorts, her weird grey eyes. I didn't like her much at all, and I wouldn't have asked her for dinner if I hadn't noticed the way she breathed. Like she was sucking air along a sandpaper throat, holding it in clogged lungs. Like each inhale was an effort, like it was earned.

The girl offered a quick smile. Gap in her teeth, but she was probably considered pretty, and she probably knew it. "Hi," she said.

It wasn't warm, but the sun glinted off her hair. That's what I remember most: the cool sun, the dropping pressure. Rain was coming, and it was giving me a headache.

———

I INTRODUCED THEM. Father, I said, this is Rae. It was unfortunate, but I couldn't have known.

I met her on the last day of school, when the bus dropped me off near where she walked along the highway. I recognized her even though she was new to the school and two grades above me. I asked if she was lost, and she said she was lost on purpose. She said she likes to go for walks when the air is clear. She also said that her boyfriend's an asshole and when she told him so, he'd opened his car door and left her on the side of the road. She looked angry and like she might have been crying. She asked me, You're Edith, right?

I told her she could come to my place, for a snack or something. I said I was certain my father wouldn't mind. She looked irritated, like I'd ruined her plans. But then she said, Okay. Sure. Thanks.

———

SHE STARTED COMING OVER nearly every day. Suddenly my daughter was sitting beside that girl in front of the TV, bowls of soggy cereal resting on their knees. Or the two of them would lie in front of the house, moving their towels around the parched grass to follow the sun. They greased themselves in oil, and the girl would wave to Jerry and the guys as they walked by. Edith started wearing her hair down and a borrowed bikini, her body too young for it. Edith, who was usually locked in her room with her books and her mother's old tapes and an attitude. What my wife called "an innate aloofness."

That girl wasn't the kind of friend I'd expected my daughter to make. She wasn't the kind I'd hoped for.

———

THAT FIRST NIGHT, she opened our screen door and strode in like she already knew her way around. This is a cool place, she said.

When we had dinner, she bounced her knees under the table and took huge helpings of potatoes and corn. She'd seen rodeo on television, so she had questions about bull riding and calf roping. At first my father answered with one or two words and he looked shy when he spoke to her. She leaned on the table and kept her eyes on his tanned face, like this was a challenge or a game. I was sure he was a joke to her, someone she'd tell stories about later: a cowboy with greying hair and the top two buttons of his shirt undone. My poor, idiotic father.

By dessert, he became less quiet and seemed to enjoy answering her questions. He told her about branding parties and moose hunting, and when she wanted to know how cattle auctions worked, he asked me to put the kettle on for coffee. Then he told her how loud an auction was and how it smelled like someone had trucked their whole farm into town and dumped it in one building. Which a lot of guys did. He explained feedlots and weights and weaning. He told her about the spring, how busy calving was, but beautiful. He used that word: *beautiful*.

———

I EVEN CAUGHT THAT GIRL sneaking into our house after Edith had gone to bed. She'd party with other friends—her boyfriends, as far as I could tell, changed with the weather. Then she'd get them to drop her off at our place so her parents didn't meet the guys she was with, didn't smell the beer on her breath. If she saw that I was still up—looking out the window, trying to find something decent on the radio—it never bothered her. She just passed me on her way to Edith's room doing an exaggerated tiptoe, her finger to her lips, as though this was our secret. Which I guess it was, since I never called her mother, though I meant to.

To teach a lesson, a couple of weeks ago, I woke both girls up one morning and forced them to watch the sun rise above the tall grass. Edith came out of her bedroom pissed off, exhausted.

The girl had slept in a pair of my daughter's old pyjamas, and the material was creased, thin as water. "Are you kidding me?" she said.

I kept a straight face, walked them out to the herd, and listened to her teenage whines about dew soaking through her socks. My daughter didn't complain the whole time, so I figured she was seriously angry, seriously humiliated. But then Edith said, "I remember this from when I was a kid. It was my favourite part."

She pointed out the calves who were sickly, or whose mothers wouldn't produce. Then she took the girl's hand and showed her how to lead the calves out of the field and into the loafing pens, walking backwards and letting them suck on her fingers.

One calf suckled the girl's hand and slobbered down her wrist, and another pushed its head against her thigh, looking for milk. "This is the nastiest fucking thing I've ever done," she said when she caught her breath from laughing.

Edith looked at me then as if to say, "City girl." I nodded and gave her a wink. It felt good to see my daughter like that, smiling.

—

RAE CARRIED AN INHALER in one back pocket and a pack of cigarettes in the other. She saw the irony of this, but she didn't care. Once, when she gave me a drag off her cigarette, I thought I was dying. My eyes watered and my throat felt like it had been torn.

God, Edith, she said. You're such a baby.

She laughed and passed me her inhaler and I pumped the powder into my mouth. It made me feel the same way I did when I saw her walking up our driveway: light-headed and spinny.

—

ONCE, SHE SNUCK IN so late that I was already at the kitchen table. The sun wasn't up yet and the kitchen was dim. She leaned in the doorway, then sat right down across from me. I should have said some adult thing—got mad, got worried—but her clothes were wrinkled, her eyes tired, and I remembered that kind of morning. I got her a mug from the cupboard and took the milk out of the fridge.

"Sugar?"

"Yeah. Please."

When we spoke, we whispered. A little agreement to keep this quiet.

"Don't your parents worry about you?" I sat across from her. "Wonder where you are?"

"No." She stirred four heaping spoons of sugar into her cup. "Not when I tell them I'm at Edith's. They moved me out here so I'd breathe clean air and meet wholesome people like her. So I'd join 4-H."

She poured milk into her cup, holding the jug high so it fell in a thin stream. I looked at her puffy eyes, her blotched skin.

"You look like hell," I said.

"Well, this coffee tastes like hell."

"It should sober you up."

She looked at me, smiled. "Why aren't you married?"

"I am."

She leaned toward me. "That's a story."

"There's no story." I passed her the sugar. "My wife wouldn't stay, and I wouldn't go. That's all."

I sipped my coffee, still too hot, and she slurped from her spoon.

"Nina lives in Victoria now," I said, even though I don't normally like to say her name aloud. "We don't talk much anymore."

"No kidding."

The girl lifted her cup to her lips and blew at the steam. I stirred my coffee, even though it was black.

"It was supposed to be temporary, her leaving," I said. "Nina called from Calgary and said she just needed a couple days away. But then she kept driving." I leaned back in my chair. "Edith really misses her."

The girl nodded, folded her arms on the table, rested her chin. I didn't expect her to say much, but it was nice to sit there with someone. No matter that she was half awake, sleepy-eyed.

———

LAST WEEK WE MADE CINNAMON TOAST, then tried on the clothes my mother had left behind. Neither of us could fit into the tight jeans or the small, high-wedge shoes. But Rae filled out the thin sweaters and the silky, sleeveless tops. She loved the scoop necks, and when she looked in the mirror she said, No wonder your mom left.

She wore one of the shirts—it was pale gold, a shimmery sun-on-wheat—to the dinner table. It was nearly ten at night, but since it was summer, my father had just come in and cooked steak and sweet potatoes. He'd already folded up the cuffs of his sleeves and served himself. He was sitting; Rae was standing. And when he saw the shirt, he looked in her eyes. There was nothing she or I could say. No reason we should have been in his bedroom, rifling in his closet. And no reason we should have found my mom's stuff. No reason he shouldn't have gotten rid of it years ago.

When I saw his face, I thought he might pick up his plate, his fork and knife, his beer, and quietly leave the kitchen. But he just shook his head. And Rae smiled too. It was as though they were sharing a joke. As though they were the only two in the room.

That was it, the only hint I got. Then Rae pulled out a chair and sat down. My father nodded toward the stovetop for us to grab some food, and I got myself a pop. I opened the fridge door and it breathed cold air on my face. Then my father said, just loud enough for us to hear, It fits all right, that's for sure.

❧

I POURED MYSELF MORE COFFEE and the girl drank the sludge in her cup. The house was chilled and she curled up in the kitchen chair, held her knees.

"When did she leave? Your wife?"

The girl was hungover and wanted entertainment, a good story. So I took a breath and told her about the storm. How it had been nearly dinnertime and I'd wanted to head home, but the cattle were acting funny. Whining and lying down, then standing up, being strange.

Once I started telling it, I couldn't stop. I talked about how hot it'd been that day, and how it'd cooled so suddenly the sweat on my shirt made me shiver. Lightning shattered the grey sky every few seconds, and clouds spooled and unspooled themselves. The rain hit hard, but I didn't move from the field. Not even when the funnel cloud dropped and skimmed my neighbour's land. Not until it blew the hip roof off his barn.

Then I climbed into my truck, pulled it over to a bluff of trees, sat and listened. That's what I remember most. The colour—that grey—and the noise. Rain and hail against a metal roof. The wind shot nails and boards past me, hail cracked the front windshield and smashed the side window. Glass landed in my lap, hailstones clattered onto the floor. And then it was over.

The quiet was as hard to take as the storm's noise. I watched the weather spin along the prairie, leaving as fast as it had come. The only sound was water that streaked into the cab, pooling around my boots. The funnel had touched down for less than two minutes. It was nothing. It wouldn't even make the news.

THE TWO OF US like to imagine my mother's new life. Rae invents episodes that remind me of television soap operas: romantic dates and exotic travel. But from the two times I visited, I know my mother lives in an apartment and works in a college library. What I like to picture are the details. I see her with shorter hair and makeup. I imagine her coming home from work and taking off her coat. Unzipping her high-heeled boots and shaking water from an umbrella.

WHEN THE WIND CALMED, I climbed from my truck and walked to the house. The front door had been ripped off its hinges and it lay in the front yard, near the saskatoon bushes. Edith stood in the doorway, her arms crossed against the cold. When she saw me, she turned toward the kitchen. Even then, she used that cold tone. "He's here, Mom. He's fine."

In the kitchen, one of the windows was broken and shingles from the neighbour's barn had embedded themselves in the wallpaper. My wife sat at the table and stared at two hailstones that sat like a centrepiece. Maybe she or Edith had picked them up from the yard. Maybe these were the stones that had broken the window. They were as big as my fists.

"You're both all right," I said, and maybe I sounded too rough about it. Maybe I sounded like a businessman checking his stock, a cattleman counting head.

That's when Nina said it: "I hate this place." She pressed her forehead against her hand. "I hate it here, Braden."

I figured it was shock. I figured it would blow over. "Come on now," I said, and started to unbutton my shirt. Water glued it to my chest, and now that I knew my family was safe, my body let itself feel the cold.

"I can't stay here." Her voice was like that moment after the storm, so quiet it spooked me.

The hailstones were soaking into the tablecloth, and I don't know why that made me so angry. I picked them up and threw them out the broken window. Some glass dropped into the sink and Nina flinched.

"I'm going to check the field," I said. My wife didn't answer, so I turned to Edith, put my hand on her shoulder. She looked at me like she hated me. "Stay here," I said. "Keep your mom company."

DURING THE STORM, my mother pushed me against the kitchen door jamb and held my hands. I could feel the house shake against me, and I remember thinking this must be hard on her. I have my father's bones, my father's flesh, and even at thirteen I was taller than her. She could be wild: she was always dancing to the Rolling Stones in the kitchen, or speeding along the highway. But right then she reminded me of the sick calves my father nursed, the ones he kept in pens and bottle-fed warm, glutinous milk.

I felt the house creak against the wind, and my mother's sweaty hands. Then there was a crack and the front door blew off its hinges. I watched it float and waver in the air, then drop to the grass. My mother squeezed my hands until her knuckles went white. Her face was empty. It was like something my father once described, a blankness he'd seen on some animals. An injured horse determined to stand and survive, or a calf too scared to wail before slaughter.

AFTER SHE FINISHED her first cup, the girl didn't even bother with coffee. Just spooned sugar into her mug, poured milk on top, and ate it like soup. The sun was rising, and Edith was still asleep.

"I should take you home," I said. "You're going to make yourself sick."

"I feel fine."

I didn't want to sound fatherly, because I didn't feel it. Whispering like this, ignoring work and the radio, I didn't feel like me at all.

She reached across the table and tapped my hand. "Show me where you were," she said. "When it hit."

So we left the kitchen. Midsummer, but the grass was crisp with frost, and you could still see the moon through the clouds. I pointed out the silvery birch that blocked some of the wind. Then I took her to the pond where geese land every spring and she picked some water-parsley. I showed her the three hundred head of cattle, the morning air rising out of their big soft nostrils. All the things that charmed my wife, at first. The things Edith used to love too.

When we got to the fence that's separated my property from Jerry's for nearly thirty years, I said, "That's all she wrote. Might as well turn back."

But she squinted and walked forward. She'd seen the lush place where we throw the bones, and the white glint of them.

"It's just the yard," I called out. My wife had always hated it there. The high grass, the smell.

She stopped a few feet away from a bull's rib cage and I stood behind her, back a ways. I watched her neck, her shoulders. Tried to imagine the look on her face. "It's not much to see."

The girl nudged a piece of the bull's torso with her toe.

"I throw them here for the coyotes," I said. "Feed them so they don't bother the herd."

She stepped forward again, her sandalled feet disappearing in the green and yellow grass. She knelt, almost facing me, full of bravery. Then she lifted a cow's skull that was old enough to be picked clean. So heavy it strained her arms.

"I don't take people out here, normally."

She slid her pinkie finger through the bullet hole I'd had to make, can't remember when. Must have been a few years ago, maybe a calving that went wrong.

"Come on. I'll drive you home."

She ran her hand along the forehead. Feeling the rough bone, I guess, against her palm. This is when I figured out she was beautiful. Something about how calm her face was, how curious. She held up the enormous head, looked it right in the hollow eyes.

—

SHE NEVER INTRODUCED ME, but I'm sure that every one of her boyfriends was an idiot. I called them all by the same name: Kyle. That was the one she was with when I first met her. The one who dropped her off outside my door, some miracle working through him.

How's Kyle? I'd say, and she'd reply, His name is Joel and he's not my boyfriend.

Bullshit.

You're bullshit.

Then she'd smile in a distant way and I'd know her life was made up of endless possibilities, her life was complex and golden. This was while we were flipping through one of her magazines, or while I braided her hair so it would be wavy the next day. I adored her tangled, complicated hair, so many shades of blond and brown all at once.

—

I OFFERED TO TAKE HER HOME. "You need some sleep and a shower," I said, and we walked to my truck. We climbed in, and the bench was already warm from the sun. There was still a web of cracks through the windshield, and light splintered through it.

From what I can tell, most city people think it's boring to talk about the weather. But here, it's important. Every morning, Nina and I used to look out the kitchen window to see what was coming: heat, sudden cold, or the possibility of worse. Talking about the weather, you talk about everything that matters—what you want, what you're scared of.

There was a pause—after I turned the key in the ignition, before the diesel engine turned over. The girl and I stared straight ahead, through the cracked glass.

"Beautiful day," she said, and I knew exactly what she meant.

—

ONCE, I ASKED HER to tell me what it was like.

No way, she said.

Please? Since you've done it uncountable times?

She slapped my face then, but not hard.

Okay, listen. She pressed her forehead against mine and I smelled the nicotine on her breath. It's different every time, she said. Sometimes it's passionate, and sometimes it's sweet, and sometimes it's just sad.

I tried to imagine having direct contact with those: passion and sweetness and sadness.

But I'll tell you one thing, she said. It's not like it is on TV. People don't actually scream like that.

—

I ALWAYS KNEW what that girl felt about me, even if I didn't get it. I've known since she came into my kitchen wearing my wife's shirt, and that gold material caught the light from the fixture above the table.

It took me a few seconds to recognize it, to understand what she'd done. To understand that the girl had been in my closet, handling my shirts and pants and belts. Clattering the hangers as she searched through my stuff for the one thing that would catch my eye. The one thing that would make me look at her, look at her different. Then she put it on, knowing exactly what I would feel, exactly how it would hurt. To see that shirt filled out, to see a body move and breathe inside it.

And then one night, so late it was almost morning, she came into my house. She walked up the stairs, through the hall, then opened my door. She stepped into my room.

"Hi," she said.

"Hi."

She sat beside me on the bed and I smelled rain on her, exhaust.

I didn't look at her, just asked, "What are you doing here?"

"I walked over from my place." She whispered. Aware, too, of Edith sleeping down the hall. "I've been thinking about the story you told."

I lay on my back and stared at the ceiling. "You should go home. I'll take you home."

"My parents talk a lot about right and wrong. But I don't believe in that."

And I thought of all of it—my wife, my daughter, the sky's frosts and floods. I looked at her, and she touched my arm. Her hand was cold from the air outside, and I said, "Me neither."

She nodded like she already knew that, and pulled out her ponytail. Her hair hung damp and knotted down her back. Then she unlaced her muddy boots and placed them beside the bed. She unbuttoned her shirt, folded it. Paused, as if thinking it through, then unzipped her dirt-hemmed jeans and slid them from her legs. She stretched herself out and lay beside me. Touched, carefully, the hair on my chest.

She was nervous too. I heard it in her breathing.

—

MOST NIGHTS, she came into my room, then peeled off her T-shirt and jeans. I sat up and watched her do this, squinting through the dark. Then she'd climb into bed, put her arm around me, and say, Shh. Go back to sleep.

Not that night. That night, they thought I was warm in my bed, deaf and dumb. They didn't think the rain woke me. But I heard it. I heard her walk through the house and then I heard her open the wrong door—his, not mine. A mistake, a funny mistake. I expected her to burst into my room, gasping and laughing holy-shit-guess-what-I-just-did.

That night, my bed felt as big and cold as the sky. And if there was one thing I knew, it was that this wouldn't get easier. It would ache for years. That's what I've learned. That's what my father taught me.

—

AFTER, WE DIDN'T KNOW how to talk to each other. She lay on her back and breathed, air scraping along her throat. I picked up some of her hair, felt its weight, but she wouldn't look at me. The moon shone through the window, and I could see her pale lashes and the pale hair between her legs. She looked skinny. She looked seventeen.

I took a breath, as pained as hers. "Rae—"

"Don't say anything." She stared at the ceiling. She must have been used to these kinds of things being quick and rough—at a party, in the back of a truck. She'd probably never done that before. Been in a bed, beside a man.

She sat up and turned her back to me—embarrassed, now, to be naked. "I should go." She tied up her hair.

"You don't have to." I knew she'd never be in this house again. "You can stay awhile."

She put on her shirt and buttoned it. Then zipped her jeans, buckled her belt. I wanted to touch her arm, take her hand. But she pulled on her socks, laced her boots.

She walked down the stairs and I heard the front door open, then click shut behind her. The same door that flew off its hinges during the storm. The one I replaced with a tarp the next afternoon, the afternoon my wife left. The tarp didn't do much to keep out the cold. I sat at the kitchen table and listened to the wind catch and snap it all day. As I waited for the school bus to pull onto the highway's shoulder. As I wondered what I would tell my daughter, when she came home.

escape

WHEN HIS WIFE DIED, Tom started going to the casino. The first time, it was by accident. He'd driven for hours, past the stylish downtown condos that resembled his own, the Costco and the Home Depot—where he would never shop—the suburban houses and then the patches of rainforest that had yet to be developed. He didn't know where he was going. He only knew that he didn't want to sit in a bar or restaurant—that would make too pathetic a spectacle. He drove out of town, along the highway, and into the small city where his wife had been raised. She'd escaped this place as soon as she could, and he could see why. It had a casino, a mall, and a bus station. He pulled into the casino's lot, went in to use the urinal, and ended up at the blackjack table for three hours. This is how he lived his life now: everything was accidental. Everything was inevitable.

These days, he goes every night. He knows the roads well, and can make it in less than an hour. He could go to the casino in town, but he likes being far from home, far from colleagues and well-meaning friends. And he likes the drive: the rain-darkened highway, the sudden light from passing cars.

He leaves work at six and arrives at the casino at seven—seven-thirty if he remembers to stop for dinner. He parks in the north side of the lot, and it's never difficult to find a space. It has been nearly a month, and he goes to the same cage at the beginning of each night. But the cashier—a young man with eyes the colour of kelp—never treats him like a familiar. Tom appreciates this disdain for small talk. The staff deal with people the way they deal with money: with immunity, without judgment. Tom buys a hundred dollars' worth of chips and, as he walks to the tables, enjoys the feel and weight of them in his hand. He stays an hour, two at the most. This is a habit, not a compulsion. Other than a few poker nights he participated in as a student, he's never been a gambler, and he has no special talent for it. He simply wants company in his solitude.

He craves a certain kind of crowd, the kind that cares nothing for him, and he feels at ease with the people in the casino. They are not the kind of people he's used to: he doubts that they know what a polypeptide is, or care about cellular receptivity. Most are quiet, habitual gamblers. Many are older and less fortunate than he is. Men at poker tables who wear sunglasses and stare at screens. Elderly women who wear cards around their necks and plug these into the slot machines, like patients taking oxygen from a tube. These people don't seem to hear the dinging and beeping of the slots, or mind the dry air. Tom likes the way their worn faces look under the blue-tinged light. They remind him of a school of basslets, shy but aware of each other.

His favourite card dealer works the blackjack table. She is from China, or maybe Japan or the Philippines—someplace Tom rarely gives any thought to. She looks to be a few years older than he is; he guesses late forties. She rims her eyes with blue makeup and has a perm in her hair that's growing out. She's professional but not friendly, and she runs her table with a serious efficiency. It's a fast, rhythmical game, and she speaks only in service of it. When she says certain numbers—eleven, thirteen, and seventeen in particular—he can hear a slight accent in her voice.

He knows little about gambling, but enough to know that it's a waste of time and money to play at her table. She uses four decks, accepts only high bets, and a quick calculation tells him that he loses approximately seventy percent of the time. He knows he should stick to poker—he has a good instinct for the game, and lately his expression has hardened into a permanent poker face. But he likes her. He especially likes her hands. They're not a young woman's hands: the skin is creased, and veins reach down her wrists like dark ropes. And it's not that these hands are capable of anything remarkable; she is not, for example, a surgeon or a concert pianist. But her hands are slim and bare—she doesn't wear jewellery—and he likes to watch them pull cards from the shoe and drop them on the table. It's pleasant even to watch them sweep his chips away from him. Her hands, he decides, are golden damselfish—understated, graceful. But he would never tell her that. She probably wouldn't know what a damselfish was, and if she did, she might not like the comparison. And he doesn't want to ruin his routine by offending her. She works every night, from Tuesday to Saturday. She is a relief and a pleasure he can count on.

KELLY HAD BEEN SICK for four years, and for much of that time they believed she would recover. She was thirty-six when she died. Tom was thirty-eight.

In the months after, Tom dismantled the bed they'd set up in the living room so she could look out the window. The condo was on the fifteenth floor, and she'd had a view of the sky, the distant ocean, the gulls that occasionally rose that high. Now, he rarely takes in the view. He moved the couch and coffee table back into their normal positions, cleared away her magazines, and gave her clothes to charity. He keeps up with work, goes to the gym, and cleans the condo himself. He continues to put money away for retirement and to pay his credit card bills on time. And he remains fastidious about the aquarium.

Each day, he sprinkles food onto the surface of the water, and watches the fish nudge each other as they open and close their mouths over the pellets. He also cleans the inside of the glass and replaces the evaporated water. Once a week, on Sundays, he removes the waste. He tests the calcium, magnesium, alkalinity, iodine, phosphate, salinity, and nitrate levels. Once a month he changes the filter's pouch, and once every four months he checks the components of the skimmer, lights, air pump, heater, and hydrometer. This allows him to maintain emerald and sea corals, a hermit crab, a blue damselfish, a jawfish, two mated gobies, a flamefish, a convict tang, a blue *Linckia* sea star, and seventy-five pounds of live rock. He keeps the temperature at seventy-seven degrees and maintains the pH at 7.8. He records any changes in the water's parameters in a log, which Kelly used to call Tom's

Bible. As a joke, she'd hide it around the house—sometimes under the bed, once inside the fridge.

"You have to find it." She kissed his neck. "That's the game."

"I hate games, Kelly. You know that."

Memories this clear are rare. Kelly's presence in his mind is shadowy: she drifts in and out, but never in any form that he can smell or touch. That part of his mind has gone dark, and is lit only in patches, like the highway at night. It's as though Kelly disappeared in a puff of smoke or stepped behind a curtain. She must have passed easily into some sort of afterlife, which is what she would have wanted. He'd expected grief to be engulfing. He'd hoped that she wouldn't vanish so quickly. He'd hoped that she would haunt him.

⁓

AFTER THREE WEEKS of watching that woman deal cards, he follows her outside. It's nine o'clock and she's being relieved for a break. A muscular, bald man takes over the game and she walks away from the table. Tom follows her past the roulette wheels and the slots. Down a dim hallway and out a streaked glass door marked No Exit. She must sense him, but she doesn't turn around and she doesn't look at him when they're outside. She watches the heavy, drowsy rain fall onto the cement. This must be the staff parking lot: cars are parked next to a Dumpster, and there are two metal chairs against the building, sheltered from the rain.

She sits in one chair and puts her feet up on the other. She wears practical shoes—black and thick-soled—and she loosens the laces. It occurs to Tom that her feet must ache. She's not young and has been standing for hours. She closes her eyes and he sees that her makeup has begun to crease and flake. She lights a cigarette and offers him one, which he accepts.

She's the one who talks.

"You could be doing better than you are." Her eyes are still closed, and she rubs her shoulder with one hand.

"Pardon?"

"There are strategies." For the first time, she looks at him. "It's mostly luck. But there are ways of increasing your luck."

"I don't care about that." It's been years since he smoked a cigarette and his voice comes out gravelled and dry. "I'm not here for the reasons you think."

He would like her to be curious about his reasons. He would like her to ask, the way barmaids in movies do, "What's your story, mister?"

Instead, she closes her eyes and rolls her shoulders to get the kinks out. "Most people aren't."

"You have beautiful hands."

She smiles like she's used to this from men like him. *Men like him*. He's not sure what kind of man he is, or what kind he is becoming.

She pulls a deck of cards from the inside pocket of her blazer. "Choose a card," she says. "Memorize it, but don't show it to me. Then put it back in the deck."

He pulls out the seven of hearts then slips it back.

She shuffles, and the sound of cards landing one on top of the other merges with the sound of falling rain. She fans the cards out on the chair beside her, face down. There is no flourish, just her usual professionalism, as she brushes her hand over the deck and pulls out the seven of hearts. "Here." She hands it to him. "Keep it. Maybe it's lucky."

Then she lifts the sleeve of her blazer—a stiff navy jacket that all the casino employees wear—and exposes her slim wrist and a cheap, plastic-strapped watch. He can tell from her face and the tired way she lifts herself out of the chair that her fifteen minutes are up. She stands and strides past him. It's not only her hands that are graceful—it's every movement of her lean body. She leaves him outside, and he watches through the clouded glass as she slips away.

<hr />

HE WATCHED HIS WIFE disappear piece by piece. First, the exterior that had attracted him: her left breast, then her right. Her hair, eyelashes, eyebrows. Then her insides: her lymph nodes, her lungs. Death progressed with slow, methodical determination.

He took a leave from work to nurse Kelly, and lived off the savings they'd meant to spend on a vacation in Italy. He bought her magazines, cooked whatever she felt like eating, administered morphine when she needed it, and even read to her from the Bible—a book he'd always studiously ignored. In the last months he washed her with a sponge and hot, soapy water that ran down her skin and onto the towel he'd laid over her bed.

During this time, he kept a record. He wrote down her symptoms, pain levels, and the drug side effects in a lab book he'd taken from work. He took her temperature three times each day and he monitored her heart. He did it because it might help the oncologist. He did it because he believed in accuracy and rationality and solutions. He did it because it was the only thing he could do.

———

THE CARD IS NOT LUCKY. The next night he keeps it in his breast pocket but loses more than ever. It's nothing spectacular, just steady losses, hour after hour. Twice he stands up to leave but never makes it to the door. She watches him with something that might be empathy.

On her break, he follows her outside.

"What do you do? In your other life?" She speaks too loudly, as though she's in front of a crowd. "How do you make all that money you lose?"

"I'm a doctor."

"Ah."

"Not the kind you're thinking of. A researcher." He pictures himself at work, his eyelashes against the microscope's glass. He has spent his life developing drugs for diseases even more aggressive than the one that took Kelly. The job used to consume him, but now he shows up late and is careless. The work seems too hopeful, too optimistic. He no longer believes that inevitabilities can be staved off. "I run a lab," he says. "I don't deal with people."

"You remind me of my ex-husband." She pulls the deck of cards from her pocket. "He hated people too. And he gambled too much."

"I don't gamble too much."

"Paul and I used to have this exact conversation."

"I don't hate people either."

"What's your name?"

"Tom. What's yours?"

"I feel like I've known you my whole life, Tom." She flirts like a woman who has practised and mastered the art. "It's like we've been married for decades."

"That's probably not a good thing."

"You must not be married." She shuffles, Vegas-style. "Or you'd know that marriage isn't good or bad. You just fall into it, like any habit." She holds the deck on her palm like a waitress holding a tray of drinks. "See this? A regular deck, right? But I bet I can find all four aces in the next half-minute."

"That accent—where are you from?"

She fans the cards and two of the aces are face up. One appears in her hand when she snaps her fingers, and the last one—the spade—he finds in his shirt pocket.

"How did you do that?"

"A party trick," she says. "Always goes over well."

"Where did you learn this stuff?"

"I used to do it for a living." She tucks the cards back into her pocket. "I toured the country with my husband. My then-husband."

"A past life."

"It wasn't much of a life. The show never did well. People didn't like the reversal—a woman magician and her husband, the assistant."

He can imagine her onstage. She is all angles: ribs, slim hips, long tendons of the neck. He can imagine her in a sequined jacket, her hair slicked back, face covered in a mask of makeup.

"I used to cut people in half. Pull roses from my sleeve." She speaks as though she is remembering a former lover. "My stage name was Miranda. Miranda the Conjuror."

"That suits you," he says. "Miranda."

"If you think so, then that's what you should call me."

He recognizes this as an invitation. That night, for the first time, he follows her home.

HE STAYS FAR BEHIND HER and keeps his headlights off. It rains and her car's lights are blurred by the water. She turns down a badly lit street and parks in front of an apartment complex that looks nothing like the tall glass building where he lives. From a distance he watches her walk from her car to the lobby, and a few minutes later a light flicks on in a room on the third storey.

From that window, she must have a view of the highway and not much else. He imagines that her apartment is small and tidy, and smells of air freshener. The walls are painted a pale blue, and they are bare. The kitchen is simple and clean. There are dishes in the dish drainer and no magnets on the fridge. A fluorescent bulb gives off a bright, blue-tinted light.

But despite the apartment's cleanliness, there would be details that prove she is not the kind of woman with whom he would normally associate. The carpet in the hallway lifts in the corners, and the kitchen linoleum has yellowed. He can imagine what Kelly would say about Miranda's place. She would notice unmatched dishtowels, cheap kitchen cabinets, worn carpeting. He can imagine, too, what Kelly would think of this card dealer—when he is honest about her memory, Kelly wasn't always sweet. But if there is an economic disparity between himself and this woman, it's being slowly eroded by his habit. And if there is an emotional disparity, he hasn't seen it yet.

⟋

THE LIFE HE SHARED with Kelly has begun to slip away. The friends they had—mostly other couples—are busy with jobs and young children. His parents live in another province and they call on weekends, but Tom is no good on the phone. Then there's the church where he went each week because Kelly asked him to. He had never been a religious man but had secretly enjoyed the Sunday routine. He liked the readings, the music, the sermons delivered by a good-natured rector. The tea and muffins afterward.

But it wasn't until Kelly was admitted to the hospital that he prayed. It took him a while to get the hang of it. He tried to pray to the God of Light that Kelly favoured, but as her condition worsened, that god satisfied him less and less. The god Tom knew was a darker thing. A murky, underwater god. A god who said, *Sometimes there is light*. A god capable of beauty and cruelty and—Tom prayed for it, every night, on his knees—magic.

⟋

THIS BECOMES THEIR ROUTINE: for fifteen minutes each night they take shelter from the rain and wind, and she performs. She changes aces into kings. She makes a ten-dollar bill disappear, then reappear sticking out of the collar of his shirt. She asks him to kiss a card, and when she shuffles, the card his lips have touched is at the top of the deck. He's seen most of these tricks before, but that doesn't matter. When she performs them, there is nothing of the usual weariness around her eyes. None of the boredom that slackens her features while she works. And nothing of the poker face she wears when they speak. She is full of cunning and joyful underhanded-ness. She is alive.

"How did you do that?" He asks this each night, and each night the answer is the same.

"A magician never reveals her secrets, Tom."

On his part, there is an easy pleasure in being had. And there's something else too. He can recognize bereavement in others now. Miranda was once a performer and he imagines that a life dedicated to this kind of artistry is not always kind. It results in a jackpot or in great loss—nothing in between. Whether a person is rewarded or punished is a matter of luck. He can tell by looking at Miranda's hardened, tired face that her luck has been bad.

So he allows himself to be seduced by her grace, her hands, and what she calls magic. This is his kindness to her. He allows her to be onstage again, to wear a glittering suit and white gloves. He allows her to pull doves from her hat.

THERE IS ANOTHER ROUTINE, and she is ignorant of it. Each night, he waits for her. Sometimes she has to work an hour or two of overtime, and while she does, he sleeps in his car. This is the kind of man he is becoming, the kind who gambles away his earnings and who sleeps in his car. But it doesn't matter, because he likes the sound of her shoes on the pavement, stepping around the puddles. It invariably wakes him up.

He follows her home, squinting through the rain. He stays far behind her, and keeps his lights off. He doesn't mean any harm. He only wants to watch her step out of her car, shut her door, toss the car keys into her purse. He wants to watch her unlock the door to her building and disappear inside. Then he likes to imagine her in the elevator, and inside her apartment. Washing the makeup off her face, climbing into a dark bed, sleeping well.

He has trouble sleeping. When he arrives home, he is often up for an hour, sometimes two. He sits in the dark and watches the aquarium. The convict tang, with its silver body and black bars, skims the rock for food. And the nocturnal flamefish is always up. Its red body is easy to see even in the dark. It is a slow, methodical swimmer. Following its cautious movement is the only thing that eases Tom into sleep. He wakes most mornings on the couch, in front of the aquarium. His body jerks as though he's emerging from a dream, the kind where he is continuously, endlessly sinking.

⁓

THEY SIT OUTSIDE and listen to rain hit the Dumpster.

"What do you do in your other life?" he asks. "When you're not at work?"

"I try to get some sleep. I clean when I have to. I cook."

He imagines she eats her meals the way he takes his: alone, in front of a flickering television. "I'm not much of a cook. It's depressing to eat alone."

"My father used to run a restaurant in Grande Prairie, so I'm happy in the kitchen."

"Grande Prairie? I imagined somewhere more exotic."

"Trust me, Grande Prairie is exotic." She laughs. "My parents wanted me to take over the restaurant and I wanted to be a famous magician. You can imagine how that went over." She rolls him a cigarette of loose tobacco that gets stuck in his teeth—"How's that for exotic?" she asks—and shuffles her cards.

"Let's start over," he says. "Let's get married."

"You're just like my ex-husband. Out of nowhere, Paul would say something hilarious."

"What happened to this husband? Did he die?"

"If only."

"At least tell me your name."

"I've never liked it. My parents heard it on TV and it sounded perfectly North American to them."

"It's Lucy, isn't it? They named you after Lucille Ball?"

"There are ways you could find out." She drops the end of her cigarette to the cement. "Ask any of my co-workers, for example."

"Let's get out of here. I mean it. We could take your show on the road. I'd make a good assistant."

"No, you wouldn't. You're too morose."

"You said it seems like we've known each other for decades. I just want you to tell me your real name."

She smiles, closes her eyes, and massages her neck. Her body leans, slightly, in his direction. She is so close to him that he could reach out and touch her hair. She has forgotten herself for a second, forgotten her desire for distance and privacy. He could wait for this to pass—and it will, quickly. She'll look at her watch and walk away. He knows this because he too knows solitude. He knows its pleasure and its power. He knows it is a home you can occupy, a place where you can watch your pains shimmer around you like a school of fish. It's also a habit, and he knows how entrenched and addictive it becomes. She might hate him if he pulls her out of its dark waters. It would hurt at first. And maybe always.

Still, he reaches out and takes her hand. She lets him hold it for a second, maybe two. Then she slips it from his and checks her watch. "Look at that." She stands to leave. "Time's up."

—

HE LEARNS TO RECOGNIZE the ones who play for money and the ones who play to find God. The first play to win, and they stop once they do. They pick up their chips and they walk out. The other kind of gambler, the kind he is becoming, sinks into the game and disappears. This gambler plays because he loves the rhythm and routine. He loves the moment—a breath—between winning and losing. To be made or broken within seconds. To live or die—the choice made each minute, by luck or some other careless god. He loves the risk, and cares little for the reward. He plays to lose.

—

"WHY DO PEOPLE SEE MAGIC SHOWS?" He asks her this after she has torn a twenty-dollar bill in half and magically restored it. What he really wants to ask is this: Why do people touch each other? Why do they fall in love?

"That's easy," says Miranda. "To escape."

His friends and colleagues would pronounce that word differently, and it's not just the accent, so faint it must be left over from early childhood. *Escape*. Others would emphasize the word with a tone she doesn't use. They would mean a certain kind of irresponsibility. His friends and colleagues would see his actions—gambling, associating with this woman—as irresponsible, dangerous. He's noticed the concerned looks they give him at work. He's noticed the way they avoid him, out of fear or sympathy.

But his time with Miranda is as generous, as religious, as he's ever felt. As she performs what he knows are false shuffles and crimped cards, he is himself, and he is not himself. He is her attentive audience, and he is Miranda the Conjuror. He is the pleasure she takes from her own competence and the joy she feels in revisiting her repertoire. He is the grace that lives in her hands. To let go, to disappear, to forget himself. To exist in another's skin, and then—on the long, dark drive home—to return to himself, with another's knowledge. To escape. It was the only way to live.

———

HER VOICE AS SHE COUNTS OUT his chips. Her laugh, brittle from tobacco and the casino's air. The way she smashes his watch to pieces then restores it to him as good as new. Her hands as they hold the watch in front of his face, a hypnotist's hands. That's what haunts him.

He has heard of men who resign themselves to loneliness and begin to visit whores. He imagines that they often visit the same woman, perhaps every night. They grow fond of the routine. Then they grow fond of the woman.

Inside the casino, Miranda treats him like nothing more than a customer. When he sits at her table, she doesn't look him in the eye or use his name. When she drops cards in front of him, he can almost believe they are strangers. It reminds him of Kelly's last weeks. He had to move her from her bed beside the window to the hospital. There, she was cordoned off from him by tubes and wires and painkillers that made her mind and speech fuzzy.

Only once in those last days did she really look at him. She woke up and he leaned forward and took her hand. She focused on him for one or two seconds and said, "I miss the fish."

So even then, she could surprise him. She'd never liked the aquarium when she was healthy. She used to joke that she only liked the sea star because it matched the throw pillows. But she must have grown fond of it during her illness, when watching the fish was all she had the energy to do.

And now, Tom stares at Miranda as though she were a fish in a tank, beautiful and trapped and not meant to be touched. He tries to stop, for his own sake as well as for hers. He tries, at least, to keep a discreet distance. He often sits at one of the slot machines and watches her, pressing and repressing the button, losing ten cents at a time.

⁓

HE LETS THINGS FALL APART. The condo he shared with Kelly has become chaotic. Dishes pile up on top of the dishwasher, dust lines the electronics, the hardwood is never swept. When he needs to do a load of laundry, he drops clothes into the machine then forgets them. He finds them days later, damp and smelling of mildew.

He smokes inside now, and doesn't care if the smell gets into his clothes or the furniture or the bedsheets. He likes the craving for nicotine that pulses in the back of his neck—a sure sign that he is alive. He smokes when he can't sleep. He smokes in front of the aquarium, and if the fish and corals didn't need fresh oxygen, he wouldn't bother to open the window.

The aquarium. For an entire week he doesn't clean the sides of the tank and the glass becomes sticky with algae. There are other problems: The lights have not been switching on at their regular intervals and he needs to repair the timer. And he hasn't replaced the water, so the salinity has gone up to 1.27.

It is late Saturday night—no, early Sunday morning—when the goby dies. Tom is on his third cigarette when it turns softly, weightlessly, on its side. It is a dark fish with a blue stripe that begins above its eye and continues the length of its body. The second before, it had been eating from the sand bed. Now it floats—the word *leisurely* comes to mind—toward the surface. Its eyes and mouth are open, and its face looks no different than it did in life. It drifts upward, and as it passes another goby, the live one tries to sink tiny, translucent teeth into its flesh.

When it reaches the surface, it bobs there until Tom scoops it out with his bare hand. He should have put the rubber glove on; not to do so is a risky manoeuvre that could contaminate the tank. He has never before behaved so rashly. But he wants to touch the aquarium's water and feel the fish's cool skin against his own.

———

THAT NIGHT, he goes to the casino with flowers: two white orchids that have been dyed blue. She refuses them. She refuses even to look at him. He stands beside her, under flashing lights and surrounded by the slots' din, with the orchids in his hands. "They're just flowers, Miranda. Take them. They'll be dead in a week anyway."

When security arrives, she says, "I don't know this person. He keeps calling me by some other name."

A man who has a phone piece clipped to the side of his head grips Tom's arm and says, "Come on, friend."

So this is the kind of man Tom has become: the kind who is broke, frequents casinos, falls for cold women, and gets dragged to a parking lot by a man who calls him *friend*.

The guard speaks into Tom's ear. "What's your name?"

"Paul."

"Listen, Paul, I'm going to remember your face."

Tom shakes his arm loose from the guy's grip. He drops the flowers on the pavement and walks off into the rain. Is this how she felt in her last moments? This free? This frightened? This far from herself?

HE WAITS IN HIS CAR for her shift to end. The night is cold, and after a couple of hours he has to cover himself with the emergency blanket he keeps in the trunk—a precaution he took when he believed in precautions. Finally, she walks out the casino's door and to her car. Her purse looks heavy on her shoulder, and she moves slowly despite the rain. She must be tired. She has not noticed him. He can tell by her walk that she doesn't believe she has an audience.

She gets into her car and he turns on his own ignition. When she pulls out of the lot, he follows. He doesn't keep his distance. He keeps his headlights on.

She drives for less than five minutes before pulling over onto the highway's shoulder. She cuts her engine, steps out of her car, and stands in the middle of the road. She watches him come toward her as though she doesn't care whether he runs her down or not. He keeps his speed up. His headlights hit her face, but she doesn't look away. Her age shows under those lights, and she looks nothing like a woman who once commanded a stage. He slows, then stops in front of her.

He gets out of his car without turning off the lights or the engine. "I didn't mean to frighten you."

"You didn't. I'm old enough to know who I need to be scared of."

"I just want to talk to you."

"Are you a crazy person? Are you going to kill yourself and blame me for it?"

"I don't think so."

"You're probably going broke." She crosses her arms. "That makes people behave badly."

"I just want to disappear. Can you do that?"

"Don't you ever sleep? Don't you have a job?"

"Please, Miranda."

"It's not that simple. You need props and a rigged stage and dry ice for that kind of thing."

"I just want to know what it feels like."

"Go home." She speaks as though she is used to men like him. "Go home to your wife or whoever buys you those nice clothes."

"My wife is dead."

"Okay." She looks up at the sky then closes her eyes. "I don't care. Do you understand? I don't care, because it's not my job to care."

"Because you're the dealer and I'm the player?"

"Good guess."

"Because you're the performer and I'm the audience."

"Leave me alone, Tom."

"I wasn't joking about the two of us running off together. I wasn't joking about taking your show on the road."

"You want to lose it all?" She smiles the kind of smile she must once have used onstage, before juggling knives. "Some of us don't have that luxury."

"We should escape. We should be brave. You should have seen how brave my wife was."

"I have rent to pay. I have an ex-husband who owes me over four thousand dollars—but maybe that's nothing to you."

"This time we might be lucky."

"I have a son. Okay?" She runs her hands through her dark, wet hair. "And I have to be up in less than five hours to get him to school."

He hadn't imagined a child, another life that filled her own. He looks at her exhausted face and sees, now, how poor his imagination had been.

"I'm sorry," he says. "You should go home." But she doesn't move. He steps closer to her and she doesn't walk away. "Just tell me one thing."

"It's Mabel, all right? My name is Mabel."

"Really? It's cute."

"It's terrible."

"I can see why you don't like it."

She smiles, and he touches the hair that sticks to her forehead. She lets him brush it out of her eyes. He wraps his arms around her shoulders and she allows this. She leans into him, for one second, maybe two.

WHEN HE GETS HOME, he scrapes the algae off the glass. He distills and cools twenty gallons of water, and replenishes the tank. When he sprinkles food onto the water's surface, the convict tang, damselfish, and flamefish swim up to it. Tom presses his palm to the glass and touches the place where, on the other side, the sea star has attached itself. Then he lies on the floor, on the spot where Kelly's bed had been, as though he's beside her. He watches the fish until he falls asleep, and he sleeps until the next afternoon.

That's when he finds the seven of hearts. It's in his wallet, which had been empty before.

t r a c e s

ALL I KNOW OF YOU is in traces: the musky smell of lavender and molasses in the house, his rushed phone calls when he thinks I'm not listening, the look on his face. Maybe if we met, I could explain my situation. *Explain my situation.* As if situations can be folded into the neat boxes of words, as if the word *situation* can define this. Define *this:* you are fucking (fabulous word, perfectly shaped box!) my husband. And for four months, you have occupied my mind, a presence I can't place.

I'm not sure how I know of you so clearly. I sense you in the house, something foreign, spicy, and warm that permeates the hardwood floors, dark walls, leather furniture. And Peter is quiet, though not in the brooding way I'm used to. He is calm and distracted, as though some new, bright thing has caught his attention. The two of us are trying too hard to be ourselves. I shower, paint, take rambling walks; Peter comes home with cheese and bread from the market. His book proceeds. He doesn't discuss it much, doesn't wrestle with it, simply writes. But he no longer watches me paint, and I paint thoughtlessly now, without concern for building a series for a show, or for what galleries might term saleable. I don't even use my oils, just dab recklessly with watercolour.

━━

TONIGHT, APRIL AND I sit on her cedar deck as we do most evenings, sipping her homemade wine from Mason jars. We lounge in her deck chairs, our sketchbooks resting on our crossed legs, and face her backyard. With her Baroque Red and Indian Gold pastels, I draw the sun that drops below the horizon. April plays a chaotic colour game in her sketchbook, and smudges the waxy Terra Rosa, Vermilion, and Prussian Blue with her fingers. I flip my sheet of paper, pick up my black pen, and begin to sketch the broad outlines of her features. It has been months since I attempted a face, though they're my favourite subjects. This book and many others are full of Peter: the dent of his cheeks, lines of his eyes, his slim jaw, the changes of his skin and expression recorded over twenty years. I capture April's long nose in one stroke and say: "I want to paint her." April knows I mean you.

She's the only one with enough balls to talk to me about you. She gathers information, a big friendly dog digging for bones, then runs back to me out of breath, excited, proud. But April knows only certain details. She once saw Peter with a young woman in the Roasting Company—we assume it was you—but she was unable to describe her to any satisfaction. Long red hair, but she couldn't tell if it was thick or thin. A body that was not fat or skinny. A white sweater. April saw you from behind, she said, so she doesn't know your smile, doesn't know your eyes. I have a canvas that sits blank against my kitchen wall, waiting for you. It will be a dark piece, I'm sure, but I can't even begin, because—surprisingly—I can't picture you. I can't see you whole, so I try something simpler (imagine: an ankle, a freckle) and can almost get you in focus. But the images scamper away like the rats that harvest our compost box. Like everyone else, I content myself with rumours.

April stares at my sketch, her hazel eyes following my pen. I stop and flip the page. My hand has fallen back into its abstract college days, and she might be insulted by the harsh black lines.

"I'm not sure if I should tell you this." April leans over the varnished arm of her chair. She gulps wine. "I found out where she lives. I saw her hitchhiking last week in Fulford and I followed, saw where she got dropped off."

I raise my eyebrows, and April takes this as a pat on the head ("What's that you got there, girl? An address? Good girl"), gains confidence, grabs my hand, and pulls me from my chair. My sketchbook falls and I trip down the deck's three steps.

"What if she's home? What if she sees us on her lawn? What if she calls the police?" I pull on April's sleeve as she drags me around her bungalow, toward her matte yellow Tercel. I feel pressure in my chest—the same as when, at thirteen, I stole a sweater from Woolco (lilac, acrylic)—and then we're in the car. "April, this is a bad idea."

"Have some fun, *p'tite*." She backs out of her crooked park job and we swerve onto Vesuvius Bay Road. April was once married to a police officer, and since the divorce papers were filed she drives too fast, drinks too much. We speed along the narrow asphalt past a scattering of houses and the evening glitter of St. Mary Lake.

"I have a good feeling about this," she says. In the back, a bottle of her wine rolls and thuds against our seats.

Within minutes, April and I are at the other end of the island, south, twisting around Reynolds Road. Then she takes a sharp right up a gravel driveway. The yellow Tercel bounces on rough rock. Broom and the arms of pine trees scrape against the car. The driveway seems to twist for miles, and after each corner, when I think we must be close, it's more dusk and trees and gravel. Nerves and drink warm my cheeks as we get nearer to you, your house, and I reach around for the wine bottle, fish the corkscrew from April's glove compartment. A corkscrew: I marvel at her foresight.

We find your place, surprising considering the geography. The island: winding, crumbling roads and mile-long driveways that lead to houses layered in moss. Peter and I are staying in such a house, folded into such moss. We've tucked ourselves away for the summer, like in a bed. Or rather, Peter tucked us in, covered us with leaves like blankets, old man's beard, the falling ash of arbutus, under the guise of *getting away from it all.*

"This is what we've always wanted! Our dream!" Peter said last winter, exclamation points at the ends of all his sentences. For weeks he'd talked about islands and had taken out glossy books on the West Coast from the library. We were standing at our apartment window, eating salami and hot mustard sandwiches, watching snow spit over Toronto high-rises. Peter's hand was on my back, under my grey wool sweater. This was after his first infidelity, a period of desperate, clinging affection between us. I tried to remember if I'd ever given the impression that this—an island that can be driven end to end in half an hour—was my dream. "You'll find new subjects! You'll like it! You'll see." He spoke as though he was thinking of me, not for me. But we are here for Peter: Peter who needs a place to think, Peter who has a book to write.

"This whole thing makes me nervous," I say to April, a last-ditch attempt at responsibility, sobriety. The cork pops. Beyond the pine and fir and cedar, there's finally an open clearing, short, uneven grass spotted with tiny yellow flowers.

We're still hidden by the earth-green shadows of trees that line the driveway. Fifteen feet away is the field you must call your yard, inside that a small fenced-in garden, then the barn-like house, painted a burnt ochre. A blanched wood fence surrounds the field, its boards fallen in most spots. More traces: laundry floating on the line (green drawstring pants, thin white T-shirt), strawberries in the yard, a deck painted Naples Yellow. Behind the garden, the house leans to one side, somehow orange and off-centre, like a rotting and caving pumpkin. The windows have pale blue trim (peeling), the door is white: paint jobs of different qualities, likely reflecting different tenants. Faded plaid curtains float in the windows.

"She shares this place with four others. A commune or something," April says. The car is still running, old and shaky.

"A commune. Of course." We have reason to believe you are about twenty-four, twenty-five. I climb out of the car and take a few steps forward, careful to stay in the cool shadow of forest.

April rolls down the window. "I didn't mean for you to get out, honey, just for us to have a look."

The wine bottle is in my hand.

"What are you going to do, Mimi? Hike around the property?"

I ignore her, take an elegant sip from the bottle, and walk toward the yard. All I can think is: This is where Peter comes to see you. He has parked his car on the flattened grass, walked in without knocking, looked out from those windows. One of those windows is yours. One of those rooms has a bed, a lamp, a bookshelf, whatever else you keep. In the garden I notice a boy, twenty at the oldest, and stop walking. He hasn't seen me, but I'm close enough to watch him pop green beans off their stalks and lay them in a flat basket. He wears a beat-up leather cowboy hat and takes bites from some of the beans, throws others over his shoulder. I can't distinguish much of his features except for dark hair that falls over his eyes in a wavy, undecided way. His arms are muscular but too long and his jeans don't fit right along his legs: too tight at the ankles but nearly slipping off his hip bones.

"She could be here. Behind those curtains." April is beside me, her chin on my shoulder. She left the car running, her door open. "That's probably her roommate. Get back in the car. I shouldn't have brought you here."

The boy finishes picking, then leaves the garden through a wire gate and heads toward the house. Even from this distance, I hear the clump of his boots on the hollow porch, the creak of the screen door as he passes inside.

"Hello? Mimi?" April whispers. "I'm agreeing with you. This was a bad idea."

"I want to see her." I hand April the bottle. For the first time, I feel as though I can picture you: the green pants on the line would fit a woman with narrow hips, though the shirt proves broader shoulders, likely freckled with sun. And I picture your hair the same rust shade as the house, imagine you pedalling down your driveway on the old bicycle that rests against the porch. Your hair flies behind you in a tangle of auburn. Is that how Peter first saw you, on your bicycle? Muscular calves, bare feet. I can picture it.

Then I feel fur rub my sandalled foot: a small white cat scratches at my toes, and I bend to pet its head. He rubs his wet nose into my outstretched hand. "Hey? Hey, who are you?" These days I feel a tipsy affection for anyone who touches me, no matter how accidental. "Look at you, mister. Look at you."

April presses the lukewarm wine bottle to my shoulder and passes it to me. "Apparently she's a cat person."

When I look up, I notice an entire litter. They idle under trees, sleek across the fence, pounce half hidden through grass. Some are white like the one who now obsessively licks the hairs of my arm, but there are a couple of golden tabbies, some greys. Feral, but friendly enough. As they walk, the movement of their bones shows under their coats. Eyes depthless and crystal, amber or sap green.

"Give me a minute." I scoop up the small white cat and walk to the chicken-wired garden. Your garden is nothing like April's. Hers is cluttered with bursts of showy, non-indigenous colour: irises, rhododendrons. Her orchids have won prizes. Your garden is muted greens: peas, beans, herbs, unripe tomatoes, a corner of strawberry plants that shoot out slim legs. I've never had a garden, though Peter and I do keep and name potted plants. Next to these neat rows I feel off balance, useless. I turn back to April and throw the wine bottle behind me, over the deer-proof fence and into the garden. An arc of Shiraz sputters through the air. "Okay. Fuck it. Let's go."

AS I SAID BEFORE, you are not the first. There was that Heather girl: Irish, an exchange student. Peter came home from work one evening and cried into my lap until my black pants were soaked through. He repeated over and over the banal words the girl spoke. She had said, "I admire you," then unbuttoned her coarse blue sweater in his office. I stroked his back and made him tell me everything: how she wore her hair, what she smelled like, the angle of her cheekbones, the shape of her chin and nose. It was how I forgave him.

Months later, I met her at a faculty and grad student party. I shook her hand. She was a quiet girl, with a thick body and still eyes. I've tried to imagine how it felt to be her, the girl, or to be you for that matter, the "other woman." Of course, as Peter would point out, you can only be defined in relation to "the woman." Without me, you disappear.

I MET APRIL the day after Peter and I unpacked our suitcases. She was to be our neighbour. Her acre is next to the stout brown house Peter had arranged to rent for four months, *a place where we can get some quiet*, he called it. He hadn't bargained on the shaky bleats of April's goats, her chickens' chatter, or the lowing of her Jersey, Marilyn. April arrived on our doorstep with a plastic bucket of brown and blue eggs and a zucchini as long as my forearm, though not as skinny. She never goes anywhere without gifts. We have a fridge full of her eggs, their shells like pastel chalk.

I was opening and closing cupboards in the kitchen, to see what plates and pots we'd been provided with, while Peter flipped through the island's weekly fifteen-page newspaper. He read the best headlines aloud to me from our screened deck. "'Garage Sale Draws 200.'" He smoked a cigarette, an occasional habit we both refuse to give up. "Two hundred. Just imagine that."

"Gracious."

Then April, in neon pink flip-flops, slapped her way up our porch steps and stood in front of the screen door. "Hello! Welcome wagon!"

I came out of the kitchen in leggings, one of Peter's collared shirts, bare feet. Peter stared at her but didn't move to the door, didn't say a word.

"Have you been to Vesuvius Beach yet?" April held up her hand, her stretched and faded bathing suit hooked on her thumb. Purple and white flowers. "Warmest on the island!" She pushed open our screen door, stepped onto the deck, and handed me the eggs. She wore a white dress of eyelet lace and a sheer magenta shawl. She is the kind of big woman who believes she can wear anything, and so, miraculously, she can.

I said, "These eggs are blue," and ten minutes later I was seated on the duct-taped upholstery of her car (which we would later name Lemon). As we left Peter behind in the brown house, I remembered to introduce myself: "I'm Mimi. Who are you?"

Now she arrives nearly every morning with cappuccinos she makes herself, and some afternoons we paint together, it doesn't matter what: Fulford's streets, the view from Mount Erskine, or Marilyn, who stands dull and quiet for hours behind April's violet bungalow. For me, a studio painter, this is not the kind of work I do. But for April, art is a social, drunken, unserious business. She goes to the mainland to buy red-sable brushes, scrubs them lovingly with walnut oil, but hardly knows how to use them. When she can scrape together the money, she buys primed canvas like paper, wastes it on first attempts.

April and I spent that first afternoon at Vesuvius Beach. It was May, not warm enough to swim, but we did anyway. She brought a six-pack of frothy, malty beer I'd never heard of, and we plotted to seduce the young sons of tourists once July came. April manages to have a sex life, though we don't discuss it much. And she doesn't know, for example, that Peter and I only make love in the middle of the night, when the room is dark. I wake to his fingers sliding down my arms, then the sex is hard. We grip each other like strangers, hot breath on our faces. Then we fall asleep, my cheek pressed to his wet, bony chest. By morning he's gone, reading the paper or already in the kitchen with April, drinking a cappuccino.

After our trip to Vesuvius Beach, I came home to Peter, who was still on the deck. I rushed up the steps. "We're having dinner at April's."

"So you like it here." Peter had moved on from the newspaper and the Bible was open on his lap.

"The Bible?"

"Research." He uses either too many or two few words. There is no in-between.

"April's that woman I went swimming with. She suggested dinner at her place, since we haven't unpacked yet." I tried to hide that I felt giddy, being the first to make a new acquaintance.

"April? She sounded Québécoise. I wouldn't be surprised if she changed her name from the French."

"She expects us by six. We don't have to knock."

APRIL COULD HANDLE PETER, his initial silences and then, later in the evening, his lectures, his educated anecdotes. She fed us pasta with seared scallops in a dill sauce (dill from the garden, of course) and poured wine into preposterously huge and heavy glasses that she had hand-painted. She told us never to buy blackberries, since she had more than she could eat in a year. Though we didn't know the names she mentioned, she fed us island gossip (apparently, everybody fucks everybody else) and Peter, like any academic, was enraptured by her tales of scandal. April pointed to the clumsy realism on her walls and explained that, though her income came from selling bread at Jana's Bakery and the Saturday market, her real love was painting.

"Painting anything. Walls, houses, canvas, wood. I'm just colourful." She laughed too loudly, and shook her long, grey-streaked hair. Her eyes folded shut in a blissful, childish way, wrinkling her temples.

"I can tell," said Peter, not altogether kindly.

April wore a loose olive tank top that showed her body of contradictions: soft but tanned shoulders, hard, knotted knuckles, and red fingertips. At fifty-three, she is thirteen years older than me but seems younger, bustling. Peter was right: she came from a small town in Quebec, but left at sixteen.

"*Mais je peux encore faire une tourtière fantastique—la recette de ma mère.*" She had a harsh accent that clashed with Peter's Parisian French, one of three languages he knows inside out.

She buzzed about exhibiting her work at a hole-in-the-wall gallery in Fulford, how ferry tourists loved her Island Houses. I told her about Toronto: the agents, grants, shows, reviews. Peter complimented the wine.

"So you're a linguist," April said as we ate tiny dark chocolates from a glass bowl. "If it's not too boring, doctor, tell me about your work."

"It is too boring," he answered, sternly but in good humour, though he rarely spares me from discussion of his latest class, chapter, lecture, or the thoughts that cram themselves into his days. He was, I assume, bored by her.

"Do you sell these?" he asked, and held up his wineglass. "We would love to have a set."

───

WHEN WE RETURNED (overfull) to our small house of unfamiliar smells and furniture, Peter didn't go to the narrow room that would serve as his office. We went to the bedroom and I flicked on the dim bedside lamp.

"I had fun," I said, though I meant it as a question. I wondered if he had enjoyed himself.

"Yes," Peter answered, and sat on the other side of the double bed, a bed much smaller than our own queen-sized. "She has character, I suppose."

I kicked off my sandals and began to unbutton my shirt. "And she's a marvellous cook. Sometimes I wish I could cook—though not often." I was chattering. For the first time in years, in this strange room, his eyes on me felt new. In Toronto, we rarely went to bed at the same hour. Before sleep, I was used to seeing the light of his study shine through the crack in the door.

"You're burnt." Peter touched his finger to my shoulder and I felt a pulse of pain.

"We were at the beach all day." I went to the suitcases we'd left open in the living room and fished for moisturizing cream, tossing clothes and books on the floor. I checked my reflection in the bathroom mirror: my neck and shoulders were splotched red, the skin already puckered white in places.

When I returned to the room, Peter sat me on the bed and slipped the bra strap from my shoulder. "This might sting." He pressed the cool cream onto my skin, gliding his hands along the angles of my back. "I looked over some of my notes today. I outlined the second chapter."

We have discussed that his new book will be a return to his doctoral thesis, but employing more subtle thought, more mature theory. Perhaps, he will argue, naming is not simply a process of organizing the world, of owning the world, or of knowing the world—but of sundering oneself from it. Perhaps, I had said, though I always felt the opposite.

His face was so close I could smell April's wine on his breath. I touched his knee. "Maybe this was a good idea, coming here," I said, and my skin peeled into his hands.

❧

I SCOOP UP THE WHITE CAT and climb back into April's car.

"You're stealing a cat?" April, in her too-dramatic way, sounds shocked, horrified.

"Let's see how the hussy feels when she's the victim." My words are slightly slurred and I'm using April's vocabulary. The cat jumps from seat to seat in the car, smelling the torn upholstery, Kleenex box, crumpled clothes. He is young enough to be totally trusting, the same as I imagine you to be. I rub behind his ears, and his eyes seal shut in a euphoric feline smile. "A husband for a cat. It's a good deal."

April doesn't bother to turn around. She throws the car into reverse and speeds backwards down the long narrow driveway. Her wine has worn off and the adventure is over. We drive back in silence, her car being too old for even a functioning tape deck. When we reach our gravel street, she drops me at the mailboxes.

"So I took a cat. Do you really think that's wrong?"

"Do you love him?"

"The cat?"

"The husband."

I take April's hand. She has told me of her relationships, her brief marriage, and often asks these types of questions, fascinated by the idea of commitment, of prolonged sharing. She points out words that Peter and I pronounce in the same odd way, the sayings we employ, our constant use of "we" even when we are most distant from each other.

"Evidently," I say. I hold April's hand, but I don't know how to explain my marriage to her: lying in bed and hearing the scratch of his pen in the next room, or the daytime routine of coffee, work, my long walks. "I'll show you my books, the sketches I've done of him."

"Yes. Please." April looks out at the purpled sky, the grey horizon. She squeezes my hand and I squeeze back. My new cat digs his claws into my T-shirt as I climb out of the car and push the door shut with my hip.

I walk into the house with the cat nestled in one arm, and Peter sits in the living room, a mug of tea made with April's dried mint leaves beside him. A book open on his lap. I stand in the doorway and imagine how he must see me after so many years: my leggings emphasize my bony hips, my hair hangs limp. You must think this is the time of confrontation, when the wife's jealousy bursts out in unfinished sentences and exclamation marks. The cat licks underneath my chin.

"Sorry I'm late. I was with April. We walked down Price Road, looking for sand dollars." A lie so perfect and poetic I want to wrap it in a tiny blue ribbon. If the study of words has taught Peter—and therefore me—anything, it's the ease of lying. Each word is a sham, a small, meaningless collection of sound that pretends to be what it is not: cat, house, husband. All fops at a costume ball. And everyone accepts this banter as if words, dressed in their masks and cloaks of consonants, were not pretending. We are all complicit, Peter once told me: just by saying good morning to a neighbour, one participates in the great lie. And then, of course, there's the pun on "lying." But maybe you know this.

"Evidently," he says.

"What?" I hold the cat tight to my chest.

"You were with April. You're drunk."

I raise my hand to salute him, his statement suddenly making it true. It occurs to me that perhaps you were at this rented house while I was at yours. But everything is in its right order: the quilt Peter's mother made as a wedding gift, folded on the couch; the empty fireplace, its blackened grate; Peter, in a corduroy chair, a book on his lap, his grey hair combed. And me, in the doorway, in my paint-stained men's shirt. "I'm going to bed."

"Good night."

"Thank you."

I bring the white fluff of a cat to the bedroom with me and place him on Peter's pillow. He circles and smells the bed, then settles next to me, lets me rest my hand on his warm rising-falling stomach.

I drift in and out of sleep and hear Peter brush his teeth. I've spent too long imagining your form drifting through our rooms, and I picture you at our bathroom sink. When Peter comes to bed, I'm hardly sure if it's his weight beside me or yours.

He slides under the covers and I say into the dark, "I stole her cat." As if he knew he was called, the cat crawls over me, his paws sinking into my stomach. Peter doesn't reply, and the cat licks my temple. Then my husband does something: he wraps one arm around my shoulders and pulls me to him, his hand on the back of my head. The cat scrambles and squirms between us.

I speak into Peter, my lips against his collarbone. "Can't you just tell me her name? Can't you just say what she looks like?" Over Peter's shoulder, through our bedroom window, I see the silhouette of the garden we let go to seed, and the huge shared yard where Marilyn grazes. Beyond that, April's lights are on, and I see her outline move outside. She is efficient and domestic even at this hour—picking blackberries. She has changed into the lace dress I first saw her in, a yellowing strap fallen off one shoulder. The white material has a faint green glow in her house lights.

She drops berries into a metal bucket and from where I lie I hear the soft *plink* of each one hitting the bottom. No, of course not. I'm too far away. I imagine the sound. And I imagine April will make a pie, leave it steaming on her windowsill. I imagine, too, in that instant, that she'll feed it to Peter, who still presses the back of my head with his palm, whose smell is familiar, whose heart is against my chest. I understand. I see.

"I suppose it's April." I whisper each word, then hold my breath and watch her glowing dress move outside. The dark outline of her arm reaches for and retreats from the blackberry bushes. I imagine she might invite me over for a piece of pie, or she might not. I suppose I wouldn't mind going, watching her—you—slice perfect triangular pieces. It would be pleasant; it would be summer. What I can't survive is this imagining: tomorrow's afternoon kitchen light, flour on your forearms, Peter's smile as he licks purple from your fingertips.

PETER ASKED ME TO MARRY HIM while we lay on my single bed and chewed black licorice. He was explaining that he believed—truly believed—words could be accurately compared to boxes.

"Ill-made boxes, of course." He was within a year of completing a Ph.D. in linguistics, still entirely thrilled by ideas and their explanations. He spoke too fast through the bedroom's pale cigarette smoke. "Boxes with holes in the bottom, squeaky hinges, a lid that won't close. No meaning ever quite fits inside."

"Ornate boxes," I agreed, partly because I loved when his quick blue eyes lit up. "Gorgeous nonetheless."

We had met on a particularly picturesque day (thick falling snow) in the middle of a Toronto winter of slush and crowded streetcars. Three weeks later, Peter moved into my apartment with four pairs of socks, five boxes of books, and a collection of shirts he buttoned unevenly. He wrote his thesis and I painted sad city landscapes—I was trying very hard, in those days, to be an artist. Peter would sit at a small metal desk, I would spread my canvas and paints on the kitchen floor, and we would work. In the evenings he handed me typewritten pages to proofread. His last chapter. Life was flawless.

"Why don't we get married? Why not now?" The licorice had blackened his teeth, and I ran my hand through his hair. I had been asked this before, by less sober and sillier men, but this time it wasn't funny. As a boyfriend, Peter hounded me: letters in my apartment mailbox, unexpected visits to my art classes, phone calls at midnight. In the first week I knew him, he climbed in my window to leave a miniature rose on the desk, a flower that still reminds him of me. I was twenty to his thirty, and his age and education made him seem foreign, as though he had an accent I couldn't place. He taught me wine, dictionaries; I taught him colour coordination, sparse rooms.

I pressed my thumbs to the small lines beside his eyes and said, "Why not now?"

I PULL MYSELF QUIETLY from Peter's grip and take the riled-up cat with me. I slip on my leggings, my painting shirt. I don't bother with shoes.

"Wait." Peter sits up in bed—I can tell, though it's too dark in the room to see. "Mimi. I've lied. I've broken promises. At least say something." He climbs out of the bed, finds me in the dark, and holds my wrist. "Talk to me. Let me talk."

I slip from his fingers, grab the keys to the cool-grey compact car we rented for our months here (it still smells of air freshener), and leave the room. I know this house well now, and stride through the cramped living room to the door without flicking on the lights. The August nights are getting cooler, and I feel rain held in the air, almost visible, waiting to drop.

I drive back to Reynolds Road, back along the driveway that is now dark. I don't care about the hair scratches from tree needles that Peter will find on the car tomorrow morning. I know he won't ask where I went. He'll forgo work for the day, drive to Stan's to buy a small jar of wax, then spend hours rubbing the car clean.

I drive up to the rusted-orange house, not concerned this time with staying hidden. The porch light is on, and a mosquito coil burns, letting off a blue smoke. The boy I saw earlier sits on a fraying lawn chair, one leg propped on a milk carton. Three cats sit on the porch. I turn off the engine and climb out of the car.

I say, "This is awkward," though I don't feel it. "I stole your cat earlier. I thought it belonged to someone else." I nod to the white fluff that clings to my shirt.

"You can keep her if you want her." The boy is smoking a pipe.

"It's a her? I've been referring to her in the masculine."

The boy nods. Up close he looks older than I thought— twenty-three, twenty-four—and his eyes are calm.

I make a last-ditch attempt at hope. "Does a young woman live here? Red hair?"

He shakes his head no. "Just me and my dad."

"Whose bicycle?"

"Mine." The boy squints, tilts his head. His tobacco smoke smells warm. "Do you want some tea?"

The cat claws at my shirt, nips my ear. "Yes. Please."

He disappears inside for a full five minutes, then emerges with a cracked pot that drips from the bottom. He has a large dish of milk in the other hand, and sets it on the wood planks of the porch. The three cats jump to the dish and bend their elegant heads over it. My white cat squirms, begs me with her eyes, then pushes herself from my arm. The boy pours weak ginger tea into a metal cup for me, none for himself.

Neither of us is very talkative. I sit on the chair and he takes the milk crate, places his now-unlit pipe beside him. His face is already becoming leathered from sun, like the hat he wore earlier. The hairs of his arms are more fair than his skin. His eyes are green, the same glassy shade as my cat's.

"I saw you earlier today, picking beans." For years Peter studied small talk, the words people use when they're thinking very hard about the words they're using, or when they're hardly thinking at all. Peter's informal conclusion, the philosophy this work built into his life, was that all talk is unfinished, inexpressive, small.

"I saw you too. Your wine bottle." The boy smiles, wider and more openly than before. He leans toward me, his elbows on his knees. Other cats have moved quietly onto the deck, and they brush up against his calves, leave fur on his jeans. I can see why they like him. "Did you name her?"

"Who? The cat? No."

Again the smile. His forearms' long muscles move under his skin and his hands are callused and scraped. I sip the tea, still too hot, then lean toward the boy and kiss his smile, his lips, a kiss that takes only seconds. He doesn't move, doesn't reach to touch me, just kisses back, adept and slow. I imagine the summer he's had, the work and the romances. My cat paws my bare ankles. This kiss surprises me. It doesn't feel like revenge.

The boy flips hair from his eyes, and I know I'll never tell Peter of this moment. And he will never tell me of his time with you. I imagine waking tomorrow morning beside my husband—no cappuccinos. I'll curl up in the kitchen and flip through my sketchbook to see page after page of Peter, and, on the final sheet, you in ink. The last summer sun will stream into the kitchen, and I'll sit in a pool of it on the floor, my canvas in front of me. I'll open my tubes of oil, dip my liner brush.

And Peter will sit at the kitchen table, mesmerized by brush strokes. When he stands and slips out the door, he won't have to tell me he's gone to see you. To say goodbye to you. He'll come back bewildered, as if he never imagined consequence. I too will visit you and listen to your brief, nervous chatter. Then hand you an unfinished, unflattering sketch in ink. At night, Peter won't talk. He'll reach across the cold bedsheets and hold my tired hand.

The boy fingers a wisp of my hair and tucks it behind my ear. After a few quiet minutes, I hand him the hot metal cup and stand. He walks me to my car, opens the door, and the cat follows, leaps in. Tomorrow I will paint this: the boy's tan, mouth, tangled hair. Before leaving, I ask his name.

this other us

THE THREE OF US lived together for six years, in a two-bedroom suite on the bottom floor of an old house. We had a deck, a compost bin, and a herb garden we neglected. Like most young people in that coastal town, we rode our bikes everywhere, ate tofu, and went to bed early. We had two cats, many shared appliances, and we'd forgotten whose dishes were whose. We never kept track of who paid the biggest share of the hydro bill—it all evened out in the end, we decided—or who had cleaned the bathroom last. In fact, we hardly cleaned at all. We were used to each other's unruliness.

We also had routines that we shared. On Thursdays, Lawrence would bring home a Polanski or a Kubrick and we'd have a movie night with popcorn and vodka sevens. Karen had travelled for a year in India, so sometimes she'd get dressed up in a sari and cook curry in a big pot on the stove. She used whatever was in the fridge and every spice in the cupboard. It didn't always taste great, but

Lawrence and I loved her so much that we ate it anyway. For days we'd eat it for breakfast, lunch, and dinner, so the three of us even shared digestion problems.

Sometimes we'd have friends over, or Karen and Lawrence would try to set me up with a boyfriend. But for most of those six years, it was just the three of us. It was as though we were all married to one another. Except that only two of us slept together. One of us—that one was me—slept alone.

—

WE'D MET BECAUSE we'd all studied impractical things at the small university that was just outside of town. Karen had studied conceptual art, Lawrence political science, and I'd studied comparative lit. We continued to live together after we graduated, and into our mid-twenties—a time of anxiety and self-indulgence and poverty. Karen worked at the M•A•C makeup counter in the mall, Lawrence worked for Blockbuster, and I got casual hours at the library. None of us knew what we wanted to do with our lives. We only knew that we didn't want to return to the big eastern cities where we'd been raised—places where the air was not as clean and the weather not as warm. We considered our little suite home, and we considered one another family.

It's hard to explain what a perfect match we were, just like it's hard to explain what makes you love your boyfriend or your girlfriend. We were so different that people often said they couldn't believe we managed to get along at all. Karen wore fake eyelashes that made her green eyes look as perfect as the kind of doll's eyes that roll shut when you tip the toy backwards. She accentuated her nose with a gold ring, and her heart-shaped mouth with perfectly applied lipstick. She had red hair that she dyed even redder, and she looked improbable. Her skin was improbably pale and her hair was improbably red and she was improbably tall. She was the kind of person you never forget and you never get over.

Lawrence was one of those slouchy urban guys who wears tight jeans and witty, used T-shirts. He was skinny in an intellectual way, his 140-pound body a protest against conventional forms of masculinity like manual labour, going to the gym, and eating steak. His hair hung in his eyes, his jeans were frayed, and his sneakers were falling apart. He liked to watch cult movies and read the newspaper and take long naps in the afternoon. He was a hipster who was probably meant to become an instructor in a small-town college somewhere. If I were to imagine his future—though I've learned not to make predictions anymore—I would guess that he'd eventually trade the ironic T-shirts for sweaters and corduroys and unkempt, receding hair.

If you were in a room with the three of us, I would be the last person you'd notice. You might notice our cats, Percy and Beau, before you noticed me. I was almost a foot shorter than Karen, and I had dull brown hair. It brushed the tops of my ears in a style someone's kid sister might have. I wore flowing skirts and blouses because I was not proud of my body. It was—it is—scrawny and flat-chested. Sometimes generous people would say that I had a dancer's body, but I'd never been able to dance. And I didn't like to look in the mirror because, when I did, it seemed that all my features—my eyes, nose, mouth—were of one nondescript colour.

But somehow, we were all happy together. At least, two of us were.

I HAD PREPARED MYSELF for something bad to happen, because I'm the kind of person who thinks ahead. I'd imagined that, one day, Lawrence and Karen would sit me down and tell me that they were engaged or they were pregnant, and they wanted to live alone, as adults, as two people in love. I had never been in love, so I didn't know much about love's progression. I thought it might increase, grow until it got so big that there wasn't room for it and me in one house.

I was not prepared for what actually happened. I was not prepared to come home from work one afternoon and see, parked in front of the house, a pickup truck with the words *Revolution Now!* spray-painted across the back. I was not prepared to find Karen and Lawrence and the owner of the truck—a big guy with a goatee and a polite smile—in Karen and Lawrence's bedroom. I was certainly not prepared to see Karen shoving clothes into a backpack as Lawrence watched, and as the *Revolution Now!* guy scratched Percy behind the ear.

"Hey," I said. "What's up?"

Karen looked at me. "Oh god. Oh god, Lise, I'm sorry."

I picked up Beau. He was fat and cross-eyed and the best thing to hold on to when there was a crisis. The cat and I stood in the bedroom doorway and watched Karen grab things from the closet—a pair of flip-flops, a handful of underwear—and stuff them into the backpack. I held Beau so tight that he started to squirm and dig his claws into my arm, but I didn't let him go.

Karen also took her pillow and her sketchbook, and she held up a T-shirt that said *I am a sports fan.* "This is mine, right?" She was asking Lawrence, because sometimes they shared clothes. I guess sometimes they forgot whose was whose.

"I don't know." Lawrence said this so quietly that I hardly heard him. "I don't remember."

Karen looked at him and blinked. "I'm pretty sure it is." Then she put the T-shirt in the backpack and said, "Okay, babe, let's go." This time she was not talking to Lawrence. She was talking to the other guy, the *Revolution Now!* guy.

The two of them walked out of the house while Lawrence and I stared after them. We heard Karen kick the door shut with her boot, and we heard their steps on the deck. Then we didn't hear their steps anymore. We didn't hear anything. Then it was just me, Lawrence, Percy, and Beau, who had scratched me so deep that I was bleeding.

THAT FIRST WEEK after Karen left, Lawrence and I were sure she'd come back. We said, "She probably just went to Seattle to go shopping." We said, "She'll come in here dressed like Rita Hayworth and holding Chinese takeout and it'll be hilarious."

Because she had done hilarious things before. She had once come home holding a gigantic white wedding cake with the words *Happy Common-law!* written across it in pink icing. This was to celebrate the second anniversary of when we'd all moved in together. And she had once found an old electric guitar on the road, had it repaired, and learned to play a very fast, very rock-and-roll version of "Puff the Magic Dragon." She and I had also shared a secret love of Rod Stewart. When Lawrence was out, Karen would take her boyfriend's artsy CDs out of the stereo, put on Rod Stewart's greatest hits, and say, "Take that, Radiohead! Fuck you, Mercury Rev!" Then we'd dance in the kitchen to "Tonight's the Night" and "Da Ya Think I'm Sexy?"

Karen was the only person I'd ever allowed to see me dance. Sometimes she'd take my hand and spin me, and I'd twirl through the kitchen without worrying about how dumb I looked, or that I might kick over the cat-food dish. When Karen danced with me, I felt like myself, or like the self I wished I could be.

And almost every day, I'd come home from work to find her wearing something outrageous—she might be dressed as a goth Barbie or a sad clown. She had all these M•A•C samples that she was allowed to take home—lipsticks and foundations and eyeshadows—and each day she looked like a different person. It was as though there were a lot of Karens living inside her body. In a way, it scared me.

It didn't scare Lawrence. When Karen dressed up, he would say, "You look great, sweet pea." Then he would take her hand and they'd go into their bedroom and I would have to turn up my music.

⁓

THE SECOND WEEK AFTER KAREN LEFT, Lawrence and I didn't go in to work. He told the manager at Blockbuster that he'd had a family emergency and I faked a scratchy voice and told the librarians that I had laryngitis. Then we spent the whole week in our pyjamas. We ordered pizza, drank all the beer in the fridge, and smoked hash from an old, sticky Sprite can. We let the cats crawl all over us, we didn't shower, and we didn't smell very good.

THE THIRD WEEK, we did go to work because we realized that there were now only two of us to pay this month's bills. We picked up as many extra shifts as we could and we ate canned beans or Ichiban noodles for dinner. We didn't have enough money to go out, so we spent every night at home, watching *Seinfeld* on DVD.

Once, during the Bizarro-world episode, Lawrence started to cry. I had never seen Lawrence cry before, but I remembered that Karen said he sometimes did.

"At least you know you'll be okay." He wiped his eyes and nose on his sleeve. "At least you were just the roommate. I thought I was going to marry her."

I knew this wasn't true. I was not okay. I wasn't good at making friends, so even if such a thing existed, I wouldn't be able to go out and find a Karen-replacement. My heart was broken, like Rod Stewart's when he sings "I Don't Wanna Talk About It." And like Rod, I didn't want to talk about it, so I didn't say any of this. Instead, I said, "If Elaine left—I mean, just up and walked out— what would Jerry do?"

Lawrence did that thing where you start to laugh even as you're crying. "'What Would Jerry Do?'" he said. "That would make a great T-shirt."

But then, as the credits were rolling, he said, "He would kill himself." He said this as quietly as he'd said *I don't know* when Karen asked him about the sports-fan shirt. Then he said it again: "Jerry would kill himself."

Of course, Jerry wouldn't. But still, I took the Advil and Sinutab and Gravol out of the bathroom, and all the knives except for the dull one out of the kitchen drawer, and I hid everything under my bed.

———

KAREN WAS GONE FOR WEEKS. She was gone for months. She was gone so long that it started to seem like she'd never lived there at all. The stuff she'd left behind—the clothes and half-used tubes of lipstick—started to seem like it'd been forgotten by some previous tenant whom we'd never met. Her stuff seemed like it was up for grabs, so I began to wear her weird architectural shirts and her vintage skirts and her wool hats. I didn't fill them out properly, but they made me feel like a different, glamorous person. And I only wore them around the house, and only when Lawrence was out. That is, until one Tuesday he got off work early and came home to find me in a pair of Karen's purple tights, a long shirt Karen used to wear with a belt, and Karen's little beret. Lawrence stood in the doorway and let his eyes travel up and down my body. I was so ashamed that I couldn't move. I couldn't even make a joke out of it. I felt like a man who'd been caught trying on his wife's underwear.

Lawrence said, "You look hot, Lise."

No one had ever said that to me before. People had told me, "You look pretty today." Or, "But you're so cute." Or, "Nice shirt." But no one had ever used a word like *hot*. So I started wearing Karen's stuff more often. Just around the house at first, then on the occasional errand, then to work. I hemmed the skirts and pants that were too long for me, and I wore extra socks so I could fit into Karen's tall boots. I even started to wear her pyjamas and her lacy bras. And in secret, I would lock myself in the bathroom and apply her makeup: the iridescent pressed powder, the Pleasureful blush, the Cinnamon brow finisher. That's what I was doing one evening when Lawrence knocked on the bathroom door.

"Lise, can I come in?"

We were the kind of roommates who were so used to each other that we could pee with the other person in the room. We could shower—the curtain was not transparent—while the other person was brushing his or her teeth. So when I said, "No," Lawrence was understandably annoyed.

"What? Are you popping a zit in there or something?"

"No. I'm tweezing my private part."

"Stop being weird, okay, Lise. I need to take a piss."

I had lined my eyes with Karen's black Liquidlast liner and brushed on the Sweet Lust shadow. I had used a concealer under my eyes and, most importantly—most sacrilegiously—I'd put on Karen's Lady Danger lipstick. This was her favourite colour—a bright, deep red. Wearing her clothes was one thing, but I knew this was too much, this was too far. When I opened the bathroom door and Lawrence saw me, he looked like he'd been smacked in the face.

"I'm sorry," I said. "I was just goofing around." I took some toilet paper and started rubbing the lipstick off. It looked like blood on the paper.

"Stop it," said Lawrence.

I kept slapping at my mouth with the toilet paper, but no matter how much I rubbed, there was still a stain on my lips. I thought of when I'd visited Karen at work and heard her use her salesperson's voice. *It's such a great colour on you, and this product is very long-lasting.*

"Stop it." Lawrence put his hands on my shoulders. "Please."

Then he turned me around to face him. It was weird to have him touch me—we'd only ever touched when Karen was around, when we gave each other group hugs. His hands made my shoulders feel tingly, and I only let them stay there because I was wearing the makeup. With all this stuff on my face, I felt like a different person. And this person, this other me, was not afraid to be touched.

Lawrence picked up the Lady Danger lipstick and looked at it. It had been worn down to a stub and I wondered how Karen was managing to live without it. Then I wondered if maybe she wasn't. For the first time, it occurred to me that maybe Karen was dead. Or rather, it occurred to me that maybe I could act like she was.

This thought must have occurred to Lawrence too, because he said, "Stand still." Then he held my face with one awkward male hand and held the tube of Lady Danger with the other. Slowly, gently, he reapplied it to my lips. He didn't do a good job, and we both laughed when we looked at me in the mirror. But that didn't matter. We both knew the lipstick would get smudged anyway. He took my hand and led me to their—his—bedroom. That first time, and every other time, we didn't bother to take Karen's clothes off my body.

———

MONTHS PASSED, and I stopped wearing any of my own clothing, using my own meagre hair and beauty products, or sleeping in my own room. I couldn't even stand to look at my old, single bed. So I went to a garage sale and bought a set of vintage wooden chairs and a lace tablecloth. Then I pulled my bed out from the wall, covered it with the tablecloth, and arranged the chairs around it.

"Now we have a dining room," I said to Lawrence. "Now we can have dinner parties."

We put candle holders in the centre of the mattress and came up with an imaginary guest list for our first dinner party. This list included, but was not limited to: David Lynch, Frida Kahlo, Lord Byron, John Wilmot, and Jane Jacobs.

We talked about these dinner parties while we lay in bed—our bed—and I rested my cheek on Lawrence's chest. I was used to his smell now, and the taste of his skin, and the way one of his ribs dug into the side of my head. I was not only used to these things—I liked them. I liked them so much that I thought about them all the time. As I shelved books for eight hours every day, I thought about Lawrence's body and his laugh and the way air whistled through his nostrils very quietly while he slept.

It was while we lay in bed and talked about whether Van Gogh would accept our dinner invitation that I said, "It's better now. It makes more sense. Two rooms, two cats, two people."

"For sure," said Lawrence, and he reached his hand under the pink negligee I'd found at the back of Karen's old closet. "For sure it does, sweet pea."

───

I'M NOT SAYING there weren't things that bothered me. I didn't like to come home and find Lawrence listening to "The First Cut Is the Deepest," and not just because of the song's implications. Karen and I had loved Rod Stewart. He'd been our thing, our guy, and I didn't want to share him with Lawrence.

One other thing that bothered me was this: Lawrence never told his family that Karen had left. He said he didn't want to worry them. So when his parents phoned, he'd say, "Yeah, Mom, everything's fine. Same old, same old." He said that while he was beside me on the couch, his hand resting on my leg. I sat completely still and completely silent, even though I'd started to cry. This was something I had always known how to do: I could cry without making any noise. My eyes would form only a few tears, and these could be blinked back before my liner got smeared.

"Yup, Karen's fine," Lawrence would say. "She says hi."

But Karen had not said hi. And I had not said hi, even though I wanted to. I wanted to get on the phone the way Karen used to. I wanted to say, the way Karen used to, "Hey, Mrs. T. How are ya?"

Also, I was getting sick of Karen's clothes. None of her shirts fit right, I didn't like walking to work in high heels, and I felt a little stupid in all that makeup. But I'd noticed that when I wore my own clothes—things that seemed so soft and girlish now—Lawrence's eyes passed over me as though I wasn't really there. If I wore my own flowing skirt or my own argyle sweater, at night Lawrence would run his hands through his hair and say, "I'm wrecked. Today's shift was hell." Then he'd go into the bedroom and fall asleep before I'd even had time to floss.

That wasn't all. Things got worse that winter, and maybe winter was to blame. Those coastal Januarys are awful in their mild way: there's no sun, there's always rain, and the mould along the windowsills really starts to assert itself. Maybe that's why Lawrence started to act funny. He called in sick to work so many times that his manager had to talk to him. He never did dishes or picked his dirty laundry up off the floor. I had to work so much at the library to make up for his lost shifts that I didn't have time to clean either, so our place went from being pleasantly disordered to plain disgusting. He had no desire to see any of our friends, and he didn't care about our dinner party anymore. When I suggested that we add Leonard Cohen to the list, he said, "Who cares? Who cares about a stupid fantasy?"

And once, I came home from work to find him at his computer in only a pair of boxers and unzipped jeans, scrolling through pictures of models on the M•A•C website. He was looking at the Fall/Winter Trends, jerking off to girls with sculpted eyebrows and glossy, open mouths. He was so captivated by those Perfect Pouts that he didn't hear me come in.

"Lawrence," I said.

"Hold on." He didn't even look at me. He wanted to finish. So I took off one of the stilettos I was wearing and threw it at him. The heel caught the side of his head and he jumped up, tucked himself back into his jeans, pressed one hand to his temple. "What the fuck? What's your problem?"

"My problem? My problem is that we have bills to pay! My problem is that we have dishes to do!"

I'd never screamed at anyone before. I'd never even raised my voice. It felt even newer and stranger and better than sex.

"My problem is that I'm the one who does everything around here!" I took off the other shoe and threw it, but he managed to duck. "Do you think it's easy? Do you think I like looking like this?" I tore off a set of fake eyelashes, dropped it, and ground it into the carpet with my toe. "It's like I'm ripping off a layer of my own skin, Lawrence. Every single day I'm ripping off a layer of my own skin."

This was true and it was also not true. There was part of me that loved looking the way I looked, loved wearing those clothes and those eyelashes. But there was another version of me who couldn't breathe under all that foundation. This was the me that was screaming. The me that was crying so hard she could barely breathe. This me didn't give a shit about her eyeliner.

"I wish you had killed yourself." That wasn't true, but I liked saying it. "I wish you'd killed yourself the way Jerry would have."

Lawrence didn't say anything. He just slid his jeans down—he hadn't had a chance to zip them up—and kicked them off his feet. He did the same with his boxers: dropped them down his legs and left them on the floor. He wants to fuck, I thought, and I hoped he would spontaneously combust.

But then I realized this was the first time I'd seen him without anything on. He slept in underwear and a T-shirt and that's what I was used to. It was the first time one of us had been in front of the other entirely naked. He stood there, slouched and quiet, and let me look at all the flaws of his body, all the things makeup could never hide: patches of uneven hair on his abdomen, arms that were too skinny, feet that were too big, and that stupid-looking thing between his legs.

"I'm sorry," he said.

Then he bent and picked up a pair of tights I'd left on the floor. They were red, and Karen used to wear them with flats, an A-line skirt, and her beret. Lawrence put them on and pulled them up along his calves, over his thighs, above his hips. He was about the same height as Karen, so they fit him better than they fit me.

Then he slipped on the shoes I'd thrown at him, placing one red foot in, then the other. They were too small for him, and he looked pained and wobbly in them. He looked idiotic in the whole getup. He looked like a pale, straight man in drag. A pale, straight man in drag who missed his girlfriend. "Lise," he said. This was the first time in months he'd used my name. "Lise, I'm sorry."

And he might have said other things too—other sweet, kind things—but I interrupted him. I walked up, stood on my tiptoes, and pressed my mouth against his so hard that I thought our teeth would crack.

THINGS GOT BETTER AFTER THAT. Spring arrived, the rain was replaced by sunshine and cherry blossoms, and we scrubbed the mouldy windowsills with bleach. Lawrence got fired from Blockbuster, but that turned out great because then he got a job at the independent video store. This video store was beside a farmers' market, and he would bring home something delicious every day—heirloom tomatoes or goat cheese or local pears. I gained a bit of weight, but Lawrence said he liked that, and it meant that I was beginning to fill out Karen's clothes. In fact, I didn't even consider them Karen's clothes anymore. They had been worn against my skin so often that they even smelled of me.

And I think Lawrence felt the same way about me as I felt about him. Sometimes he woke me in the middle of the night, gripped me in his sweaty arms, and asked, "You aren't going to leave me, are you, Lise? Promise?"

Of course, I promised. I had spent six years on the outside, excluded from this kind of love, so I knew I would never leave. Especially because I couldn't foresee any serious problems for this new, other us. I knew that Karen would eventually come back for her stuff, but I imagined that Lawrence and I would greet her together. I imagined that we'd hold hands, invite her in, and seat her at my old bed. "This is our dinner table," we'd say. "This is our life."

I was not prepared for what actually happened. I was not prepared when I came home from work one evening and saw Lawrence and Karen in the kitchen, drinking Slurpees.

"Holy shit," said Karen when she saw me. "Great outfit!"

I was wearing my own denim shorts with her green velour blazer and her ankle-high boots. I was also holding two bags of groceries. Inside these bags there was enough pasta, eggs, tofu, apples, and canned cat food to last two people and two cats for exactly one week.

Karen came over and hugged me. I didn't hug her back because I was holding the groceries and because I couldn't breathe. She said, "I missed you guys so much."

"Karen called from the ferry," said Lawrence. "She asked if I could pick her up."

Then he gave me a look. I don't know what that look communicated. It might have been apology. It might have been collusion. He might have been begging me to keep my mouth shut.

Then I noticed that the living room was full of wooden chairs. So he had dismantled the dining room and turned it back into a— my—bedroom. He must have taken the chairs out, pushed the bed against the wall, and thrown the tablecloth in the garbage.

"Where's *Revolution Now!* guy?" I said.

"What?" Karen tugged at the sleeves of the blazer. "This is a bit big on you."

She was wearing a layered skirt, a tank top, and a fake red flower in her hair. She must have stepped off the ferry like that—looking like the hottest, most badass flamenco dancer in the world. Lawrence must have forgotten all about me. Karen looked so great that even I wanted to make out with her. She looked so great that I wanted to cry.

"I know." I looked down at myself—my narrow hips, bony knees, all the evidence that I was still the old me. "Nothing fits right."

Then I did cry. I dropped both grocery bags, not caring if I broke the eggs or bruised the apples, and Karen said, "Oh, no—your mascara."

Lawrence obviously hadn't told her anything, and that's why she put her arms around me. She held me, pressed her cold Slurpee cup against my back, and I cried into her improbably red hair.

"It's okay," said Karen. "It's okay, Lise."

And the way she said that made me think that maybe Lawrence had told her. Maybe he'd told her everything. And maybe she wasn't upset about it. She saw it as something that could be fixed or painted over. *It's okay*. She'd said it with confidence—confidence in herself, in her ability to make everyone in the room feel happy and lucky, her ability to bring beauty to life.

"I'm back now," she said.

Then Lawrence came up and put his arms around us both, and it was just like before. Except better, because Karen held me the way Lawrence never had. And I stopped crying so ostentatiously, so passionately. Instead, my tears came out in that small, silent way. I could hear Percy, or maybe it was Beau, batting one of the fallen cans of cat food around on the floor. And when Karen said, "Everything's going to be okay," I thought maybe she was right.

the fiancée

WHEN PENNY STUMBLES OFF THE TRAIN, she has the drunk look of someone who's spent too long absorbed in a book. For three days she travelled from Montreal to Calgary, reading *Madame Bovary*. Not that she'll be allowed to teach nineteenth-century books, or any books at all, since Calgary's university is too small to offer those kinds of courses. She has come to teach grammar and pronunciation to students who don't speak a word of French.

She carries a green, hard-sided suitcase, the same one her mother took to Paris. She insisted on minimalism before she left, partly to impress Andrew with her socialist packing skills.

He stood in her bedroom and watched her fold cardigans into the suitcase. "Why do you have to go?"

"It's only for a year."

"It doesn't make sense, Penny. West of Kenora, the world ends."

"The world doesn't end." She nudged his leg with her foot, tried to catch him on the spot that tickled. "It just gets flatter."

Penny feels as lost as her mother must have felt during her first days in Paris. She watches the train pull away; it will continue to Vancouver, a place she never before bothered to imagine. A sign tells her she's on Ninth Avenue, in front of the Palliser Hotel. The few passengers who got off with her have been picked up by relatives or friends and are driving away along the grid of downtown roads. Under the bright sun, the cars have a dreamy quality as they cross the tracks and swerve into the quiet heart of the city. There's a thinness to the air here, a dry heat that makes Penny's skin itch and will probably give her nosebleeds. She smells dust, or maybe pollen. She sneezes twice, and no one takes any notice.

⌒

THE FIRST TIME Penny was engaged, she and her fiancé were ten years old. His name was Adam—appropriate, she now thinks, considering the purity of their romance.

Their engagement lasted an afternoon, when they folded wedding invitations out of paper torn from their spellers. Penny's best friend, Donna, performed the ceremony behind the school. It was winter in Montreal, and snow soaked through the leather of their shoes. The bride and groom exchanged mittens instead of rings.

But the next day, Penny went to hold Adam's hand and he skipped away from her.

"I've enlisted," he said. This was during the last year of the Second World War, and the schoolyard games centred on imagined battles and deaths. "You'll never see me again."

Penny ran home, burst through the door, and threw herself against her mother's legs. Katherine was reading on the couch, the unfolded laundry in a pile beside her. She bent the corner of her page down. "What are you crying for?"

When Penny explained, her mother said, "Is that all?" Then Katherine lifted Penny into her thin, ballet-trained arms. "Hush, now." She held her daughter, stroked her hair, and Penny smelled cigarettes and lilac soap on her skin. "You'll meet plenty of Adams. The choosing will be the hard part."

———

PENNY STAYS AT THE EXPEDITION MOTOR HOTEL, and her room is directly above the motel's sign. It advertises *Great Monthly Rates!* under a picture of a camel with lewd-looking humps. In the distance are snow-capped mountains and the river she can barely glimpse from her window. All around her is dust and desert heat that rises from the pavement.

The motel's other guests are young men from places with incredible names like Carstairs and Medicine Hat. Some are in town on business, some for rodeo, and none can comprehend that she is a woman travelling on her own.

"So you came here by yourself?" they ask over and over. "Where're you from again?" They strain like they can't quite hear her, or as though she speaks with a difficult accent.

Only one of them says, "Montreal. I've been there. Nice

place." He is as young as the others, tall, and with the broad, innocent face of someone raised in the country. He wears a suit, carries a briefcase, and looks like a boy wearing his father's clothing. They stand in the hotel lobby and he leans against a wall covered with photos of men on horses, the brims of their hats throwing shadow over their eyes.

"You know Montreal?" Penny craves a memory of home, hers or someone else's. "When were you there? For how long?"

"A few days." He has an accent Penny can't place: British, but with a rollicking, rhythmical quality she's never heard before. "Enough to see it was a fine old place. Which isn't my kind of place."

He smiles, and this is the first time in days someone has looked at Penny warmly, not in the guarded way of strangers. He invites her to join him at Phil's Pancake House. "It's terrible. But you're welcome to dine with me."

"Pancakes for dinner?" Penny has been living off sweet-and-sour pork from the Silver Dragon, the only decent restaurant she's found in the city. "I can't."

"You have stomach problems?"

"I'm engaged."

"Good for you." He holds out his hand. "I'm David."

———

A MONTH BEFORE LEAVING MONTREAL, Penny stood with Andrew in an empty apartment on Craig Street. They were looking for a place to rent, a place that would be their own once they married. Without meaning to, they seemed only to consider apartments in their neighbourhood. This place—part of a crumbling Victorian row, with a bay window and two dim bedrooms—had exactly the same layout as the one Andrew grew up in.

"This could be the study," he said. "We could set up two desks, side by side."

Penny smiled, because fiancées were supposed to be happy. She was supposed to look forward to her quiet, studious life with Andrew. She would write her thesis and he would finish his studies. They would listen to classical music; he likes Shostakovich, she Berlioz. They would read to each other in bed.

"We can paint the walls any colour we want," Andrew said. "Or hang pictures."

But Penny was thinking of Andrew's mother—her anxious voice, wool skirts, the cuffs of her blouses that she scrubbed each evening so they stayed white. And her own mother, who still wore her old silk dresses and sweaters with pearl buttons. Penny and Donna had laughed mercilessly at their mothers, had believed their own lives would be different.

"I've been offered a job," she said. "As a French teacher—a professor."

"Our own kitchen, Penny." Andrew gestured grandly at the grimy counters and oil-splattered walls.

"The pay is good. But I'd have to move away. To Alberta."

"The windows face south, so we'll get good light."

"It's a year-long contract. It would only be for a year."

"And look at this." Andrew turned the sink's faucets—first the hot, then the cold. "A kitchen sink, Penny. Our own kitchen sink."

PHIL'S SERVES BREAKFAST ALL DAY, so she orders the Cowboy Two-Step: two pancakes, two slices of bacon, two eggs any style. When the plate arrives, she says, "My mother would disown me if she saw me eating like this."

"That's the purpose of parents," says David. "To disapprove of what you do, so you can enjoy doing it."

He tells her he's from Wales and moved to Canada three years ago.

"I'm over a foot taller than anyone in my family," he says between bites of an omelette. "It was how I knew I didn't belong at home. I looked an imposter. Everyone in Swansea called me Dai Tall."

He tells Penny that his mother hoped he'd become a preacher—a tall man commands authority, she'd said—but the Church wasn't for him. Now he's in real estate: he buys houses, fixes them up, resells them. He has property in Mount Royal and Sunnyside, and is thinking of getting into development. He can't be more than a couple of years older than Penny, but she guesses he'll soon be wealthier than anyone she knows in Montreal.

"I can't keep up with business," he says. "The oil in Leduc helps."

"You own houses and you live in that motel?"

"It's easier—I don't have to worry about furniture. I can pick up and go any time."

His foreignness is obvious: he orders tea, not coffee, and is disappointed when the waitress doesn't scald the cup. But other than that, he's pure Alberta: capitalist, inventive, decisive. Next election, he tells her, he'll vote Social Credit.

Penny thinks of the earnest disapproval Andrew would show him. But David—he tells her to call him Dai—has a musical quality to his voice, and she loves it. He reminds her of a song-and-dance man, an entertainer, someone who tells lies for a living. She feels the way she did as a child, mesmerized by her mother's French.

"She thinks I'm crazy. She keeps writing and telling me to come home," he says of his own mother. "She lives in a tiny stone cottage in Llan. It doesn't have heat and the roof leaks." He eats quickly, as though he's got somewhere to go. "I tell her that, out here, if there were houses that old"—he finishes his eggs and pushes his plate away—"we'd just tear them down."

PENNY HADN'T KNOWN ABOUT her second engagement. When she was fourteen, a boy joined her class in the middle of the year. He was from Boston, and had been sent to Canada to stay with an aunt after his mother died. He was a shy, absent boy who always seemed to be falling ill.

Katherine insisted on having him over for dinner. She prepared a roast chicken, one of the only times she managed much beyond sardines on toast. During the meal she pressed the boy to talk about Boston. He couldn't tell her much, but Katherine gushed over the details he gave about the weather and the street where he lived.

"It sounds divine," she said. "Doesn't it sound divine, Paul?"

Penny's father didn't answer. He hunched over his plate and ate quickly, as though he'd been starving. His napkin was tucked into his shirt, his tie flipped over one shoulder.

"You don't need to eat so fast," said Katherine. "We have a guest. A foreign guest."

Paul looked at the boy and nodded, then returned to eating.

Penny and this boy said nothing to each other, which was about as much as they ever said at school. After dinner, to rescue him from Katherine's questions, Penny showed him her stamp collection. She had stamps from as far away as India and China.

"Wow," he'd said.

A year later, long after he'd been shipped back to Boston—it was said his father had already remarried—Penny received a letter from him, calling off an engagement she'd never been aware of.

I was wrong, he wrote, *I never loved you.*

There was a loneliness about the letter that stopped Penny from laughing. She didn't show it to anyone. She just peeled off the stamp and pasted it into her collection.

———

PENNY SPENDS THE FIRST WEEKEND in her airless motel room, preparing her lessons. She takes breaks only to eat, sleep, and once, to write a letter to Donna. *I've arrived!* she begins, then continues with tales of mysterious, dark-haired men she met on the train, men who glanced at her "achingly." The letter is witty and ironic, but in the end she doesn't send it. Perhaps it's childish. Perhaps Donna has outgrown that sort of thing, since she's to be married in less than a month. Her fiancé is well off, and she is considered the lucky one because she'll never have to travel across the country for a job.

When Penny arrives for her first class, she feels sweaty and short of breath. She picks up a piece of chalk to steady her hands and writes her name on the board. This gives her confidence: her own name. She introduces herself, then goes through the class list. She'll never be able to tell her students apart: nearly all are women, and there are two Margarets, one Maggie, and four Jennys. Almost every one of them is blond. Also, the students' skin is different from hers—tanned. They are people who have grown up outside, and remind her of animals. Cute but unpredictable animals.

"*Bonjour,*" she says, and waves a chalk-dusted hand. "*Ça va?*"

They stare at her without interest or malice, as though she is not really there. She wears a green skirt and a blouse that matches. Her outfit is the same colour as the chalkboard, and it's possible she is camouflaged and the students can't see her at all.

She thinks of when Katherine taught her French—to speak, not with the accent of a Québécoise, but *comme une petite Parisienne.* As a child, Penny sat with her mother in the kitchen and they practised vocabulary with flash cards Katherine made by cutting pictures from magazines and catalogues. Her mother would hold up a picture of a chair and Penny would say, "*Une chaise.*"

She quickly outgrew simple vocabulary drills, and Katherine quizzed her imagination too. She might hold up a clipping of a face, a woman who had recently been in the news, or maybe an actress, and Penny would say, "*Une femme. Son visage.*"

"Yes. And what about her face?"

Penny studied the features. "*Elle est triste? Malheureuse?*"

Katherine looked at the picture. "Yes. She might be sad. Or maybe she's angry."

"*En colère.*"

"Sometimes it's hard to tell the difference."

Penny looks out at the faces of her students, faces she would describe as looking sleepy or sweetly bored. "By the end of the semester," she says, "you'll have a good grasp of vocabulary and be able to speak in the present and past tenses."

One of the Margarets raises her hand. "What about the future?"

"The future?" Penny is so grateful to this girl for listening that she could kiss her. "We'll try to get to that too. But the future is complicated."

—

PENNY'S MOTHER LOVED TO WALK through Montreal's wintry streets. She'd put on her coat and scarf, draw a thick line of lipstick over her mouth, and take the curlers from her dark hair. She had a small fur hat, a white puff of a thing she'd inherited from a wealthy, distant aunt. When she placed it on her head, she always said the same thing: "A woman must make an effort, even if she's just going out to buy eggs." She adjusted the hat and admired its angle in the mirror. "It's a tyranny, but also a truth."

From the time she was twelve, Penny accompanied her mother on these walks. Sometimes they stopped at Morgan's so Katherine could admire a mink coat in the window. Sometimes they bought a quart of milk on the way home. Katherine wore heels and had to take her daughter's arm to steady herself on the frosty pavement. Her shoes clicked over the ice, and Penny associated this sound with adventure. She heard its rhythm along the rails while she travelled to Calgary.

They moved east, crossing the unmarked border of St-Laurent. The city became noticeably poorer—the houses closer together, the snow unshovelled. Montreal was a place of categories, a city mapped by difference and prejudice. Most of the adults Penny's parents knew—and by extension their children, whom Penny grew up with—didn't speak a word of French and rarely went to the other side of the city.

But Katherine's time in France had made her brave. She felt she was at home anywhere in Montreal, in the same way she had walked through the many *arrondissements* in Paris. She had the same disdain for French Canadians as any other Protestant Anglo. But there was a part of her that worshipped and envied them—her idea of them—for their ties to Europe. They were nothing like her stifled, British-bred husband.

Penny and Katherine often got lost in these foreign parts of the city, and had to find their way back by negotiating streetcars and strange, curving streets. After an hour, Katherine's pace would slow and her knee would weaken. She leaned more of her weight on her daughter, and Penny steadied and held her. Katherine's face flushed from the effort, and Penny never saw her look so beautiful.

"This is how I met your father," Katherine said. "I asked him for directions."

Penny knew this story: her mother was home from dancing in Paris due to a ripped tendon in her knee, and she spent her days wandering through the city. Her knee was swollen and the doctor recommended a cane, but Katherine ignored advice. She wore heels and walked every day. She was determined. She was putting on a show.

"Your father insisted on driving me back to my house. He thought it was too far for a woman to walk."

And with this, her life was given sudden direction: marriage, motherhood. They honeymooned at Niagara Falls, which Katherine called the perfect place for a suicide.

"What did you imagine it would be like?" Penny asked. "When you got married?"

"Imagine? I didn't imagine anything." Katherine raised a dark, sculpted eyebrow. "When it comes to marriage, imagining is the worst mistake a woman can make."

❧

NEAR THE MOTEL there is only one grocery store, which stocks bruised apples and cheese that grows mouldy in an open cooler. There are pawnshops and a used-book store that sells the kinds of paperbacks Katherine never allowed in the house. When Penny hears a knock on her motel door, she opens it cautiously, the chain still bolted.

David is in the same suit but without the briefcase. His tie is loosened and the top button of his shirt undone. "Came to see if you wanted to go for a walk."

"A walk?"

"It's what I miss most about Wales—wandering the hills. Here everyone owns a car, don't they? I'm starved for walking."

"Where would we go?"

"The world is ours." He gestures beyond him, toward the wallpaper that curls away from the hallway's corners and leaves a mess of dried yellow glue. "Come on, love. Let's go."

They end up at Nose Hill, an expanse of prairie. Wind hits them from all directions and brittle grass sways and pricks Penny's nylons. She is thankful for her glasses, which keep the dust from her eyes.

When she walked home from school with Andrew, there was conversation. They discussed Soviet history and the books Penny read. They gossiped about mutual friends and laughed over the insanity of their parents. Walking with David is different. He points out bits of nature he finds important—June grass, purple clover—but that's all. They walk downhill until they find shelter from the wind, then sit with their backs to the slope. Grass reaches their shoulders, and the sides of their bodies almost touch.

"Maybe it wasn't the best weather for this." There is a pout to David's voice, a youthful disappointment. He plucks a blade of switchgrass, peels the seeds away, and watches them fly from his palm.

Penny looks at the low, monochromatic hills. "It all seems the same. How do you find your way out?"

David puts his arm around her. It's a proprietary gesture, and there's something comforting about this, about being owned.

"I'm going to be married next year," she says. "His name is Andrew."

"I know." David smiles at her. "I haven't forgotten."

She should stand up and leave. The virtuous characters in novels would do that. But his lack of artfulness is charming. He is as straightforward as this place he's taken her to. The sky is blue and clear, and the grass moves with the wind. It's nothing like the tangle of buildings and streetcar cables she's used to.

"Look," he says. "A coyote."

"Where?"

He directs her gaze to a thin doglike thing farther down the hill. The coyote stares at them, and its bony, disapproving face reminds her of a certain kind of woman she often saw in east Montreal. The kind who watched Penny and Katherine through her window, with arms crossed, and who could tell they had stumbled into the wrong neighbourhood.

Penny inhales, feels the air in her lungs. She lets David's arm stay on her shoulder, and the coyote jumps, disappears into the grass.

HER THIRD ENGAGEMENT was to Andrew, who lived only two blocks away. They played games on the street with other children, and later walked home together from university. During these walks they compared childhood memories. They found that they'd shared a faulty, childlike understanding of the war they'd lived through. When Andrew heard people speak of Occupied France, he thought it had something to do with his own family, since they often received letters addressed to Occupant. The thought that he was somehow to blame gave him years of stomach cramps and bad dreams. Penny had similar nightmares. As a child she dreamed she was a soldier, knee-deep in snow and unable to move. The war she fought was on St-Laurent, and her parents were on opposing sides.

Finding these similarities made them giddy, because most of the time they seemed to live in different countries, raised by families so unalike they could have been oceans apart. Andrew's mother had none of Katherine's glamour: her clothes were ironed but shapeless. And unlike Katherine, she never retreated into books or her own cantankerous nature. She served hot cocoa and biscuits when her son arrived home from school. She cooked full meals, and the dishes were washed promptly after dinner. Her home was tidy, without any dark, messy corners that could be explored. Penny and Andrew had to remain in the kitchen or living room, and Penny was not to stay late.

It was easier for them at her house. Penny's father ignored Andrew much of the time, and Katherine had a laissez-faire attitude to her daughter's sexuality. If there had been a mistake—even the unthinkable, a pregnancy—Katherine would likely have crossed her arms and said, "Well. What do you suppose you'll do now?"

Andrew and Penny spent most of their time in her bedroom, whispering and finding reasons to touch each other accidentally. Penny would lean on Andrew's shoulder or he would brush his hand against her leg. The rest of the time they did homework in the kitchen. Andrew was studying to be an engineer—his specialty was refrigeration systems—but as an elective he took a Russian class. Penny helped him study, though she didn't speak a word of the language. She held up flash cards with simple phrases spelled out in Andrew's sloppy Cyrillic.

"Here is a banana." He read slowly from the cards. "Here is a pencil. Here is a catastrophe."

"You'll never be allowed into Russia," Katherine called from the living room. She had the ability to read a novel and eavesdrop at the same time. "They have no use for modern refrigeration over there. It's cold enough as it is."

"I don't need to go there," Andrew said. "Freedom and justice will come to us."

If Penny loved him, it was partly for his politics and the romantic nature they betrayed. It was while helping him with his Russian at her kitchen table—in view of her mother, if Katherine had cared to glance up from her book—that Penny first kissed him. That was the beginning: her initial victory. With every subsequent advance she allowed him—to put his hand over her shirt, then under it—the more devoted he became.

◦

THE MOTEL SERVES WEAK COFFEE and muffins and calls this the Continental Breakfast. Every morning, the business and rodeo men shuffle into the lobby. They look hungover or homesick or both. They eat standing up and speak to each other in clipped, joking sentences. For Penny, it's like another language.

"Heard you got blitzed with that girl—the Saan clerk."

"She was all show and no go."

When they notice Penny enter the lobby, they stop talking. Only David smiles at her. He pours her a cup of coffee and drops a sugar cube into the cup. The other men watch this silently. Penny can only guess what they say after she's gone.

◦

OTHER THAN THE SECRETARIES, she is the only woman in the French department. Most of the professors are men from France. Others are from Spain or Italy, but speak enough French to get by in a classroom. These Europeans, she can't get enough of them. They invite her for lunches in the university's cafeteria. They hold doors for her. They look her up and down, though she wears nearly the same outfit every day.

One of them—a man named Gérard, who got out of France during the war—invites her to a party, to which she wears her usual green skirt and blouse. The professors are too busy drinking and pursuing each other's wives to notice her clothing anyway. Perhaps because she's young—just twenty-five—they gently exclude her from their sexual arrangements. They understand that she is unmarried and therefore still a child—or the equivalent, a virgin. They ask her about her research and make sure her wineglass is full. Only late in the evening, when everyone has had too much to drink, do some men dance with her. They press her body so close that she smells tobacco and wine on their breath. One says he likes her perfume, despite the fact that she's not wearing any.

Don't believe what you hear, Penny writes to Donna after she stumbles back to her motel. *The Bible Belt is full of sin and debauchery.*

AFTER THREE MORE WALKS—beside Fish Creek, along the river, and once along Bragg Creek—David and Penny go on a different outing. She wears a wool suit she bought with her first paycheque. In the store she thought she looked like Jackie Kennedy: a skirt cut above the knee, and big buttons. The wool is pink, a summery rebellion against the coming winter. Now she regrets her choice. She feels conspicuous. On her left ring finger she wears the slim gold band with a squint-diamond her parents gave her when she finished her studies.

David looks at it. "What's that for?"

Penny sits with her hands in her lap and doesn't answer. As her mother used to say, there are certain indignities a woman must avoid.

They stop at a pharmacy, where the saleslady has a blue rinse through her hair. Penny would have used the dignified Latinate word *contraceptive*, but David leans against the counter and asks for a box of Frenchies. It costs $1.05, and Penny can't believe it's this cheap and easy to change your life.

On the way back, he drives fast. Penny feels a gentle carsickness but nothing else. She knows that some decisions don't make themselves felt right away. No revelation, no pang of regret—just a slow discovery, later, of what you've done. A minor injury that worsens.

"You know what this means, don't you?" Penny watches the blur of houses out the window, and the first scraps of snow that hit the windshield. "Now we have to get married."

She sounds like a child explaining the rules of a game. And maybe that's why David laughs.

———

WHEN HE LEAVES in the mornings, Penny tries to mark papers but can't concentrate. Most often she ends up squatting in the bathroom, staring into her garbage can. The contraceptives aren't perfect. She's heard that sometimes they tear. Sometimes they slip off. Penny picks them from her garbage and examines them. She thinks: We trust our future to this? They are smoky white and thin-skinned. She holds them to the light and they look sad, as though they are weeping.

INSTEAD OF GOING FOR A WALK, David drives Penny along roads she's never seen. They are heading to the edge of the city, away from the restaurants and office buildings. Out here the houses are square and simple, and look as though they've been assembled by children. No one cares for their lawn and the grass comes up in patches.

"This used to be an army town," says David, and there is entrepreneurial lust in his voice. "It's nothing now, but it'll change."

He stops the truck in front of a bungalow with faded blue siding, his newest acquisition. One side of the porch has collapsed, and there's no walkway, only the frosted ground.

"This is it." He unlocks the door and shows her around the empty rooms. He taps on walls and tells her to ignore the carpet that lifts away from the rooms' edges.

"What do you think, angel? It's heaven, isn't it?" He shows her one of the bedrooms. "This room'll be your study," he says. "This the nursery—for Dai Junior."

Penny knows he's joking. But still, she lets herself imagine. Their homes would be like this one, in a constant state of renovation. She would continue to teach for a while, but soon she would get wrapped up in David's ideas, his schemes—maybe become his partner, or his bookkeeper. Maybe she'd be good at it. They would have lots of children, and these kids would grow up with practicality as well as the brash confidence of the nouveaux riches. On weekends the family would go for brisk walks. They would probably own dogs.

"It's nice," she says, and steps into the master room. She presses her face to the large south-facing window. There is a view of other houses that look like this one, some empty lots, and roads without sidewalks. Penny wonders what this property says about David. She is thinking with her Montreal mind, a mind that associates place—not only street, but precise location on that street—with identity. She hasn't yet understood the freedom of this city, the way it allows David to move from place to place without bestowing judgment on him, without locking him into a grid of language, religion, ethnicity. Nothing labels his past or decides his future. She hasn't yet realized how quickly he can move on.

<hr/>

PENNY RECEIVES A POSTCARD from Donna, sent while she was on her honeymoon at Niagara Falls. It's as full of half-truths as Penny's letters. *We're having a great time! I didn't want to come here at first—you know me and heights—but I'm getting used to it. Our hotel is super.*

Penny stares at the postcard's image. The water looks cold and dangerous. She imagines leaning against the railing and feeling the spit in her face. Marriage, she thinks, must be lonely too.

She doesn't know how to reply to Donna, so instead she writes Andrew a letter. Then she walks along the frosted sidewalk to the mailbox. Snow fell the night before and the city is hushed. The lid of the postbox creaks from the sudden cold.

She imagines Andrew in Montreal, at the desk in the bedroom he's slept in since he was born. It faces the window, and is made of dark, scratched wood. His hair hangs over his forehead and he continually brushes it out of his eyes. Penny can see grooves in it from his comb. He is surely reading. In his last letter, he wrote that he had discovered Tolstoy's later, short works. His elbows rest on either side of a book that he has nearly destroyed with love, underlining phrases and folding over corners.

I was wrong. I never loved you.

She doesn't mail the letter. Instead, she tucks it into her pocket, a possibility she'll carry with her.

———

A PHOTOGRAPH OF PENNY'S MOTHER hung on their kitchen wall. The glass was coated with dust, but the photo was stunning: Katherine *en pointe*, her arms in third position. She wore a white bodysuit and a skirt that fanned out broad and white. Her chest was as pale as her tights, her legs as slim as the leafless, winter trees outside Penny's motel window.

Katherine has remained as thin as in the photo—she lives off toast and marmalade—but her body has a brittle look now. She spends her time on the couch. She reads and nurses her injury, which is as haunting and unpredictable as a ghost. Apart from her walks, she rarely moves. Her digestion is slow and painful, so she dislikes eating and has taken up smoking instead. Her teeth are edged in black. "By the time I reached twenty-six," she has said, "my body was dead to me."

It had been years since Penny noticed the photo. But two weeks before she left on the train, she stood in the kitchen and stared at it. Katherine was at the table, drinking coffee from a stained cup. Penny's father was in the living room, listening to the radio.

Penny touched the glass, traced the outline of her mother's body with her finger. She used to beg her mother to speak of that graceful, former self. Katherine had told her of the studio where she danced: its crumbling brick walls and the exposed piping that leaked onto the floor. Even in winter the rooms were too hot, and the dancers' sweat formed condensation that dripped down the mirrors. There was a smell of hair lacquer, rosin, and blood that seeped from the dancers' blisters onto the silk of their shoes.

"Tell me about when you were in Paris," said Penny.

Katherine looked up from her book and seemed pleased. "What do you want to know?" Then, just as she did when Penny was younger, Katherine imitated her dance instructors. *Mesdemoiselles, des tendus, s'il vous plaît.* She stood, paraded through the kitchen, and snapped her fingers. "Light footwork, please! You sound like a pack of elephants."

This had always made Penny laugh, and it still did. But now she saw something dark in her mother's imitation of these women. Women who had once danced onstage, and who still hungered for that light. Who lived with the bitter knowledge that their bodies had betrayed them, that time had betrayed them. Women who understood, already, what it was like to die.

"I'm going to get married," Penny said. "Andrew and I are going to get married." She had meant to do this properly, with Andrew and her father present, all of them at the table.

Katherine's face took on its usual expression—an almost theatrical sternness. It was the expression of a woman who felt wronged: denied a life of grace and beauty. Given, instead, a two-bedroom walk-up, a broken body, and a host of chores that made her feel bored and incompetent.

"Things are different now," said Penny. "Things for women are changing."

Katherine only laughed at that. She reached for her novel, but Penny grabbed the book before her mother could hide herself in it. "You worry he'll disappoint me?"

There was the sound of the radio in the other room.

"Of course he'll disappoint you. But that's not the worst part." Katherine stepped toward Penny and touched her daughter's hair. "Disappointing him. That's what'll kill you."

She slipped the book from Penny's hands, then walked out of the kitchen. When she moved slowly, her limp was more noticeable.

Penny went to the doorway and watched her father. He was so absorbed in the news—the Cubans and Americans were having a standoff, the world frozen in a moment of choice—that he didn't notice her. He still wore the suit he'd worn all day at the bank, and leaned with his elbows on his knees. He looked worn from standing on his feet, performing the underpaid, bureaucratic duties of a clerk.

For once, he didn't seem distant or unknowable or strangely quiet. Penny felt as though she understood him. He wanted a peaceful house. A bright, cheerful child. A wife who could love him and who could cook. Like Andrew—who wanted an orderly, contented home, the kind that keeps childhood nightmares at bay—he had the simplest desires.

———

PENNY SURVIVES THE ENTIRE YEAR, despite having to fail her favourite Margaret. The faculty party this week is to celebrate the end of term. One of the European professors orders a crate of wine and uncorks every bottle. Penny doesn't keep track of how many glasses she drinks.

She has been teaching the subjunctive all week—*que je sois aimée, que tu sois aimé*. None of the Margarets and only one of the Jennys is clear on the use of this verbal mood. And she and David haven't been for a walk in over a month. He is making big sales and rushing renovations. When he does return to the motel—to shave, shower, eat—he kisses her forehead roughly and says things like, "How's my girl?" He is distant, like a husband returning from time with his mistress.

Now she eats cheese cubes and talks to Gérard. He is a good listener and, to her surprise, he doesn't laugh.

"A similar thing happened during the war," he says. "Women got engaged to two or three soldiers at once, to hedge their bets."

"What did they do?" Penny leans against the wall, which is keeping her steady. "If more than one of their fiancés survived?"

"Good question." Gérard sips his wine, which has tinted the inside of his mouth purple. "I suspect they rarely faced that issue. I suspect they had more pressing problems."

Penny nods. "More pressing problems." She thinks of the contraceptives in her garbage. She'd spent the entire afternoon on her hands and knees, picking through them to see if any had torn. She thought—she almost hoped—she would be punished, like the heroine of a cautionary tale. But everything seems to be in order. She will return to Montreal at the end of the month. Her ticket is booked, and Andrew expects her.

"I'll probably just keep going west," she says. "Get on the train and go all the way to Vancouver."

And then she starts to cry, holding one of the host's napkins to her face. Gérard puts an arm around her, and no one at the party seems to notice.

"We should get married," says Penny. "We get along."

"Possibly." He touches her hair. "We should at least have a dance."

They move awkwardly to music that is said to be popular in Europe now. The tempo and rhythm are like nothing Penny has heard before, but the lyrics tell the same old story. Penny leans against this man and he presses her to him. He holds her the way he held his young fiancée during the war, as they listened to the boots and trucks outside their Paris window. The way Katherine held her daughter after that grade-school heartache, a first disappointment. As though it might change something, they hold each other and dance.

r e l y

PEOPLE JUST DISAPPEAR. My wife's gone. My mom made it to a sturdy old age then faded away. And I hardly see my daughter anymore. Alicia's in Vancouver now. She lives with her boyfriend— they're both in med school, that's how they met—and she's usually too busy to call. When we do talk, the conversation is rushed. It's like she's practising her doctor's voice with me: concerned but efficient, just checking in.

So when she calls and says, "I hate this city," she sounds like a different person.

"It never stops raining here," she says. Her voice has the rawness of morning, but it's five o'clock at night. "It never, never stops."

This is her first phone call in over a month, but I hadn't been worried. People are always spiralling off in other directions, like twigs knocked around by a river current. I try to be the still point, a rock on the bank. I stay put, so that when my daughter calls to say, "I hate this city," I'm right here to pick up the phone.

"I can't stand it here," she says. "All the rain and the grey make me want to kick the wall in."

Her voice echoes, and I figure she must be in the bathroom to get some privacy. She's probably in the empty tub with the shower curtain drawn. Her mom used to do that when we were married, when she was having all kinds of conversations she didn't want me to overhear.

"Gavin's always at the clinic and I'm always in the library," Alicia says. "We don't even have time to buy groceries. We live on ginger ale and cereal."

Out the window, I see patterns of frost on the windshields of parked cars.

"I haven't slept in weeks, Dad." Alicia whispers this. "I can't even sit still."

"You should come out here," I say, and that surprises me—I never ask her to come home. I'm not one of those fathers who are always calling and sending emails, talking about how much they miss their kid. I don't wear my need on the outside. "You should stay as long as you want."

I hear her exhale. She sounds done for. Maybe that wet Vancouver air is making her sick.

"Yeah," she says. "Okay."

And that surprises me too.

THE THING IS, people also come back. They return just when you thought they were gone for good, when you were finished even missing them.

Take all the boyfriends my mom had. They were men who'd seen lots of the world, who were worn down by it, and they never stuck around. There was this one guy, George. He was the best of them, the one I hoped would stay. A decent, slow-moving guy. He liked caramels, the kind that come wrapped in clear plastic. When I was a kid, he taught me how to toss them in the air and catch them in my mouth. "You two are a pair of wackos," my mom would say. She used words like "wacko" when George was around. She laughed a lot too.

Mom wasn't with George for his looks. He was balding and had a sac of skin that hung under his chin. He also had a belly that seemed to move on its own, like it was alive. I used to pretend it was a soft, furry animal that had curled up next to him and that he hadn't bothered to shoo away.

I haven't seen him in years, decades even—not since I was seven—but lately I meet him every day. Especially when I look in that little mirror at work, the one above the sink that runs only cold. The mirror is so small that I can only see one section of my face at a time, and there's a bit of George in each part. I don't have that soft, swaying stomach yet, but he's there in my face. My tired, unshaven skin—that's George. The crease along my forehead: George. The pouches under my eyes, like I've been storing my disappointments there. That's George too.

I'M A FINISHER. I do handrails, boat hulls, car parts. I spray them with powder then bake them in an oven. There's some skill to it—getting the colour on evenly, and setting the temperature right so there aren't any bubbles. I like the work. The monotony is lulling, almost addictive. And I don't mind being alone. I like having time to think.

Mostly I think about Alicia. I try to picture her in Vancouver. She lives on Cambie, in an apartment. I've never seen it, but I've looked Cambie up on a map. She takes the bus to the university, I know that. She says it takes about half an hour.

I don't know what her classes are like, but I guess they sit in desks and take notes. They also carve up bodies—cadavers. She described a cut-up hand to me over the phone: the skin, bones, nerves. And last year she called and said, "Dad, guess what?" She was out of breath. "I helped deliver a baby!"

That's why I work six, seven days a week—to hear Alicia happy. To help her pay her tuition and go off and live her life. She appreciates it. She told me so last time I saw her. That was over a year ago, because she didn't come home this past Christmas. She spent the holidays in Puerto Vallarta with her boyfriend and his family. The boyfriend's mother had called me up a couple of months before, to see if Alicia could go with them. They rented a house and the whole family went every year. Grandparents, uncles, kids.

"We'd love it if Alicia could join us." The mother had a sunny voice, the voice of someone who's never had to earn a living. Her husband is a radiologist, and Gavin plans to be one too. "It's always such a fun time."

I wanted to tell this woman that Christmas is my only holiday. Christmas Day, Alicia and I go for a skate, make a simple dinner.

We take it easy. With Alicia in Mexico, I knew I'd spend the day in bed with a bottle of champagne and a pizza I'd order from any open restaurant I could find.

The mother—Diane is her name—said they'd pay for the ticket. "Airfare is next to nothing these days," she said, and I almost hung up on her.

That was over five months ago, and now Alicia's coming in for three days, maybe even four. I'm leaving work early to pick her up from the depot. I wash my hands and face in the sink, the one that only runs cold. I've been spraying Matte Blue, and the powder sticks to my eyebrows, my hair, the insides of my ears. I leave this stuff everywhere—on my clothes, furniture, the soap in my shower. I usually don't think about it, but with Alicia coming I see things differently. During the drive to the bus depot I notice it under my nails, on the dash of my car, embedded in the plastic of the wheel.

GEORGE USED TO GIVE all kinds of hugs. Bear hugs, alligator hugs, elephant hugs. If he was being an elephant, he'd swing his arm like a trunk and pick me up. The bear hugs were my favourite. He'd pick me up, squeeze me to his chest, and growl in my ear. His breath was warm and cavernous, coming from deep inside that body.

That's how I want to hug Alicia. I see her before she sees me. She hops off the bus and picks up a half-empty backpack. She wears a flimsy raincoat and jeans. She's thin and jumpy, and her movements remind me of the magpies that skip around on my balcony. I want to pick her up and hold her, but she's an adult, a woman, and maybe too old for that sort of thing.

She sees me, waves, and walks over. "Dad." She laughs. "You're blue."

She rubs her hand through my hair the way she liked to do when she was a kid. Blue powder sprays from my head and floats between us. "Snow," she says, which is what she used to call it. I notice her skin: it has a grey tinge, the same colour as the slush piled at the curbs. I give her a quick hug, pat her shoulder, and she smells like she needs a shower.

"I didn't have time to get many things together." Her eyes are glassy, like scraps of ice. "I didn't know what to bring."

Her coat is unzipped and she wears a T-shirt underneath. On her feet she has blue canvas shoes, bad for this weather. "You'll need a better coat," I say.

"No, I'm fine." To prove herself right she takes my hand and presses it to her forehead. "See?"

Her skin is hot and damp, and it reminds me of when George held me so tight that I couldn't breathe and I'd start to sweat. Sometimes it felt like my ribs were cracking. When he put me down, I'd wobble foot to foot, catching my breath. I'd be dizzy, light-headed, and I'd look up at him and he'd seem different— bigger, almost dangerous.

Alicia sees my car and walks toward it, ahead of me. She nearly slips on the ice, then regains her balance. And I remember how, when I steadied myself, caught my breath, George would go back to being George—that sweet, soft-spoken guy. And I'd grab his sweater. "Again," I'd say, and pull his sleeve. "Again."

WHEN WE GET TO MY PLACE, Alicia kicks open the door as though she still lives here. "It's exactly the same," she says.

We used to live as a family in this place, a two-bedroom off Memorial. I didn't move after Claire left because I didn't want to upset Alicia even more. She was only seven years old, and I thought too many changes would confuse her. Anyway, it took me years to believe that Claire wasn't coming back. By the time I understood that, I'd lived this way so long it didn't seem worth changing.

Now that Alicia's here, the first thing I want to do is feed her. Then sit her down and ask her questions. Why she's so thin. Why she's so wrecked. But she throws herself onto the couch and adjusts one of the green, craggy cushions under her head. The stuffing is worn down, which I didn't notice until now. Alicia used to trampoline all over that couch.

"You look tired," I say. "You look like you could use a nap."

"I know I shouldn't sleep in the middle of the day." She closes her eyes. "But I don't give a shit."

And with that, she's asleep. Her breath makes a wheezy sound like the spray gun I use at work.

I tiptoe through the apartment, then sit in the kitchen and try to read a magazine. I go onto the balcony and stand there until my toes lose all feeling. Then I go back inside and try to read again. It's a business magazine, with news about oil and all the other money in Calgary that I'll hardly touch.

I can't remember when I've had so much time to fill. After work I'm usually so wiped that I heat a can of soup, spoon it from the pot, and go to bed. It's been a long time since I had anyone else in the house, and it makes the place feel strange. There are things I've never noticed: the squeak of the bathroom door, or the sucking sound the fridge makes when you open it. I'm afraid to make a noise, can't remember whether Alicia is a light sleeper or not. So I just sit in a chair I never normally use and watch her. Then I cover her with a blanket. Under it, her body looks like a pile of bent hangers.

—

ON HER DAYS OFF, my mom and George liked to go for drives in her Volkswagen Rabbit. It had been a lipstick red, but that must have been a cheap paint job because it faded to a paler, milky colour. The Rabbit was small but could travel fast, and that's how my mom drove.

"This city was built for me," she'd say as we blasted down wide roads, past subdivisions. "One big highway."

George didn't drive anymore, but he loved being on the road. He talked about the BMW he used to own. "I lived for that thing," he said. "It was a beaut."

Sometimes we drove all the way to Cochrane, where we bought ice cream, even in winter. I was allowed to buy a double scoop of chocolate, I remember that. We ate in the car, and had to turn the heat up to keep warm. We ate the ice cream fast, before it could melt.

—

ALICIA SLEEPS SO LONG that the sun starts to set and I can hear rush-hour traffic outside my window. I write her a note, put on my jacket and boots, then head out to pick up some pizza. I order pepperoni-mushroom but then realize she might not like pepperoni-mushroom anymore. Who knows, she might be a vegetarian, or one of those people who never cooks their food. So I stop at the grocery store to pick up some other things too. Just in case. Dill pickles, a block of cheddar cheese, precut carrots, salt-and-vinegar chips, oatmeal cookies.

When I get back, Alicia's pacing the kitchen, flipping through that magazine. "I should drop out and move back here." She's awake now and talking fast. "Here's where the money is."

"Not if you have to make rent," I say.

"Did you get food?"

"Hope you like pepperoni."

"I don't think I've eaten in a while. I don't think I've eaten all day."

While we have dinner, we play Scrabble. Alicia's clever, a bit too competitive. She makes words like *hence* and *cudgel*, and when I put down *pal* she adds *pitate*.

We drink Dr Pepper and Alicia eats only the topping from her pizza, leaving the dough in a greasy pile on her plate. I put the chips in a bowl for her, but she hardly touches those either. I want to figure her out, get inside her brain and find out what's making her antsy and sick. But I've always given her privacy. I never rummaged through her stuff or read her diary when she was growing up. And this is the first time in months my daughter's been here, at my table. I don't want to ruin it.

I try an easy question. "How's Gavin?" I ask.

"Oh, you know. The same."

"Yeah," I say, though I've never met the guy. "How's school going?"

"My supervisor says I've got a terrible bedside manner." Alicia shuffles her letters, her eyes scanning the board. "I told him I want to do obstetrics and he suggested I try surgery."

She puts down *break*, which means it's my turn, and I've got nothing but consonants.

"What was I like?" Alicia asks. "As a baby?"

"You were fat." I remember the snowsuit I used to dress her in: green, with attached feet, and rabbit ears on the hood. "Healthy."

"I was probably a cranky kid."

As soon as the water froze, I spent every Saturday morning with Alicia. I wrapped her in a scarf, mitts, toque, and we'd head over to the ice. When she was young, she loved being able to see her own breath. It fascinated her to pass her mittened hand through it.

This was before my wife left, but Claire never joined us. She liked to stay home and have the morning to herself. "I need a break," she'd say, and while we were gone she'd make a cup of tea, add a shot of amaretto, then sip it in the bath.

"Do you remember your first pair of skates?" I turn *change* into *changed*—it's the best I can do. "The ones with the double blade on the bottom?"

By the time Alicia and I would come back from our skate, Claire would be in a terry cloth robe. She'd open the door and pull us into the apartment, saying, "Hurry, you're letting the cold in." I'd grab her waist, kiss her neck. I loved her skin then. It was warm and smelled clean.

"Not really." Alicia drinks from her can of Dr Pepper.

"You always stopped fussing when I brought you out on the ice. You practically learned to skate before you learned to walk."

"It snowed in Vancouver last winter, and Gavin refused to leave the house." Alicia shakes her head. "He said he didn't want me to go outside either, in case a power line fell on me."

"You took some bad falls when you were a kid. Once, you slid across the ice and your whole face collected snow." I look at that face, see how thin it's got. "You had skid marks on your chin for a week."

All of a sudden, she smiles. It's the kind of smile my mom used to have when George was around. "This is the first time I've relaxed in months," she says. "At home, I never stop working. I have to take two Ativans just to be able to sit on the couch." She puts down *deft*, using my *d*. "An overmedicated med student. That's funny, isn't it?"

I don't know what to say to this. My daughter used to be different: driven, athletic, happy. "It's ironic, I guess."

"No. That's not quite the right word." She bites her lip as she rearranges her letters. "It's funny, that's all."

—

FOR A WHILE, my mom worked the early shift on weekends, and when she did, George cooked breakfast. He always made bacon, then fried bread in the bacon grease. I'd sit at the table in my pyjamas and watch him cook, which he said he learned to do from his mother.

"She'd be proud of me," he liked to say. "I'm the only guy in history who managed to live off powder for three years and not get thin."

George didn't mind doing the dishes either, or the laundry. He had lots of time, because he didn't work. George's work, he told me, was to stay clean. At the time, I didn't know what this meant, staying clean, but George said it was a full-time gig. Soon, when he got his confidence up, he was going to look for a job.

"I used to be in finance." He chased a bite of his toast with coffee. "I was a gambling man, a broker."

I didn't know what those words meant either—*finance, broker*—but I liked listening to George in the mornings. And I liked when my mom came down the stairs in her nurse's uniform and George would say, "There she is. My saviour, my sweetheart, my dove."

He said it in a funny way—what Mom called highfalutin—and Mom would laugh. Then he'd serve her the bacon and toast he'd kept warm in the pan. She'd sit at the table and sip coffee from his cup.

—

ALICIA'S GOT OVER a hundred and fifty points and will beat me easily.

She says she's forgotten her childhood. "My brain's so full of drug reactions and side effects that everything else has been pushed out."

She wants me to tell her a story, which means she probably wants me to talk about Claire. Instead, I talk about easy things. I remind Alicia of when the two of us cooked mac and cheese then watched sitcoms together. I remind her of when she and I played Snakes and Ladders and she was such a sore loser.

"Still am."

I remind her of how good she was at hockey, when she fought to be able to play on the boys' team. Of the time she bodychecked me to the ice and I broke my hip.

"It was bruised." She gives me a kick under the table. "And it was your coccyx."

"Alicia the Enforcer. You deserved the name."

"That's probably what made me go into medicine—repentance for all the injuries I caused." She pushes aside her plate of half-eaten pizza. "We should celebrate."

"Celebrate what?"

"The fact that we're alive. The fact that we never fell through the ice." She stands from the table and heads to the kitchen. "We should have a drink."

She seems suddenly bustling and dangerous, and it reminds me of her mother. Claire and I were always on and off, and sometimes she would disappear for days at a time. Then I'd wake up one morning and she'd be in the kitchen as though she'd never left. She'd have made coffee, read the paper, and be doing a cryptic crossword.

"Gavin and I used to make ourselves drinks with tequila and strawberries." Alicia's opening all the kitchen cupboards. "We'd pretend we were on vacation. We'd turn up the heat in the apartment and pretend we were in Mexico."

"You're on vacation now." I watch her pull two glasses down from a shelf. "But I don't have any strawberries."

"You don't have any anything." She pulls down a nearly empty bottle of vermouth and a nice bottle of Scotch one of my customers gave me at Christmas. It's still got a green ribbon tied around its neck.

"You'll want to mix that with water or something," I say. "Put it on ice." But she pours it straight. "That's not how you drink Scotch. Scotch is a sipping drink."

Alicia hands me a glass. "So sip," she says, then she puts *level* over a triple-word-score box.

———

WHEN GEORGE WAS AROUND, he was the one who usually tucked me into bed and told me a story. I was eight then and thought I was too old for bedtime stories.

"Too old?" George said. "No such thing as too old."

George's stories weren't like *Goodnight Moon* or *Peter Rabbit* or anything else my mom read me. My favourite was about a bear named Ted who lived in a forest with his wife, Louise. Ted and Louise had a small house, they ate caramels at every meal, and they were happy. That is, until Ted got laid off from his job in the caramel factory and had to go into the nearby city for work.

That's where he met a sly fox, a scout who noticed his size and bulk and convinced him to try boxing.

"So he's up against the top fighters in the world." George told this story the same way every time. "And guess what?"

I sat up in bed, because this was a good part. "What?"

"He wins every time. It's his bear instincts. He's a born fighter. He's raking in the cash, and women love him."

At first, Ted sent most of his winnings home to Louise, along with letters saying how much he missed her. But then he started spending his money on other things: drinks for himself and his new friends, clothes, a Lamborghini with leather seats.

"He parties hard and begins to lose his edge," George said. "He loses matches. He loses friends. He wakes up one morning, sitting in his own piss, and realizes what a mess he's made of himself."

"In his own pee?" This detail got me every time.

"He has black eyes, three shattered teeth, and his right ear's been slammed so hard he hears a buzzing all the time."

I shut my eyes at this part. I hated this part.

"So he packs up his bags—his trophies, his robes, his gloves. He'd had to sell the car to pay back debts, so he gets on a bus. He goes back to the forest."

"Back to Louise?" By this point, I usually felt sick to my stomach. "Is she mad at him?"

"Louise is a tough old bear. She looks after herself. She's been foraging for berries all summer."

"But she doesn't like Ted anymore."

"She likes him. But she doesn't say so. Not at first." George was a romantic, and this was his favourite part. He'd usually lean forward and whisper it. "She takes his big bruised head in her hands and makes him promise never to box again. 'Promise me,' she says."

"And he promises."

"And he means it."

"And they're happy." My eyelids felt heavy at this point. They closed on their own. "And they live in the forest forever."

"You bet." George brought the blanket up to cover my shoulders. "Forever."

AN HOUR LATER, Alicia and I are loaded. I'm drunk in a good way, right on the edge of falling asleep. Alicia keeps taking her own pulse and saying, "Holy shit." She says she wants to go outside.

"I'm serious," she says. "Why don't we go skating?"

"You've forgotten what it's like out there at night. You've forgotten about the wind chill."

"It'll be like old times. Maybe you'll break an arm."

"It's dark." I close my eyes. Open them. "And neither of us has skates."

"Come on." Alicia stands, holds the edge of the table for balance, then goes toward the closet. "I never get to do this."

"I don't know." I feel myself slipping down my chair. "I'm pretty tired."

"Don't tell me you're drunk already." She starts pulling things from the closet: scarves, mismatched gloves, a pair of snow pants I'd forgotten about. "I could give you something for that. I could give you something that would keep you up for days."

"You're nuts," I say. "You're a wacko."

"It's now or never, Dad." She starts pulling the snow pants over her jeans. "That's what we learn in med school. Do things today, because tomorrow you'll be on dialysis."

"They teach you that?"

"No." She's got the snow pants over one leg. When she tries to pull them onto the other, she nearly tips over. "It's what they should teach us."

She reaches for her shoes—the useless canvas ones. The Scotch has changed her movement, or maybe my vision, but she's not like a magpie anymore. She's got the slippery grace of a fish, those shadows under the ice.

She walks toward me, the snow pants swishing as her legs touch. I knew this would happen. I knew one day I wouldn't recognize my daughter—she'd be a stranger, someone I find fascinating and frightening. She looks at the board and puts down *rely*.

"There," she says. "I win."

—

MY MOTHER MET MY FATHER when she was eighteen. His eyes reminded her of pictures of Antarctica she'd seen in *National Geographic*—pictures of dense blue ice. Not that he was a cold man. "He was funny," Mom told me. "He made me laugh so much my insides hurt."

Now he lives in Lethbridge, where he grew up. Once, a few years ago, he drove up to have coffee with me. We met at the Lazy Loaf and Kettle, and he wore a bleached denim shirt the same colour as those eyes. His hair had gone grey and he had the shy look of a person who's wasted his life. I think he wanted to be friends. Or maybe he only wanted to tell me his story. I didn't care to hear it. Instead, I told him about Mom. She was still working as a home-care nurse. She took care of people who couldn't walk to the bathroom on their own, who couldn't cut their own toenails. "People," I said, "who have no one left to look after them."

"She's a hard worker," my dad said, and I resented that. The way he talked like he still knew her.

"My wife left me thirteen years ago," I said. "She never called in all that time. Except once, in the middle of the night, when she was feeling lonely."

But my dad—his name is Christopher, same as mine—nodded

like he'd heard this kind of thing a hundred times. He stirred NutraSweet into his coffee.

"When Claire left, my daughter was at this age where she was curious about everything. Always asking questions." I took a sip of my coffee. "She kept asking where her mom had gone, where exactly. Eventually I quit making things up and told her the truth. Which was that I didn't know."

"You have a daughter?" my dad said. He didn't seem to get that this was possible, that time had whipped past him so quickly.

WE'RE UNDER THE BRIDGE where kids like to scrawl graffiti, standing on a spill of mud that leads to the water. The cold has sobered me up a little.

There aren't any street lights here, but sometimes light from a passing car catches on the water and shivers there. The river isn't totally frozen and chunks of broken ice rasp against each other.

I'm in my workboots, my parka, and a toque I don't normally wear because it's got an Oilers logo. Alicia is zipped into one of my old coats and has a blue scarf wrapped around her neck. She's brought what's left of the Scotch, holding the bottle by the neck with a mittened hand. She leans against me, her arm in mine, and watches her own breath spill away from her. She takes long drinks from the bottle.

"This stuff is good," she says. "Once you get used to it."

Then she lets go of my arm and walks to the edge of the bank. She's drunk and full of nerve. She heads out onto the stretch of ice that's formed over the water, and I can hear snow crunch and the ice creak under her weight. She stops at the edge, where water laps at her shoes. She's far from me, her body tilting toward the river. She kicks at the water and the spray catches some light, maybe the moon, and looks like a bottle shattering.

"It's different here," Alicia calls back at me. "This used to freeze solid."

She kicks at the ice she's standing on, digs at it with her heel. And I try to imagine what happened to George, where he got to, what he's doing.

"Come on," I say. "Let's go back."

She kicks again, and a piece of ice breaks off this time. It drops into the water. Either George got fat or thin. Either he grew old or he didn't.

"Alicia, let's go. You'll catch a cold."

Alicia drinks the last of the Scotch and pitches the bottle into the river. I hear it hit the water, then it turns and bobs in the current. "I don't feel the cold anymore."

That's when I move. I walk toward her and nearly slip on the frosted-over mud, but catch myself. I don't care that I don't know her anymore, and that she's too old to be held. I grab her hand. I hold it so tight it's like I can feel the bones and blood and nerves. "Yeah," I say. "But you will."

AND THEN GEORGE WASN'T AROUND to tell me stories. I don't remember much about his leaving. I guess he might have packed up his things, but I don't remember that. I don't think he said goodbye.

I was only seven when he left, but around that time I started to look after myself. I would get myself into my pyjamas, and if there was no one home to tuck me into bed—if Mom was working, and she was always working—I'd bring my pillow and blanket down to the living room, curl up on the couch, and go to sleep in front of the TV.

But the night George left, Mom tucked me in. She called in to the hospital and said she couldn't make her shift. I had grown pretty big by then, but still, she carried me to bed.

"Where's George?" I asked.

Mom didn't say anything. She tucked my sheet around me. She pulled it so tight I couldn't move.

It wasn't till years later that I understood about George and how he could never be still, how his need would never let him rest. But that night, lying on my back with my arms straight at my sides, I didn't get it. I just imagined him in the centre of a boxing ring: a stout, flabby bear of a man, swinging and swinging his fists at nothing, and always losing.

—

"TELL ME ANOTHER STORY," says Alicia.

She's in her old bed, under the ABC sheets she used as a kid. Her room is exactly as she left it. There are yellowing posters on her wall and her closet is full of clothes she doesn't wear anymore.

I'm on the edge of her bed, and I can feel her bones through the sheet. "I don't know any more stories." It's past midnight and my head feels heavy.

"Tell me anything." She closes her eyes and I notice the sweat on her temples and upper lip. She pulls the sheet higher and says, "Tell me about you and Mom."

So I tell her how Claire and I used to stay in bed all day: sleep past noon, make love till dinner, order food and eat it in bed. There were times when we couldn't get enough of each other. When we had to be apart for more than a few hours, it was like a sickness. I tell her about when we first moved into this apartment. We repainted the place, and the yellow walls seemed warm and sunny.

"I never knew any of that. I never knew that about the yellow paint." Alicia turns on her side and holds a corner of the pillow, the way she always slept when she was a kid.

I keep talking. I tell her that Claire and I used to go skating together. That we'd glide along the river holding hands. This is a lie, but I say it anyway. I say it because I want to give Alicia something. Because she's my daughter, and because whatever she's coming down from is making her shake.

"But Mom never liked skating." Alicia opens her eyes, and for a second she's sober. "Mom didn't own skates."

I touch my daughter's hair, hair that's as dark as a river at night. "Things change, Alicia," I say, even though it seems I've been this drunk forever.

remember, relive

YOU PULL HIM TO THE GUEST ROOM by the sleeve of his tuxedo, the sheen of it crumpled between your fingers, and count the steps under your rushed breath until you both drop to the floor, one of his hands fumbling with your tiny black belt, the other pushing the green skirt above your knees, all of it so sudden and stupid there is no stopping—certainly no kissing—and his zipper slides down so easily it's like you've done this before, then he's heaving like an idiot, his breath hot on the crown of your head, and just as you think, How long will this take? he pulls out and spills himself all over your thigh in a pumping sputter, his eyes squeezed shut, his mouth making an O, and you feeling the wet of it slide down your leg to the ivory carpet, a stain, this night, and you, thirteen.

THE DAY BEFORE your sister's wedding, a Friday, your mother refuses to leave her bedroom. She lies on top of her duvet in a blue shoulder-padded suit, black nylons that cover her stilt legs, and black heels. Her room is high-ceilinged, and kept as clean and cool as a museum. The housekeeper, Rebecca, tucked the bedsheets into perfect, smooth corners this morning.

Your sister, Crystal, scowls at the sheer-curtained window. Her hair is tied up and her soft arms are crossed. You are thirteen, the youngest, and you watch from the doorway. Black-and-white photographs of your father—his glasses, moustache, the lines of his brow—stare back at you from the walls, grim and faded. It occurs to you that your father used to sleep in this room, with its perfume smell. He died ten years ago, and memories of him are like the photographs: grainy, flat, not really alive to you ever.

Your mother repairs a button that fell off one of her blouses. Sewing is a chore she enjoys doing herself because she likes to make use of her slender, elegant hands.

"God has ripped my eldest from me." The button drops into a fold in her blue skirt. "Torn her like a sliver from my hands."

"That's not logical." You know this kind of routine, these dramatics. "If Crystal was a sliver, you'd want her gone."

"Are you going to leave too, Cassy?" Your mother leans toward you. "Are you going to forget me?"

"Mother." You lean against the wall and slouch, a rebellion in itself. "You were happy about this wedding months ago. You arranged the entertainment. You chose the menu."

Crystal turns to your mother with wet, turquoise-rimmed eyes. "You're still mad about the dress, aren't you, Mom?" Your sister plans to wear a puffy, blindingly white thing, with gathers and folds and complications your mother can't abide. "It's the stupid fucking dress, isn't it?"

Your mother ignores her, sniffs. "Cassy, get Mommy some coffee." Then she almost smiles. So she is half joking, exaggerating her role of distressed mother-of-the-bride. The sun from the balcony window hits her cheeks, and her hair is uncombed and scattered over her shoulders. She reminds you of a stage actress, stunning and deceitful. "Without sugar, please."

Crystal leans against the window, her forehead pressed to the glass. Your mother's smile fades. And right now you are convinced that you're smarter than your whole family—smarter than all of them combined. Except, of course, for Daniel, who is never asked to get coffee.

Your mother picks up the button and threads the needle. "And go tell Daniel he needs to be fitted for his tuxedo." It is as though she has read your mind. "Tell him he has no choice."

⍺

FOUR YEARS LATER, Crystal and Daniel have moved out, and the house seems even bigger than before. No one ever sits in the "family room," and two of the bathrooms are never used.

As roommates, you and your mother suit each other. She wakes you in time for your statistics classes at the university. And when she misplaces her reading glasses, you find them easily. You don't hate her taste in music, and sometimes you even sing along to *My Fair Lady* and *West Side Story*. And your mother never gets in the way of your routine: nearly every night, you have drinks with men who cheerfully ignore your age. Sometimes you tell them your secret—you call it your "first time"—and they enjoy that kind of story. "You're a bad girl, aren't you?" they say, and you like this version of events. You were bad. You were in control.

Then, when the man of the night falls into a spent sleep, you crawl from his bed, find your crumpled underwear, tiptoe out the door. You never spend the night, never leave your number. You walk home alone, no matter how cold the city wind. And when you reach your dark, Gothic house, you crawl into bed, lift the plastic receiver of your phone, and dial Daniel. He is always awake.

"What are you doing?" you whisper sleepily when he picks up.

Since he left home, your brother has been a serial mover. He has a need to be portable, and owns only one, duct-taped suitcase. He currently lives in a New York high-rise, with a man who cooks excessive breakfasts: hash browns, stacks of buttery pancakes, tall chilled glasses of orange juice. You visited once, picked at the food, and felt your stomach lurch with a fear of heights as you stood on their balcony.

"Reading," says Daniel through the phone line.

"I met a man who writes kids' books today. He bought me a Caesar."

"Maybe you should marry him."

You smile, and can tell from his voice that Daniel smiles too. "Maybe you should."

"I'm going to Boston for a while." Daniel coughs gently. "Without Gareth. I'll call when I get a phone."

A list of Daniel's past area codes and home numbers is trapped in your mind for life. "When are you coming home?" You hold your breath, wait for the usual answer.

"I don't know, Cassy. Soon."

YOU HAPPILY LEAVE your mother's high-windowed bedroom to find your brother, though it is not a simple operation. The house is so large—your mother calls it *stately*—that when you count your steps under your breath from one room to another, you often lose count. From your mother's bedroom on the third floor to the back door on the first, it is approximately seventy steps, twenty-three down a winding, white-banistered staircase.

On your fingers, you count twenty-eight steps through the black-and-white-tiled kitchen with the chrome fridge, the marble countertops, the spice rack. Caterers arrange crystal bowls of caviar, stack wineglasses, garnish potatoes, chop onions. Rebecca, who has dark hair that peaks low on her forehead, stands at the stove. She is making chicken soup, because she has no patience for fancy, catered food. The room is crowded, hissing, and hot. It smells of bread dough and cut dill. One counter is piled with puffed and braided challah. You pause to count: thirty-two loaves.

It is sixteen more steps to French doors that open onto a professionally tended garden. Hired workers are laying a heavy, tiled dance floor on the close-clipped grass, and installing a tent to cover it. Tables and chairs are in piles. You don't bother with shoes, and it is ten long strides through this garden, the grass sharp between your toes. The cool air snaps at your arms, but you hold your shoulders back for the benefit of the tent men. They are older, unshaved, and you feel sweat on your neck and behind your knees. You wear small white shorts and your gym shirt from two years ago—they must notice. Beyond the gate is a slope that tumbles down to the ravine and the overgrown forest your mother calls Sheol as a joke. Your brother will be there.

It is almost thirty steps, weaving between bare birch and pine, until you see him. The winter's snow melted only weeks ago, and the mud is cold and wet on the bottoms of your feet. You step over fallen logs, skip over stones and acorns that could slice your soles, and fallen leaves that are slick from last month's snow. The ravine smells the way ice tastes on your tongue, a sweet chill of melting winter.

Daniel kneels beside the creek that skids near the unused rail track. He is focused on something, his back curved, shoulders hunched. Daniel is sixteen, three years older than you and seven years younger than your sister—a lack of symmetry that annoys you. Crystal was always your babysitter, and Daniel the only friend you ever had. Your first memory—hardly that, just a blurred image nestled deep in your brain—is of watching your brother leap from his bed, flapping his arms and trying to fly.

Now, he wears his school uniform, the knees of his polyester pants pressed into the mud and his white, collared shirt untucked. Unlike other boys his age, he hasn't grown muscles, and his shoulder blades jut like wings from his back. You take three quiet breaths and walk up to him on your toes. You stretch out your finger to the bone of his neck, a marble under his skin, and watch his breath, its slow, visible rhythm. You kneel beside him and your knees sink into mulch.

"What are you doing?" You press your cheek against his shoulder, and watch as he plucks—meticulously—the feathers from a bird.

He holds the bird's slack body in both hands. "I found her against the big oak. Already dead."

"A warbler?"

"A vireo."

"Vireo." You repeat the word and observe the remaining feathers, the bird's yellow sides and white throat, the slight hook of her beak. Her legs—stiff and slim as twigs—curl in on themselves.

"I can't tell how she died," he says. The bird's empty black eyes stare open and her body fills his palm. "Maybe she froze to death, but it hasn't been that cold."

You pull the bird's wing open to touch the soft feathers underneath.

"It could be some sort of disease." Your brother seems to know most things. He runs one finger down the bird's bare skin, which looks like a pincushion where the feathers have been plucked. He lifts your hand and guides you to do the same. The body is cold, pitted, and reminds you of your own goosebumps.

"Maybe we should bury her." This seems appropriate to you. "Have some sort of ceremony."

Daniel lifts the bird to his face, as though he means to kiss her. If you weren't there, would he have done it? If he had asked you to, you might have done it.

You stare at the blank eyes of the vireo and, because you can hardly feel your toes, say, "Our mother wants you inside."

"Maybe I should bring her to the garage, for further inspection. Maybe I can diagnose her."

"She's suddenly become religious."

"Who?"

"Our mother."

Daniel laughs his rain-on-leaves laugh, puts his arm around you. "Do you need protection in there, Cassy?"

You straighten your shoulders. "No."

Daniel smoothes the plucked feathers with his palm then tucks them into his pocket. He walks to a fallen pine and places the bird under its grey, crumbling needles, then washes his hands in the creek. When he reaches to help you up, your fingers are stiff with chill.

"You know, Cassy," he says, "you wouldn't be so cold if you wore more clothes."

———

EIGHT YEARS LATER, your mother begins to lose things. She walks through the house holding her head with both hands, as though it might lift away from her body. "Where's my toothbrush? Where did I put my toothbrush?"

You look up from your studies, which you do in the living room, on a couch that Rebecca keeps covered with a sheet. "Did you check all the drawers, Mom?"

Later, when you get up to pour yourself some juice, you find your mother's toothbrush. It's in the freezer, its bristles like tiny, delicate icicles.

———

THE NIGHT BEFORE THE WEDDING, you slip through the hallway to your brother's room. Crystal stumbled out of the house hours ago for a bachelorette party, wearing hoop earrings and a silky sweater that fell like water from her shoulders. You count to ten outside your brother's room, then turn the doorknob with both hands.

Daniel lies in bed and reads from *A Field Guide to Western Birds*. The glow from his bedside lamp shows his oak desk and the detailed drawings of birds he bends over for days. A desk drawer lies ajar, as though it has burst open, too full of the feathers he collects. Sometimes, when he opens the window, they float through the room, dancing in the chilled air.

You slide between the sheets and under the wool blankets. Daniel lets you lie over his arm, your cheek on his chest.

"My room is cold. What are you doing?"

"I'm trying to memorize the warblers." Your brother's book is open to a cluster of brown and blue birds, arrows pointing to the significant marks on their bodies: throat feathers, striped backs and crowns, white bellies, and slight lines over the eyes. "There are so many."

"Do you think we'll ever see Crystal again? Do you think she'll visit?"

"She'll be too busy being a wife." Your brother shrugs, and you feel it in your own body. "But she'll remember us at family holidays. Family tragedies."

The idea strikes your mind like a gust of wind: future celebrations, future sadnesses. You haven't yet begun to imagine further years or separate lives. "Do you think she's in love?"

"She probably believes in love." It is in the darkness of this room that Daniel speaks most. He seems to save his voice, its jumpy rhythm, for your visits. And it is here, feeling the cadence of it against your cheek, that you feel calm and warm.

"What was the bird we saw today?"

"Flip to 228." Daniel holds the book's spine in his left hand and you thumb through it with your right. The thick pages are bent and have bled from rain. You run your eyes over the shiny pictures in the faint lamplight, and your brother's wrist and hand arc shadows over the print. You eliminate the white-eyed and black-capped birds right away, but recognize the yellow feathers of Bell's Vireo.

"No, think back, Cassy. It had a grey cap." Daniel points to the delicate drawing of the Solitary Vireo, and the movement of his arm pulls you toward his neck. He smells as bracing as outside. In the picture, the bird is perched on a branch, ready to hop into the air. The earliest spring vireo.

"'Blue-grey head, olive back, and snow-white throat,'" your brother reads.

You slow your breathing to match his, your eyelids heavy.

"'Similar to Red-Eyed Vireo's song. But more deliberate. Higher, sweeter.'"

"Are you going to leave, Daniel?" The question slips from you quietly, and it's hard to say if you dream the mouthing of it. "Are you going to get married?"

Daniel doesn't answer, and his breath lifts and drops you, lifts and drops you to sleep.

TWELVE YEARS LATER, your mother's mind begins to slip so much that it requires all her charm and your help to keep it a secret. When a guest arrives—the family lawyer, maybe—she holds out her hand. "You look so handsome I don't recognize you. What's your name again?"

The lawyer only laughs, so you jump in with, "Maybe Mr. Meier wants some coffee, Mom. He must have had a long day at his law office."

"Of course." Your mother takes his arm. "Get Mommy and the handsome Mr. Meier some coffee."

Crystal and Evan are too busy raising kids to visit. And Daniel hasn't been home in years. So Rebecca ensures that your mother eats three meals each day. And every night, you write a note.

Mom, today is Thursday.
—call Mary Pettleson re: garden party
—hydro bill is due
—also: anniversary of Dad's death in two weeks. Buy Yahrzeit candle?

She reads these notes the next morning, while you sleep off the drinks you had and the man you met, trying to forget them.

—

YOU HARDLY LISTEN during the evening's wedding ceremony, but watch the rabbi's wide, bearded mouth open and shut as he sings in a language you hardly know; in Hebrew school you focused only on counting the times your teacher stuttered. Daniel reads Leviticus throughout the ceremony, and you count the candles under your breath until your mother smacks your leg with the back of her hand. The sound cracks through the stone synagogue. Your sister stands straight-backed and plump beside her fiancé. He recently converted but still doesn't seem at ease in this place.

After the glass is stepped on and smashed, your sister and mother hold each other and cry while the rest of your family—all 262 of them—eat bagels spread with cream cheese and cedar-smoked lox. This is the appetizer, and you all climb into black cars and are driven to your house. Who knows where these cars came from—this whole business is disorienting. You swear never to marry.

Your backyard has been transformed. Candle flame reflects off the dance floor, and a band with a permed singer plays as guests arrive. Tables are set with heavy cutlery and tall-stemmed glasses, and the caterers have folded the napkins into shapes that look intricate and vaguely threatening. Your mother herds you through crowds of touchy-feely relatives to your family's table.

When everyone is seated, the rabbi bows his head and recites the blessing, then slices a loaf of challah into cubes. Everybody under the open-sided tent eats bread and gefilte fish, and you watch a sea of chewing faces. Evan and your mother sit on either side of you, and Daniel is three seats away, beside someone else. Your mother says his name is Stephen.

"Who is he?" You already drank a glass of wine when your mother wasn't looking. "I didn't see that guy at the ceremony. Did we even invite him?"

The stranger wears a dress shirt, no jacket, and has three safety pins slipped through his earlobes. His hair falls into his eyes, and a blue tattoo swirls around his wrist like a heavy bracelet.

"I told you, his name is Stephen."

"How is that spelled? Six or seven letters?" As far as you knew, your brother didn't have friends at that private school of rowers and debate captains. Not friends he would invite to sit at the head table.

"I believe it's seven, with a *ph*," your mother whispers. "He's a musician."

"Of course he is."

"Now hush up." Your mother's gloved fingers pinch your leg. "Drop your head, hands in your lap."

When the prayer is over, the caterers—so many of them, and they seem to multiply—bring out plates the size of platters for each guest, though all the food is in miniature: baby potatoes, asparagus tops drizzled with white wine, and a Cornish hen.

"Hello, Cassandra." Your sister's now-husband sits beside you, looking young and confident in his tuxedo. He is blond, with a pink tone to his skin. The last time you saw him was at a family dinner, much smaller than this one. When you left the table early, he followed you to the basement. The two of you watched reruns of *The Mary Tyler Moore Show* without speaking.

He glances at your shaved legs and whispers, "You look nice."

You wear a suit your mother chose. It is muted green, with a jacket, knee-length skirt, and tiny black belt. But you tore out the shoulder pads and hiked the skirt higher when your mother wasn't looking. You spread your napkin over your lap. "So," you begin, though you are bad at conversation. "We're related now."

"You say that without enthusiasm." Evan has the smooth voice of a business executive, which he will eventually become. "I saw you yesterday leaving the yard." He speaks the way girls at school talk to you, as though they are laughing in the backs of their throats. "What is it you do at that ravine?"

You don't tell him that you pick up fallen feathers for Daniel, or that you count the branches of trees. You blush, and hate yourself for it.

Evan smiles, showing the dimple on his right cheek. "It's nice to talk with you, Cassandra."

"Nobody calls me that."

Then the prayer is over and Crystal leans across Evan, pokes food off his plate, and laughs at you. "Don't drink *all* the wine, Cassy."

Your mother whispers to the rabbi, her hand resting on his sleeve, then bursts into laughter at one of her own jokes. She stabs a fork into her hen, managing to make even this look elegant.

And down the table, muffled by the din of cutlery, small talk, and the music of the band, Daniel tilts toward Stephen. His slim fingers rest on his friend's inked wrist. Daniel smiles. Daniel laughs. Their foreheads touch.

"You don't like to eat, Cassandra?" Evan elbows you, and you turn to his smile, his cologne. This time, you don't blush. You meet his eyes.

—

SIXTEEN YEARS LATER, you have managed the unthinkable: you have slept with so many men that you've lost count.

You decide to change your life. You start coming home early, right after work and before dinner. Even at this hour, the curtains are drawn and inside the house is dim. You hear Rebecca in the kitchen, the slice of knife on cutting board. You know the house's layout of rooms, angles of walls, and skirted furniture well enough to stride to the kitchen without switching on a lamp. Rebecca cuts potatoes, a pot of split pea soup on the stove.

"Is she here?" you ask, as though your mother had parties to attend or lovers to entertain.

"Your mommy is upstairs, listening to her music."

"I'll bring her dinner." You ladle soup into a gold-rimmed bowl and take a heavy silver spoon from the drawer. Then you brush one hand along the banister and count to twenty-three as you walk up the steps. You knock once, and turn the knob to your mother's room. You notice that the pictures of your father have been allowed to get dusty.

"It's me, Mom." You stand in the doorway, and the bottom of the bowl burns your palm. "It's Cass."

Your mother has wrapped herself in her ivory duvet, draped it around her tiny shoulders and her grey-streaked hair. You walk to the bed and sit beside her, then take a spoonful, blow on it, and hold it up to her mouth. She opens her lips then swallows, graceful as always.

"It's your birthday next month," you say. "And I think we should have a party." You want a celebration, because there's no telling how long your mother's mind will last. Sometimes it sparkles and she remembers things so crisply that to listen to her stories is like looking at an album of photographs. But twice last week she forgot your name—just for a second, and she didn't admit it. But you recognized the look of bemused confusion, then terror, that crossed her face.

"What do you think, Mom? We could invite Daniel. And Crystal and Evan and their awful kids."

"Evan?" Your mother stares past you. "Why do I know that name?"

"He's married to Crystal. Your other daughter."

She smiles brightly. "Of course, that one. He was so attractive, wasn't he?"

"You hate him. Said you'd never leave him a dollar and referred to him as 'the goy.'"

"Of course." She smiles. "I hate him." Then she brightens, her face childlike and full of wonder. "Oh, yes," she says. "A party."

Sometimes you wonder—briefly and in secret—if she's faking it, if this is her idea of a joke. You spoon soup to her mouth and watch her smile flirtatiously at the wall, showing her teeth and blinking her blue-streaked lids.

CRYSTAL IS BEING LIFTED on a chair and your extended family sings and dances a hora around her. Your sister's face is red and sweating from the alcohol and the attention, and the bottom of her dress lifts and drops like a huge tulle wing.

This is when Daniel and Stephen sneak off. You watch as your brother and his friend walk away from the band, the toasts, the candles. They are going toward the dark edge of the forest, to the ravine. They keep pace with each other, their hands in their pockets. From behind, at this distance, they look like brothers. You count Daniel's steps as he moves away from you—forty-seven until you can't see him anymore. You stare at that place, where Daniel took his forty-seventh step. The same way he often stares at a branch long after a bird has alighted there, then left.

YOU HOLD YOUR MOTHER'S BIRTHDAY PARTY in the backyard. This time there are no candles or caterers, and there are only five guests.

Daniel arrives first, his tattered suitcase in his hand. He took the bus up, and maybe it's travel that has worn him so thin. The skin of his face is grey and covered in a film of sweat.

"Hey. How are you?" He speaks casually, as though he's forgotten the years that have passed since you last saw each other.

"Daniel." You say his name to reassure yourself that this man is really your brother. "Come in."

You lead him to the backyard, where Rebecca has set a plastic table with placemats and plates and glasses of wine. There is an early spring sun, though it's not as warm as it looks, and everyone wears sweaters and scarves. During dinner—cream soup, baked chicken, Rebecca's signature mashed potatoes—your mother makes up for the weather by putting on a wonderful performance. She calls everyone by the correct name and she eats with the correct fork. She tells stories of her past—of how poor she'd been as a child, of how she met her husband—and she tells jokes.

Crystal eats for two, though you are sure she is not planning on any more children. The two kids she does have run through the yard, ignoring the food she served them. "Don't go too far!" Crystal yells desperately as they run toward the ravine. "Stay where I can see you!"

Evan arrives late—a meeting ran longer than expected—but he is polite. He kisses his wife's cheek, shakes Daniel's hand, and looks you in the eye to make it clear he remembers nothing. Then he flirts with your mother.

"I don't believe it for a second. I don't believe that you're sixty-five," he says to her. "You could be Crystal's younger sister."

Everyone takes seconds and compliments Rebecca. Only Daniel doesn't eat much. As you watch him slowly lift his fork to his mouth, you think of one of your past boyfriends, someone whose name you can't quite remember. He was from Brazil, and before he immigrated, he'd been a doctor. Once, he showed you a book that you couldn't keep your eyes from: *A Guide to Tropical Disease*. There were pictures of microscopic bacteria that bloomed like flowers. And there was a photo of a man with the same thin look your brother has now. The caption explained that he was afflicted with an illness that is rare among humans. One that passes between birds, as they nest high above jungles.

"You look cold," you say to Daniel, then go inside to get him an extra sweater. The only one you find is from his days at that private school. It has hung in his closet for years, but when he pulls it on, it still fits. He's even skinnier than when he was a teenager.

"Bad memories," he says as he adjusts the collar.

———

YOUR SISTER FLIES AROUND THE DANCE FLOOR, gripping the chair. You stand from the table but don't know where to go. You want to be at the ravine, to hear leaves crunch under your party shoes and to pick up smooth stones to show Daniel. Years ago, the two of you invented a secret language of tunes and whistles. You pretended that you could communicate with birds. That's what you'd like to do now: sing and whistle. But Stephen and Daniel are down there, and you are not invited. There are different languages and different secrets to learn now.

Evan's not dancing the hora. He's not even watching his wife, though she looks happier and lighter than ever before. Evan is looking at you, where you stand with one foot on the tile floor and one on the grass.

AFTER DINNER, you hug Crystal and the others goodbye, help Rebecca with the dishes, then take the stairs to your brother's room. You knock on his door, with no excuse prepared.

"Yeah?"

You turn the knob with both hands and look into his dark room. Your brother is reading in bed. He doesn't seem to recognize you at first, but still, you sit on the edge of the mattress. You notice his protruding clavicle. The bone juts two inches from his body, covered by pale flesh.

"What's going on?" You use a voice you haven't heard in years—the voice of your younger, anxious self. "Are you okay? Are you sick?"

"I'm fine, Cassy," he says. "And look what I found. It was under the pillow." He holds up the *Field Guide*, the cover curved from so many years.

You don't tell him that you left the book there for him. That over the past years you have read the field marks and range of nearly every bird, starting with all forty-four of the warblers, then moving through the thrushes, bluebirds, solitaires. When you had trouble sleeping, you read to yourself in Daniel's voice, that steady, deliberate whisper. "'Yellow-Throated Warbler,'" you said. "'A grey-backed bird with a yellow bib. Creeps about the branches of trees.'"

Some phrases from the book have reached into your dreams so often that you don't need to look at the page. "Black-Throated

Green Warbler: a soft, lisping song." And when you were sixteen, before he moved for the first time, Daniel pointed out a Wood Thrush to you. You can still describe the bird's deep red feathers and flutelike song from memory.

Tonight, you take the book from Daniel's hands and read to him of "Exotics: Introduced Birds and Escapes."

"'Yellow-Crowned Night Heron. A straggler—'"

Most of these you have never seen, and you have no idea if Daniel has ever glimpsed a Red-Crested Cardinal or a Black-Necked Swan.

"Daniel? Are you awake?"

"Huh? Yeah." But his eyes are closed and you know he is tired and wants quiet.

You press your hand to his chest and feel the faint rhythm, the rise and fall of his webbed bones. You've waited six years for your brother to come home, so you could feel safe, take comfort, and talk to the only man who's ever been your friend. But now that he's here, it's not what you'd hoped. You think of Evan, after, when he'd looked at your skinny legs and tangled hair. Disappointment— terror—in his eyes. "Cassy," he'd said—the only time you've heard his voice falter. "Get dressed."

Daniel's breathing deepens: he is asleep, guarding his own secrets. So you tuck the book under his arm, then leave. You close the door softly, walk across the hall to your mother's room, and don't bother to knock. *A Chorus Line* bounces in the background, and your mother's eyes are as blank as snow. Her small voice rises as she sings along to "Hello Twelve, Hello Thirteen, Hello Love."

You sit beside her on the bed. "Great party, Mom."

"Thank you, Birdie."

She must have mistaken you for a friend she once had, in a past life you can't imagine. You take her hand anyway. Something about the cool light of her bedroom, the motherly smell of Chanel No. 5, and her innocent, absent face makes you confess. You tell her about your brother-in-law, the night of the wedding, the twenty minutes the two of you slipped unnoticed from the party while the bride was hoisted around the dance floor.

You tell her how you can't remember who pushed whom to the ground, how you hardly felt the blunt pain of it, how coldness rushed through you like splintering wind. How you'd wanted to be included, to be adult, but were left feeling young and ugly and alone. You even tell her of after: how Daniel was the only one you trusted, so you crawled to his room, pressed your face to his pillow, and didn't know where he was, when he would return. How you wanted to be at the ravine, singing and playing, but already that felt childish. Already, it was an old memory.

When you finish, you're shivering. Your mother looks as though she doesn't recognize you, and you worry that she's going to call you by some other name. But this time, she gets it right. "Thank God your sister didn't find out, Cassy," she whispers, as though you are both schoolgirls, getting away with it.

Then she pulls you to her chest and holds you there, warming you. She starts to sing, and her voice is high and sweet. Your secret is hers now, to keep in the jumbled drawer of her mind. It is hers now, to lose.

f r a n k

THIS WAS BEFORE THE CITY had any money, and we didn't have any either. I lived with my girlfriend in an apartment near Northland Mall, which was just a bunch of stores you'd never heard of, along with a Mrs. Vanelli's, an A&W, and the Cinerama. The building was a muddy brown, the colour that snow becomes during the last weeks of winter. But then, that day I'm thinking of, winter had just begun. The snow was new, and everything was a pristine kind of white.

We lived in a building with grey siding on the outside and mustard yellow carpeting on the inside. Our apartment was a one-bedroom that contained hardly any furniture. Simmy and I didn't do anything like decorate or paint or keep potted plants because we never planned to stay long, though we didn't have any plans to leave either. There was a couch that we'd found on the street and carried eight blocks to our place, and a dining set that Simmy's parents had given us. The furniture, the apartment itself, and the lives we lived in it never really felt like our own. I don't mean that we weren't happy. We were happy in the way that kids are happy when they're playing at pretend.

We had jobs: I worked in the Safeway—produce—and Simmy worked at a dry-cleaning place. My job was to unload boxes of cantaloupes or tomatoes or oranges from the backs of trucks, and hers was to put clothes on and take clothes off hangers. We didn't make much money, but we were too young to care. And we liked the perks: I got a discount on food, so we had a good supply of things like frozen peas and boxes of cereal. And at the dry-cleaning place, when customers forgot to pick up their clothes, Simmy was allowed to keep them. We had a closet full of power suits and well-ironed slacks, and when we were bored, we'd try them on. We were often bored, since we didn't have any money, didn't know anyone in the city, and it was too cold to go out much that winter.

I'd rented the apartment to impress Simmy, and it had worked. I was nineteen and would have done almost anything to be with a girl. That's not quite true. I'd do almost anything to be with Simmy. We'd known each other since we were kids, and for a long time I'd hardly given her any thought. But during our last year of high school, I started to notice things about her. There was her dark hair, which she kept short. Her sneakers and jeans and the sweaters she got second-hand. The tattoo of an anchor on her arm, even though she'd never seen the ocean. The fact that, as a kid, she'd done rhythmic gymnastics—ribbons and cartwheels and that sort of thing—and the fact that we both found that funny.

And since she'd moved in, there was the way she slouched around the apartment. She was like a cat, and when I came home from work I'd find her curled up asleep on the part of the couch warmed by the winter sun. She got off work earlier than I did, and slept until I came home. And even though I didn't like the city, the weather, or my job, I'd walk in the door, see her sleeping, and I'd feel okay. I knew I had a good thing going when I could lie beside Simmy and warm myself against her body.

Maybe because she slept so much during the day, she never slept through the night. That was something I never got used to. I'd wake up and the room would be dark and the space beside me cold. From where I lay in bed, I could hear her wandering through the kitchen and living room, picking things up and putting them down. I didn't know if she was awake or asleep, and I wondered what she was looking for. She reminded me again of a cat, stepping lightly through the night. We couldn't afford to heat the apartment much, and sometimes she'd be gone from our bed for so long that I'd start to shiver from the cold. I'd start to believe that I was alone in that sprawling city.

But then light would slant into the room and Simmy would be in the doorway. She'd stand there naked, with her eyes half closed. "Sim? Are you awake?" When I talked, she jumped like a startled animal. Then she came back to bed, her body slurring toward me through the dark.

BUT I DON'T WANT to talk about Simmy. That's another story and everybody knows how it ends. Everybody's been young and in love. Everybody's lived through it. What I really want to talk about is that kid. He must be about nineteen or twenty himself now.

Sometimes I still think about him, even though I don't remember his name. It was a name that sounded too grown-up for a kid that age—he was only four or five. It was something like Ernest or Warren or Frank. Let's say it was Frank. Let's say he was a five-year-old kid, with dark eyelashes like a girl's, a furrow in his forehead, and his name was Frank.

The night before we met him, it was our six-month anniversary. Six months since I'd called Simmy up and asked her to be my girlfriend. It had taken me weeks to get up the courage to call her, and I'd rehearsed my speech before I phoned. But when she picked up, I was clumsy. It seemed that I was in a dark room, and the words I said were pieces of furniture I kept tripping over. "Hey, Simmy." I took a breath. "It's Mike. Mike Sanders."

"Hi, Mike. What's up?"

I pictured her sitting on one of the overstuffed chairs in her parents' living room. I told her about my job and the apartment and I described the city. I tried to sound like a guy who had his shit together. I didn't tell her how lonely I'd been for the past two months. I said, "I'm calling to invite you down here."

"Why?" Simmy wasn't flirting—I don't think she knew how to flirt. This was a serious question.

"'Cause I think about you all the time." That wasn't exactly true, but it wasn't a lie either. "I want you to be my girlfriend." There was silence on the line. "Hey, Sim? Are you there?"

"Sure," she said. "I'll come down."

She sounded like she'd been waiting for an offer like mine all along. And maybe she had. Simmy was a smart girl, and she knew she didn't want to stay in that town forever, working at the pub four nights a week.

"Really? You'll come? That's great. That's really great."

She laughed. She was the only person who could laugh at me without it pissing me off. "I'll need a couple days to pack my stuff."

"Yeah. Of course."

"I'm just coming for a while, Mike. Not forever."

"Okay. Sure. No problem."

She arrived on the bus, and I met her at the depot, carried her bags, and used the last of my paycheque for a cab to take us to the apartment. Even though I'd exaggerated the size and cleanliness of the apartment on the phone, Simmy didn't seem disappointed. She set her stuff down, smiled at me, and suddenly everything was okay.

She'd only planned to stay a few weeks, but six months had passed. And we were so young that six months felt huge, so we wanted to celebrate. After work I went to the liquor store and brought home two bottles of sparkling wine. The wine wasn't expensive, and we had to drink it out of mugs we'd got for free at the gas station. But it was sweet and bubbly and made us feel good.

Simmy suggested that we dress for the occasion, so we put on some of the clothes she'd brought home from work. I wore a suit made for a broader man and Simmy wore a skirt, a blouse with a bow, and a sweater with gold buttons. We invented names for each other, names that suited the outfits: I called Simmy Eileen and she called me Steve. The new clothes and our new names made everything we did—heat up dinner, top up our mugs of wine—seem outside our real lives, as though we were watching ourselves on TV. And the more we drank, the more hilarious our show seemed. We used a Polaroid camera that we'd bought at a garage sale to take pictures of each other. In one, Simmy was sitting on our kitchen counter, the wine bottle in her hand, looking like an alcoholic housewife. In another, I was on the couch with the remote—a tired husband home from the office. These scenarios were funny because they seemed impossible. If someone had told us that one day we'd stop being young, that our lives would expand past that winter and that new city and each other, we wouldn't have believed them.

———

FRANK LIVED WITH HIS MOM in the apartment next to ours. I don't remember his mom's name either, but she was pretty, and might have been a natural blonde. She had a job in a dentist's office, and we passed her in the hallway when she was on her way to work and to drop Frank off at the babysitter's. She couldn't have been much older than me and Simmy, but she seemed it. When she saw us, she'd give us this wistful, loving look. People did that then. People like to see young couples, the ones who haven't screwed up too much yet. The ones who have their whole lives ahead of them.

Frank's mom must have been really desperate that day. She must have really needed someone, because we couldn't have been her first choice to babysit. It wasn't that we were irresponsible—we made it to our shifts on time and we sometimes did our dishes. We just didn't know anything about looking after a kid. But she had a doctor's appointment, and for some reason the regular sitter couldn't take Frank that day. I think it was a Tuesday, maybe a Wednesday. Whatever it was, Simmy and I both had the day off. When that happened, Simmy would sleep in for hours. I'd be up earlier, but I wouldn't get out of bed. I wouldn't even move, because I didn't want to wake her. I'd just watch her sleep. Her mouth would be open and her arms flung over her head. I can still remember the warm smell—not unpleasant—that came from her armpits.

She was sleeping like that when Frank's mom knocked on the door. Simmy opened her eyes, closed them, and said, "What's going on?"

"Someone's at the door."

At the exact same time, we got out of bed, saw the clothes we were wearing, and remembered the sparkling wine we'd drunk the night before. At least, it seemed that way to me. Simmy and I had known each other for so long that it seemed like we shared everything, including hangovers.

We answered the door like that, wearing other people's clothes and smelling like sleep.

"Did I wake you up?" Frank's mom didn't look too good either. I don't think she'd washed her hair, and she wasn't wearing the usual lipstick or the green stuff on her eyes. She explained about the doctor's appointment and the babysitter. "I'd ask someone else, it's just that we're from up near Lake Athabasca and we don't know many people here."

I was about to say no, because there was no way I was going to spend my day off looking after her kid. I was about to give some excuse. But before I could come up with anything, Simmy said, "Sure. No problem."

For a second, Simmy became a stranger, someone I didn't know or like but who was living in my apartment. Then I inhaled, and she was Simmy again.

I looked at the kid, who was in his mom's arms and seemed small for his age. He wore blue snow pants, a red parka, and boots with reflective stickers on them. He was gripping a handful of his mom's hair in his fist. His hair and eyes were a deep brown, and that must have come from his dad's side. I'd never seen his dad, and never wondered about him either—that's an old story too.

Frank's mom said she'd be back around three and would that be okay? And again Simmy said, "Sure."

After his mom kissed Frank half a dozen times on the forehead, assured him that everything would be fine, and convinced herself of it too, she left. Then Frank stood in our doorway and looked at the carpet, which couldn't have been any different than the carpet in his own apartment. He was solidly built, with hair that his mom must have carefully combed. He held a plastic bag full of toys and books. He looked embarrassed or shy, and when Simmy said, "Hey, Frank," he jumped like he'd just been woken up. She tried again. "Hey, sweetie, how about some breakfast?"

"I ate already." He said this without looking at her. Then he put two of his fingers into his mouth and left them there. He rocked back and forth on his feet, and the stickers on his boots threw light up onto the walls.

"How about I show you around?" Simmy held out her hand and he looked at it. If he'd been an animal, he would have sniffed it. "Don't worry," she said. "You should feel at home here. From now on, this is your place too."

Frank nodded. Then he took his fingers out of his mouth and held on to her hand. Simmy didn't seem to mind that he was getting spit all over her. She led him around the apartment, and he dragged the plastic bag of toys behind him. The tour didn't take long. She showed him the microwave that we'd covered in stickers and the garbage that we hadn't emptied in a while and the couch we'd found on the street. While she did that, I made a pot of coffee and poured two bowls of Frosted Flakes I'd brought home from work because they were past their best-before date.

I heard Simmy say, "You don't look like a Frank. You look like a Justin. Or a Toby."

"My dad's name was Frank."

"Those boots make him look like a superhero," I said. I'd already forgiven Simmy for agreeing to babysit. For one thing, just the smell of coffee was easing my headache. For another, I figured it'd be easy money. "If he were my kid, I'd have named him Captain Danger."

Simmy came into the kitchen, leading Frank by the hand.

"Captain Danger," I said to him. "From now on, that'll be your name."

"Okay," he said.

I poured milk into our bowls and handed one to Simmy. Then all three of us sat on the couch and watched the morning news. I don't remember much about what the announcer was saying. At that age I felt outside politics, outside history.

Frank sat very still between us, like he knew we were hungover and didn't want to disturb us. He was probably used to keeping quiet for the sake of his mom. Once or twice he kicked his boots against the couch. After a while he spoke in a near whisper. "I'm too hot."

I noticed he was still wearing the parka and boots. "Take your coat off, kid. Stay awhile."

"The zipper's stuck."

Simmy tried to help, then I tried, but the zipper was caught on something. We couldn't even get it below his neck. We tried to pull the parka over his head, but the collar wasn't big enough and the Velcro scratched his face.

"If my mom was here, she'd be able to do it." He wasn't accusing us. It was a fact, and the way he stated it reminded me of the TV announcer.

We decided that if Frank couldn't get his coat off, then the solution was for us to put our coats on.

"We'll just go outside until we get too cold," said Simmy, "then come inside until we get too hot. And we'll keep doing that all day."

"What do you think, Captain?" I nudged him. "What do you think of that idea?"

"I think it's an okay idea," said Frank, his expression steady and solemn, like the guy who delivered the news.

WE DIDN'T CHANGE out of those strange clothes. Simmy just tucked in her blouse, buttoned up her sweater, and threw on her parka and mitts. I put on that suit jacket made for a bigger man and my own coat. Neither of us bothered to shower, comb our hair, or brush our teeth. We could get away with it. When you're nineteen, going out hungover and wearing clothes that smell of chemicals and other people is okay and funny and even charming.

Simmy and I forgot to bring the toys and books that Frank had brought in his plastic bag. But we did bring a travel mug of coffee that we passed back and forth, and the Polaroid camera, which Simmy swung over her shoulder.

When we got outside, it snowed in the agreeable way it snows on TV. Thick, wet flakes stuck to our eyelashes and hair. Frank pointed out that we'd also forgotten his mittens—they were in the bag with the toys—so Simmy and I each held one of his hands to keep them warm. The cool air woke me up, and I said, "Who wants to go on a train ride?"

"I have a train set at home," said Frank.

"Forget that. This is a real train. After this, you won't care if you never see that train set again."

These were big promises, considering all I had to offer was the city's Light Rail Transit system. Riding the LRT was something Simmy and I liked to do when she first moved to the city and everything was an adventure. The fare was a little over a dollar, and Simmy and I would ride the train as far as it would go and back. We'd sit side by side, lean into each other, and watch the other passengers. We felt sorry for them because they were old, and had destinations. Most were probably commuting to and from work, and they wore the kind of clothes that we only put on as a joke. They fell asleep with their mouths open, their slack faces disintegrating into their necks, and we were sure we'd never end up like them.

My favourite part of the ride was after Sunnyside, when the train slowed to go over the bridge. I'd press my face to the dirty glass and look down at the river. Sometimes it would be high and fast and green, even brighter than Simmy's eyes. And in the winter it froze to form ice so white that the sun seemed to leap off it.

If Frank had already ridden the train, he didn't say so. He held our hands as we waited for it to pull into the station, and we let him press the button to open the doors. We gambled that no one would be checking tickets, so we didn't buy any. We just stepped onto the train as though we belonged there and sat on a bench that faced backwards, away from where we were headed. Frank sat very still between us. He said, "How fast does the train go?"

"Ten thousand kilometres per hour." I could tell Frank had been raised to be trusting and he would believe anything I told him.

The woman across from us wore a purple hat with flecks of snow on it. Her grocery bags, filled with food from the Safeway where I worked, were hooked over her wrists. She looked at the three of us, probably trying to figure out if Simmy and I were young parents to be pitied, or conscientious older siblings to be admired. Simmy, who still had the small-town habit of talking to strangers, nodded to the woman and said hi.

"Hello." The woman focused on Frank, and she made her eyes wide and spoke in a singsong voice. "Hel-lo there." Then she looked at Simmy. "Is he yours?"

Before Simmy could jump in, I put my arm around Frank and said, "Yeah, he's ours." I wanted to see if I could get away with it. I pulled Frank toward me and he tilted stiffly into my side. "I'm Steve." I nodded toward Simmy. "And this is Eileen."

"And what's your name?" said the woman, leaning toward Frank.

Frank looked at me, as though asking permission to speak, and I nodded to him. He stared at the woman's purple hat. "I'm Captain Danger," he said, in his steady, serious way.

The woman lifted both of her eyebrows, but at different times: first one, then the other. "I see."

"Could you take a picture of us?" Simmy took the camera out

of its case. "We'd ask someone else, but we don't know many people here."

"We're from Lake Athabasca," I said.

The woman put her bags down and took the camera. She held it steady, despite the curve in the track. There was no flash, but the winter light through the window was enough. The camera hummed and the photo slid out. I waved it around and we watched the picture appear out of the murk. Simmy said to Frank, "Look. That's us."

"A happy family," I said, and that wasn't entirely a lie. I was happy then, and I think Simmy was too. And who can say what was going through the kid's head. Fascinated by the Polaroid's magic, he reached out and touched the white edge with his index finger.

I don't know what happened to that picture—maybe Simmy still has it. Maybe she finds it at the bottom of a drawer sometimes, and tries to remember the kid's name, and what she loved about me then, and what exactly the girl in the strange clothes was thinking at that precise moment in time.

~

WE RODE ALL THE WAY to Anderson and back. Then we switched trains at City Hall so we could pass above the river again, and we rode to Whitehorn. Then we travelled back downtown and switched again. It took us a couple of hours, enough time for me to make stuff up about how Light Rail Transit worked and for Simmy to give Frank a tour of the train car as though it were our second home. She pointed out the map to him, and the seats that lifted to make more room, and the phone you could use in an emergency. She showed him the button you press when you want the doors to open, which he could just reach. Frank told us about his train set. He said it had belonged to his dad, and that it wasn't quite as fast as the LRT.

"It goes seven thousand kilometres," he said. "Sometimes eight."

He seemed to have stopped being scared of us. He answered to Captain Danger, and at one point he sat in Simmy's lap and lightly held some of her hair. The woman in the purple hat had got off at Thirty-ninth Avenue, and Frank stood on her seat, pressed his face to the window, and looked out. He breathed on the glass and doodled in the condensation made by his breath. When he tired of that, he settled between me and Simmy, held her hand, and fell asleep.

Over and over, the train slid to a stop and the automated voice informed us of our location. I felt cold air each time the door opened. People got on and people got off, leaving snow and mud on the plastic flooring. Then, with something that sounded like an intake of breath, the train started up again and the wheels scraped along the frozen track. My headache was gone but had left me tired and dreamy, and it was easy to make believe that this was my whole life, that the train belonged to us, and that it really was going ten thousand kilometres per hour. I could feel heat through Frank's coat, and his calm breathing made me drowsy. I kept dipping into sleep, and I slept better than I had in months. I didn't have to stay alert for sounds of Simmy climbing out of bed, because Frank was holding on to her. I only woke once or twice, when the track curved or the door shunted open.

WHEN WE APPROACHED BRENTWOOD, I woke up feeling uneasy. But Simmy was still next to me. She'd fallen asleep at the other end of the seat, her head against the window. It took me a few seconds to realize that the space between us was cold. And then I remembered Frank. He was gone.

My first instinct was to look out the window. The strip mall blurred past and made me dizzy. I turned my head and looked up and down the car. There was a guy reading a newspaper. There was a scarf that someone had left behind on a seat. I stood up and the movement of the train almost knocked me down again, but I went toward the man with the paper.

"We lost our son," I said, panic confusing my story. "Have you seen a little boy?"

The man shook his head and said something to me, but I didn't listen.

"Frank!" My voice came out hoarse, thick with sleep. "Frank!" It was the first time all day that I'd called him by his real name.

I checked under each seat, moving quickly. The train was going too fast, along a wild track. I lurched from one side of the aisle to the other, holding the metal poles for balance. Above the door, a colour-coded map bolted to the wall listed all the train's stops. I looked at it and pictured Frank reaching for the button and stepping off the train. It could have been at any one of those stops. Then a pleasant, automated voice announced that we'd reached the end of the line.

I shook Simmy hard to wake her. "Get up," I said. "He's gone."

"Who's gone?" She squinted from the sudden light hitting her eyes. "Oh shit—Frank?"

I dragged her by her arm off the train. "He must have gotten off at one of the stops. We just have to catch the eastbound and retrace our route."

"We should call someone. The police or something."

She always put her trust in other people, usually any man who seemed powerful and kind. But I wanted to deal with this myself. I wanted to show her that I wasn't a kid.

"I'm going to use that emergency phone," she said.

"Those are probably just for show." I jumped down from the platform and crossed the tracks. Then I hoisted myself up onto the platform on the other side, dragging my belly along the concrete. I stood up and called to Simmy. "He probably hasn't gone too far yet."

"How do you know that?"

She was right—I didn't know that. I didn't know anything. But I wasn't going to admit it. "Simmy," I yelled. "Let's go."

Maybe I shouldn't have used that tone. She wasn't the kind of girl who would come when called. We looked at each other from opposite sides of the track and it was like a scene on TV, except it was real. This was the first time we'd disagreed about anything, the first time we'd lost each other. Simmy turned from me and, with the agility of a cat, ran to the emergency phone. She picked up the red receiver from its plastic box, and then my train pulled in. It glided between us and blocked me from her like a door sliding shut. People got off the train and swept past me. I looked at the car, with its orange floor and bench seats. It was identical to the one I'd arrived on, except it was empty. I got on.

⌒

I FOUND FRANK at Lions Park station, where we'd started out. I'd had a feeling he would have tried to get home, and I was right about that, at least. He was outside, crouched under one of the metal benches where people toss their garbage and stick their used gum. All I could see were his boots, with those reflective stickers. I ran to him, grabbed him by the leg, and dragged him along the cold pavement toward me. I was so angry that I couldn't even yell. "Frank," I whispered into his face. "What the hell are you doing?"

"We missed our stop." He'd been outside for a while—I could tell from the snow that rested in his hair, and from his red ears and cheeks. "I tried to wake you up."

I lifted him by the front of his coat. "You scared the shit out of me."

His breathing was fast and shallow, like he couldn't get air into his small lungs. "Is my mom sick? Is she going to die?"

"What?"

"Is that why she went to the doctor?" Frank wiped at his eyes and nose with his sleeve. "Is that why I have to live with you now?"

I went cold, like those nights when I'd wake to find Simmy gone. "Hey, kid, people go to the doctor all the time." I loosened my grip on his coat and set him down. "That doesn't mean she's going to die."

"Maybe she has what my dad had."

"Listen, your mom is fine."

I didn't know if that was true or not, but I said it anyway. Because, right then, I wanted to go home. I wanted to get away from this kid and go back to my life. Because I had a good thing going. I had a job and an apartment and Simmy. I didn't want to take on Frank's sorrow. I wanted to keep sorrow from the door for as long as possible. I didn't want to think about sickness or death, just like how I didn't want to wake up at night and find myself alone.

I straightened Frank's coat. "Your mom's okay. She's coming to get you at three o'clock."

He was shivering, so I picked him up and held him against me. I took his hands in mine, to warm them.

"There," I said. "How's that? Better?"

WHEN WE GOT HOME, Simmy was on the phone to the police, but as soon as we walked in the door, she said, "Wait—here they are. Sorry," then hung up. She stared at us, then slid down to the kitchen floor and started to cry with what must have been relief. I wanted to go to her and comfort her, but I was scared. I'd never seen Simmy cry before. I'd known her my whole life and never seen her cry.

Frank looked up at me and said, "What's wrong with her?"

That made Simmy laugh, and just the sound of it made everything okay. We were young again. We could go back to being happy and safe—laughing and sleeping in and drinking cheap wine. Simmy wiped her eyes, and we could go back to being ourselves.

WHEN FRANK'S MOM came to pick him up, he wouldn't go to her. He stared at her, and held on to the sleeve of Simmy's jacket. I could tell he wanted to run and grab her legs and smell her hair, but he was scared. He was scared to love her as much as he did.

"This always happens. He always has more fun at other people's houses." Frank's mom laughed. Then she picked up her son with the ease of someone who was used to his weight. He was stiff and cautious in her arms, but pretty soon he gave in. He put his fingers in his mouth, grabbed some of her hair with his other hand, and held it like he never planned to let go.

What can you ever know about people? As I watched Frank's mom fish in her purse for a twenty, I couldn't know if she was dying or not. I'd never seen a dying person. I imagined that death might be inside her body, wandering around quietly, the way Simmy moved through the apartment at night.

"Would you want to babysit again?" asked Frank's mom. "He seems to like it here."

"Sure," said Simmy, because she couldn't know anything either. She couldn't know that she'd leave soon, run off with a surveyor who worked up north.

We didn't mention that we'd lost Frank and I'm sure Frank didn't tell either. When they left, he didn't wave goodbye. He dropped us as easily as only kids can. He clutched his mother's hair and forgot us immediately. And I decided to forget him too.

THAT NIGHT, Simmy and I took off those stupid clothes and lay naked on the yellow carpeting. The TV flickered above us and turned our bodies blue then green then blue again. The news that night was celebratory. Walls were coming down all over the world, and people were filled with a naive kind of hope.

For the first time, Simmy and I talked about the future. We talked about how much money we'd have to save to buy this place. We talked about what we'd name our kids when we had them. I don't think either one of us entirely believed what we were saying—we talked the way kids talk when they're inventing stories—but we were giddy with relief, giddy with youth. I told Simmy that I hoped we'd be together for the rest of our lives. She said, "Me too," and I don't think she knew then that she was lying. We lay on the floor and held hands. When I closed my eyes, I could feel the train's hum in my body. I could feel it pulling me, pulling me along its track. Sorrow might come, but that didn't matter. Because right then, I had a good thing going. Right then, Simmy was there, every time I opened my eyes.

c a u g h t

THERE'S MORE THAN ONE WAY IT COULD GO. Outside the office there might be the shuffle of shoes on waxed floor: students to office hours or professors to the photocopier. Inside, light through the drapes, unvacuumed carpet, stacks of lab books. There might be a half-empty coffee cup that leaves a ring on the desk, an unbuttoned shirt. A kiss and the boy's hand where the wife's leg hinges to her hip. Then the way she can't undo his belt and the way he takes her hand, shows her. The wife's weight against the lip of the desk, and the boy's mouth on her neck. There's no knock at the door, only a turn of the knob. There's the husband.

—

OR MAYBE NOT. Instead, the door is closed and there's the sound of others passing, but the wife's shirt is buttoned and the boy's complex belt is buckled. The wife and the boy don't touch, but maybe, as a joke, they've switched seats. The boy laughs because the wife—with some grey in her hair, and those angular shoulders—is too elegant for that chair.

The boy sits straight, his hand to his chin in mock-professorial thought. "Do you walk the dog, or does he?"

"This chair is awful." The wife presses her back into it.

"Seriously. I can't imagine you in that big house. Who mows the lawn? Who does the dishes?"

"I walk the dog. I take her out before teaching." The wife is thinking about his knees, cupping them in her hands.

"I want to picture you." The boy leans toward her, his elbows on his thighs. "When do you wake up?"

"At six. Liam wakes me before he leaves."

"Liam. Superman."

"Ben and I eat cereal. Sometimes toaster waffles. He gets ready for school on his own now, so I have time to walk Tasha."

"I don't even go to bed until two or three in the morning."

"I wish you could meet Tash. You'd like her."

"I bet he's handsome even at five a.m. I bet he wears a tie."

"Is that ridiculous—that I think you would like our dog?"

So when the husband turns the knob and opens the door, this is all he sees: a young man in the wrong chair and the wife with her hands tucked under her knees. The boy's wide-set eyes and the wife turning her head. Maybe the husband stands in the doorway, car keys gripped in his fist, and says to himself: This is nothing. Or maybe he recognizes that look in his wife's eyes, that blur. And he's a smart man—he knows talking can be more intimate than kissing, kissing more intimate than fucking.

Maybe he stands in the doorway and says to himself: This could be anything.

———

MAYBE THE HUSBAND SPEAKS to the boy: "I don't think we've met" or "I should introduce myself."

"I was just leaving." The boy stands, grabs his denim jacket, and brushes past the husband, through the doorway.

"I got off earlier than usual." The husband leans against a filing cabinet. "What's the matter?"

"Nothing. I didn't expect you."

"Who was that?"

"A student." She sips the cold coffee. Lying is easier than expected. "How did you get off early? A hospital doesn't need doctors?"

"I thought we could pick Ben up together." He takes a book off her shelf and flips it open. He squints at diagrams of a mackerel's jaw. "This stuff is so weird."

"No weirder than humans." They have this conversation so often it has become one of their jokes. "Imagine what fish would say if they studied our jaws, our lungs, our behaviour."

"You tell me. What would they say, professor?" The husband winks at her. "You look nice, by the way. That's a nice shirt."

The wife pauses, her purse over her shoulder. Would he normally say that?

"Grab your stuff." He jingles the keys in his hand. "We're going to be late."

MAYBE THE WIFE and the husband walk down the hallway, along the waxed floor, without talking. They cut through the campus gardens to the parking lot and the wife thinks of the boy, how she met him on a warm, blinding day like this one. Salmon were spawning in Goldstream, and she was there with three graduate students and her son, who had a day off school. She noticed the boy because he was alone. He snapped photographs of fish slipping through water, gulls and dippers lunging at them. He wore a hooded sweatshirt with fraying sleeves, corduroys that dragged in the mud, scuffed boots. The wife watched him wander along the side of the stream, jump from rock to rock, and she couldn't keep her eyes off him. His casual walk, his focus.

The boy caught her staring a few times. This woman in hiking boots and a waterproof jacket. This woman who, he had overheard, knew the Latin names of fish, plants, birds. This woman who must be fifteen, twenty years older than him: small lines around her eyes, her mouth. He could see her straight shoulders through the jacket and he imagined she'd spent much of her life outside. Her dark hair reflected the sun, and the boy would have liked a shot of that.

The wife wandered away from where her students did counts. Would her son grow up to be like that boy, clear-eyed and quiet? Probably not. He might grow to be calmer, become as reasonable as his father, but he'd always be chatty.

Where was her son, anyway? The wife looked to her students, who knelt over the water's bank. Not there. And he wasn't farther downstream. Or in the cabin they used for maps and equipment. She'd only turned away for a second.

Then the boy aimed his camera upriver, past her, and she followed the lens's gaze over her shoulder. There. Her son's pants were wet to his knees and he balanced on a rock in the middle of the river. A salmon had died on that rock, or been pushed there by the current, and the son smacked a stick against the fish's body. He raised it over his head, smashed it down, and watched the huge, limp muscle shake.

"Ben!" The wife ran toward him. "Ben, what are you doing?"

The son stared at her, the stick in his hand. "It's dead anyway."

"Get off there. Right now."

He jumped into the water and splashed to the bank. "It's dead anyway, Mom."

"I said if you came to work with me, you had to behave." The wife gripped his shoulders. "The water could have been deep there. You have to be careful."

"I had my eye on him. He was fine."

The wife turned and saw the boy, who crouched and snapped a picture of the rock.

"Thanks." She squeezed water from her son's jeans. "He's going through a bit of a stage right now."

"It'll make a good photo." The boy took another picture of the broken skin along the fish's side. "Do you work here?"

"No, at the university. The biology department." The wife pointed to the three students with their clipboards and rubber boots. "My research is on coho salmon, so we're out here observing most days."

The boy brushed hair from his eyes. "Coho?"

"They're the ones with green heads and red sides," said the son, tearing his arm from his mother's hand. "Bright red, like apples."

"What's this one?" The boy pointed to the fish on the rock.

"That's a chum salmon," said the son, and kicked water at it. "You can tell because it's green."

The boy smiled at him. "He's been paying attention."

"It's less common to see coho up here—Ben, stop that. Part of my job is to figure out why they stay away." Was she using her professor voice? The boy looked into the clear water, and it was hard to tell if he was listening. "I think there are simply too many fish in this river. Coho tend to spawn beneath logs or under overhanging banks. They're shy and secretive."

"As soon as they spawn, they die," said the son, his eyes wide. This detail had made him want to spend the day at Goldstream in the first place.

"A death wish," said the boy.

"Not really." The wife waved her hand to indicate the fish, insects, water—the whole system. "It's just the way the cycle works. It's perfectly natural."

The boy smiled, but not at the son this time. At her. "Seems reasonable, I guess." Then he turned away and held his camera to his face. Across the narrow river, an eagle lifted a mangled fish into the air. He shot, caught it.

⌒

MAYBE IT'S AN ORDINARY EVENING: the husband and wife prepare dinner, tuck their son into bed, wash and dry the dinner plates. The wife sits cross-legged at the kitchen table, as she does every night. And the husband pours the wine, as he does every night—half a glass each. Maybe the husband is calm about it, cool.

"So, this boy. How long have you known him?"

"What boy?"

"Come on, Wendy." The husband swirls the red around in his glass. "Just tell me why."

"Why what?"

"Please don't treat me like an idiot." His voice remains even. "You have a husband, a son. How can you justify this?"

The wife lifts her glass, tilts too much wine into her mouth, swallows. She shifts in her chair. "The Indo-Pacific wrasse."

"Fish? For God's sake, Wendy."

"They're gorgeous, with swirls of blue in the scales. And they're polygynous."

"Pardon?"

"Not monogamous."

"Of course."

"They live in schools of about ten females to one male."

The husband pushes his wine away. "How many lovers do you have?"

"Just listen." The wife leans across the table. "The females have a pecking order that determines breeding access to the male. If the alpha female dies, for instance, the next-biggest female takes on her role and everyone moves up a step."

"I don't get it. Who's the male in this scenario? Who's the female?"

"Would you believe me if I said I'm torn?" She reaches for his hand but doesn't touch it. "If I said I'm crazy about him and I still want you?"

"Not really." The husband leans away from her. "Explain this fish thing."

"What's fascinating is what happens if the male is removed." The wife sits on her knees. "Within an hour, the alpha female starts to court the other females. And within two weeks, she develops functional testes."

"Your boyfriend is actually a girl?"

"I'm saying, if those fish can be functional—happy—acting one way and also acting another, oppositional way, it might be the same for us."

"You think you're more evolved or something? Because you can switch your affections?"

"It just seems to me there must be more than one possibility. I'm not saying that justifies it."

"None of this makes sense."

"I'm sorry, Liam."

"Your analogy doesn't make sense."

MAYBE THE BOY IS HANDY: he can fix an overheating engine, repair broken radios, explain the inside of a toaster. He collects old alarm clocks, the kind with metal bells like ears attached to their round faces. He even once took apart his camera, inspected each mechanism, then put it back together. The wife thought at first he was practical, the kind of guy who would eventually build a workshop in his garage. Now she knows better. He appreciates machines for how graceful they are, how pure: click and whir. Though he wouldn't put it that way. He would simply say that he rents his apartment because it has an extra half bath he uses as a darkroom, and a fan from the 1940s. He likes the old copper blades, the way they cut through the kitchen air.

And he likes the wife because, when he brought her to his apartment to give her some prints, when he unlocked the door, flipped on the light, forgot to hang her coat, and showed her the fan—the wife didn't shrug, didn't laugh. She stood and looked at the ceiling for nearly a minute. This was before they had touched.

"That fan is great," she said, and rocked from toes to heels. Then the boy took her hand, held it. She watched the fan's slow spin without coming closer, without moving away. She heard her own breath. Then, as an experiment, she pulled her hand from his and touched his lower back. Underneath his shirt, her fingers on his spine.

———

MAYBE THE HUSBAND doesn't mention it, lets it go. He and the wife prepare dinner, tuck their son into bed, wash and dry the dinner plates. Half a glass each, and they sleep beside each other, their legs touching. He wakes at five a.m., and the wife hears the alarm's buzz, the water as he showers. She gets up an hour later and goes to her office until three-thirty, when she walks her son home from school. She points out birds, explains the genius of the arbutus, and lets her son hop in puddles.

When they arrive home at four-fifteen, the husband is sleeping off whatever injuries and tragedies he saw in emerg. He's on top of the blankets, in sweatpants and a T-shirt, and the wife and son crawl into bed with him. The room is cool because the husband likes the window open, and the son burrows under the blanket, snuggles into the wife. She's between her child and her husband and she feels warm, feels held. The dog jumps onto the bed and settles against the son, who retells stories he told on the way home—about an eraser fight he started, about a pill bug his classmate brought to school. He exaggerates even more for his father, and the husband tells stories too. Makes his day sound easy.

"A woman came in who broke her ankle two weeks ago. It only occurred to her today to come to the hospital about it."

"Didn't she know it was broken?" The son bangs his legs on the mattress, jolting the bed. "Didn't it hurt?"

"She was so cheerful. She said she just didn't think it was serious—not until her foot swelled so much she couldn't stretch her tights over it."

The wife looks at the hair on her husband's arm, the one he has thrown over her stomach. She thinks to herself: Everything is fine. Everything will be fine.

"She sounds stupid." The son thumps the bed.

"Ben." The wife holds his shoulder. "Enough."

"I don't think she was stupid," says the husband. "Just hopeful. Optimistic."

"What does that mean? Optimistic?" Ben pulls at the dog's ears. "Tash? Are you asleep, Tash?"

The wife runs her fingers along her husband's forearm.

"Optimistic?" He pulls his hand away and rolls from the bed. "I guess it means she's stupid."

MAYBE THE BOY arrives at the wife's office the following Tuesday, as he always does. He walks in and shuts the door with his boot. "So. He's not a bad-looking guy."

"You probably shouldn't be here."

"And he's very tall." The boy points to a framed photograph of the wife, the husband, and the son that hangs on the wall. "That picture doesn't do him justice."

"Stop looking at that." The wife is embarrassed by the quality of the photo: the sun glares in the three faces and they squint into it, watery-eyed, overexposed. "You shouldn't be here. What if he stops by again?"

"You don't often see forty-something guys who are that athletic."

"He rides his bike to work every day, and works in the yard on weekends." The wife covers her face. "He's so—maybe 'upstanding' is the word. This kind of thing—"

"This sordid affair?"

"It would be so foreign to him."

"I hate to admit it, but I think the guy could beat me up. I think he's stronger than me."

She can't help but smile. "You'd make up for it in speed."

"Is that a comment on my lovemaking?" The boy drops to his knees in front of her. "I'm already feeling young, inexperienced."

"I mean it. You can't be here."

"Hey." The boy kisses her wrist. "Don't say that."

"I'm sorry, Jamie." Out the window, students weave through the stand of sequoia, going from class to class, requirement to requirement.

"You're serious." He turns her to face him. "I'll leave if you want me to. If that's what you really want."

The wife studies his eyes—lichen green. She touches his hair. His face. "You know, I bet you're right. I bet he could beat you up."

The boy kisses under her eyes. "He's practically Harrison Ford."

She undoes the top button of his shirt and he slides his hand along the seam of her pants.

"I must have a death wish," he says, and her zipper is undone.

"Seems reasonable." Her hand against his chest. "Perfectly natural."

—

MAYBE THE WIFE continues to meet the boy in her office every Tuesday afternoon and continues to sleep beside her husband every night. And in between she marks lab exams, teaches classes. Classes on the Caribbean bluehead, for example. They begin life as small yellow fish with short fins. But at any time they can trade their shimmering yellow scales for the more threatening blue head, black and white mid-body, and green posterior. This way the fish can spawn up to a hundred times per day and defend their territory. It sounds impossible, but it's simple. They're just like us, she explains to her students, and wipes chalk from her hands. They just do what they have to do.

—

MAYBE THE WIFE starts to imagine a life with this boy. She imagines living in his apartment: low ceilings, little daylight, photographs hung like laundry from a string in the bathroom. She imagines being there when he comes home from art school, his eyes tired, his black bookbag cutting into his shoulder. She imagines it as a quiet existence, disordered but also precise, like the boy's experiments in the darkroom.

In her real life, the wife and the husband alternate making dinner and doing dishes each night. They hire a young woman—one of the wife's students—to dust their furniture, scrub their bathroom, and vacuum their floors once a week. Ben is allowed to watch half an hour of television every evening. At night the wife and the husband share a drink and whisper to each other across the table. In bed, the husband's breath tastes of red wine and toothpaste.

It's nothing like the boy's chaos. The first time the wife walked into his apartment, there were days of dishes hardened in the sink. Egg yolk stuck to a pan, ketchup skin on a plate. The bathroom: towels on the floor, mildew along the tub. And what does it matter? thought the wife, as the boy kissed her that first time. Let the dishes sit on the counter. Let the bacteria flourish. She ran her hands tentatively up his arms. She hadn't forgotten about her husband, not at all. She could hear his voice: You're being ridiculous, Wendy, idiotic. But the boy had one hand on her back, one in her hair, and he pulled her against his mouth. This boy who smelled like sand and something else, something chemical. This boy who had stood in the kitchen and listened to her talk nervously about birds—the difference between a Pelagic and a Double-Crested Cormorant—then kissed her, stopped her mid-sentence. This boy who made her feel like she was twenty again. Made her feel ridiculous, yes, idiotic. Made her feel crazy and awkward and wild.

———

BUT STILL, there are things she would miss. Her husband across the table from her, tired and good-looking, or in the yard, his shirt off as he rakes the leaves from the Garry oak. And the house: the sunny entranceway and the rhododendrons in the garden. Her son's room: yellow paint on the wall, the big window, toys on the floor, the shelf of brightly coloured books. Her son.

But maybe, if she moved into the boy's apartment, the son could come too. He would love it. No one would tell him to tidy his room. No one would tell him to brush his teeth. The wife and the boy would let him order pizza. They would let him drink pop. They would let him go to sleep when he was tired and wake when he was rested. Because how could they—the wife and the boy— how could they justify rules? What right would they have to tell someone what to do? Not only would they let the son watch television all night, but he would learn how a television worked. The boy would sit with him on the floor—that dingy carpet—and show him the insides of the small black-and-white set. The two of them would spend an afternoon taking the television apart and putting it back together, like a puzzle. Then they would move the rabbit ears around so the son could watch the screen disintegrate and rebuild itself. Nothing would be forbidden, nothing hidden. All the complexities: red wire, green.

———

MAYBE THE WIFE continues to meet the boy in her office every Tuesday and continues to sleep beside her husband every night. In between she marks lab exams, teaches classes. Maybe this becomes, like everything else, routine.

—

MAYBE THE HUSBAND is calm about it, cool.

"And you can go to your Indo-Pacific wrasse." He drinks the last of his wine. "He seems like a nice enough kid."

The wife watches light reflect off her glass. "Is that what you really want?"

"I need a break. I need to think this through." When he stands, his chair scrapes along the tile floor. "And Ben will stay here with me."

The wife feels stiff, feels caught. She can hardly breathe.

The husband dumps the rest of her wine in the sink. Then he rinses their glasses, as he does every night, so the red won't stain the bottom.

—

MAYBE SHE BUZZES the boy's apartment. "It's me."

"I'll come down."

The wife puts her forehead to the window as he takes the stairs two at a time. When he opens the door, she says, "He wants time to himself." The boy lets her press into him, dig her nails into his back. "Time." She feels his T-shirt against her cheek. "It could mean anything."

"Maybe he'll think it over and he'll be okay with it."

"He'll never be okay with it."

"Are you sure?" The boy holds her, one palm on the back of her head. "For one thing, you don't know what he's been doing."

"He hasn't been doing anything." The wife lifts her face. "I would know."

"I'm sure he doesn't mean it. I'm sure, if you went home, he wouldn't turn you away. Would he?"

"Can we go upstairs?"

"Did you tell him you were coming here?"

"Jamie, please?"

"We can't go up there right now." The boy wipes away hair that sticks to the wife's wet face. "Sara's over."

The ex-girlfriend. The ex-girlfriend who doesn't eat meat, or drink, or do drugs. That's how they met, at a "dry" party, where her band was playing. "She's sweet," the boy said when the wife noticed the picture on his wall. Then he shrugged.

"She just dropped by, Wendy. It's nothing."

"Okay." The wife nods, because there isn't much else to say. "Okay."

WHETHER SHE GETS AWAY WITH IT, or not. Whether she stays with him, or not. Maybe it doesn't matter. Or at least, sometimes it doesn't matter. What matters is this: for years the wife has studied coho salmon—their intricate bone structure, their fussy habits— and finally she understands them. And not just their sneaking around, or their risk-all sex. All of it: gestation, survival, then that mad drive upriver, toward desire and toward—away from—they don't know what. Now she gets it. But only briefly, and only sometimes, like when she suddenly thinks of the boy's quick smile, his naked hip. Maybe she'll be colouring in a book with her son, or standing in front of her grad class, and she thinks: I get it. I understand coho salmon. She wants to tell this to her students, but how can she? To those young, focused faces? They would think she was crazy, or drunk. So she lifts her hands, drops them. I get it, she wants to say: We're alive. This is called being alive.

—

MAYBE THE BOY DOESN'T ARRIVE at the wife's office the following Tuesday, as he always does. Maybe, instead, the wife finds a photograph slipped under her door: an eagle holding a fish in its talons. Sun glinting off the scales. The bird is half in, half out of the frame. A blur of feathers, flight.

—

MAYBE THERE'S A MOMENT when no one says a word. No one moves. The boy in the leather chair, the wife with her hands tucked under her knees. After she has turned her head but before the husband speaks, before the boy stands. Light through the drapes, unvacuumed carpet, stacks of lab books. A half-empty coffee cup that leaves a ring on the desk. And a pause, one second when they are still. The wife, the husband, the boy. There's more than one way it could go.

sky theatre

THE MOST BEAUTIFUL GIRL in my school was named Mary Louise. Though the name has a Roman Catholic ring to it, I don't think she was a believer. She did, however, bring out a religious kind of devotion in most of us who went to high school with her. We loved and hated and feared her with the same fervency that we might a goddess. I was at the age when I noticed feminine beauty more than masculine, because I was always comparing myself with other girls. So I can still remember that Mary Louise had long legs, ankles that were perhaps too thick, and dark eyes. She was tall and had such a confident gait that she reminded me of a horse—maybe Pegasus, or one of the lucky horses that drew Apollo's chariot. She looked as if she could have been that close to the sun.

In fact, the sun always seemed to be touching her. Her skin had a permanent tan, and even in winter the ends of her hair were bleached. This might have been because she spent each summer outside, swimming and water-skiing at her family's cabin in Ontario. I'm not sure how I knew this detail, since I was a grade beneath her and was never her friend. But somehow I'd heard about the cabin, imagined that Mary Louise spent two months in her bathing suit, and was jealous of the way she must have looked. I could picture her driving a motorboat and canoeing. I imagined that at night she and her family played board games, or took out their binoculars and looked at the clear night sky.

She might have had a summer boyfriend, some seasonal romance, while she was at the cottage. But when she came back in the fall, she returned to the only boy in the school whose beauty matched her own. Jordan Burke was so pretty that his face was almost boring. He had the cheekbones of a girl, blue eyes, and curly blond hair that frothed around his ears. I never spoke to him, but he appeared to be angelic and shy. They looked perfect together. And they were perfect: she was the star of the girls' basketball team, and it was rumoured that he was an excellent student. Every September, they walked through the halls holding hands, reunited. They had none of the awkwardness that the rest of us exhibited—sweat stains, acne, sexual fear. They seemed comfortable and happy in their bodies, like Adam and Eve before they understood they were naked. The sight of Jordan and Mary Louise was like the smell of new binders, or the sound of a book's spine being cracked. It announced the new season, and seemed familiar, unchanging, part of the natural order.

That is, until one September—it was her final year, my penultimate—Mary Louise came back from her cottage in a wheelchair.

There were different stories. She'd slipped off the dock. She'd been thrown from a horse. She'd been drunk. She'd been sober. Eventually we found out the truth: she'd climbed the steep rock that lined the lakeshore—I could picture her scrambling up, her arms reaching and her legs strong—and she dove into water that was too shallow. She'd done what all our mothers had cautioned us against, and she'd suffered the consequences our mothers warned us about too. Mary Louise had injured her spinal cord. She couldn't move her legs. She would never walk again.

When I first saw her, I was sitting on the floor outside my homeroom with my best friend, Sylvia. Syl was using a blue pen to draw a butterfly onto the knee of her jeans, and I was braiding and unbraiding my hair. We were talking about *The Bell Jar*, because we were sixteen, and we wanted to be depressed in New York. We would have even settled for being happy in New York. It was the first day of school and we wanted to be anywhere but where we were, and then Mary Louise rolled past us in her chair. I let my hair unravel, and Syl looked up from her butterfly. We stopped talking, as did the other students. The hallway had the kind of hush you find in churches.

It wasn't that we'd never seen a girl in a wheelchair before, and it wasn't just the wheelchair, either. It was that Mary Louise's face seemed to have gone still, along with her legs. Her head was bent forward, her eyes focused on the floor, and she seemed to wish she were invisible. I remember the soft noise the wheels made on the polished floor.

For the first time, I was aware of luck—that flimsy, moody thing. We existed in a world that seemed to hold to a pleasing pattern: we took the bus to school each morning, and every afternoon the same bus returned us to our safe streets. We lived in a city that was always booming, or about to boom, a city that was sunny even in winter. And we existed in a world of rules, some imposed by our parents and teachers, but more by our own sense of social boundaries. Some people were deemed attractive and some were not, some were popular and some were not. If this was unfair, at least it was unchanging.

But suddenly we saw that life was not the still water we'd believed it to be. Mary Louise had been going about the same middle-class, suburban, privileged existence that we led—except that hers was even more privileged than ours. She must have had our same unthinking confidence in the future, until her destiny swerved like a canoe caught in a current. She'd once possessed something elusive and unmistakable, something beyond even beauty—maybe charisma, maybe grace—and that something had been wrenched from her. Fortune's wheel had turned. I found this terrifying. I found it comforting.

I DON'T MEAN THAT Mary Louise was no longer pretty. But she was more ordinary. Instead of being a goddess, far above us mortals, she had become the Divine who moves among us. As she rolled past, she was both Leda and the swan. She was the Holy Ghost and she was a broken Christ.

Is this what we thought at the time? Probably not. Most of the girls, myself included, probably felt pity and a secret sense of triumph. And I can't speak for the boys. Maybe they instantly betrayed their queen and struck her from their hearts, removed her from their sexual fantasies forever. Or maybe, in her new incarnation, they found her even more desirable than before: a pretty girl who couldn't run away.

—

TO THE RELIEF OF MY PARENTS, I was an ordinary kid. I did my homework, played defence on the field-hockey team, and listened to the kind of music that got played on the radio. I had plenty of friends and had never been seriously teased or ostracized by my peers. I never got cavities, though once I had mono. And any beauty I possessed belonged to youth, not to me: I wore my hair in a ponytail, got freckles in the summer, and was of average height. This ordinariness was probably what Mary Louise liked about me, for those five minutes that she liked me.

Of course, being no different from most girls, I didn't love my body. I was annoyed by the late development of my breasts, my bad posture, and the stretch marks that scarred my hips and abdomen. But I liked what my body could do. I could easily run the laps required in gym class, and enjoyed the adrenalin of field-hockey games. When I wasn't at school, I liked to ride my bike around with Syl. We could ride and ride and feel like we hadn't gone anywhere, because in our neighbourhood each street looked like every other street: double garages, aerated lawns, pastel stucco. We never got tired, so we biked for hours and talked about moving to somewhere like Venice or Paris, somewhere we'd only seen in magazines, somewhere that was instantly recognizable.

When we got bored of biking, we'd go to Mac's and buy a bag of five-cent candies. Then we'd lie on the patch of grass beside the parking lot and talk about boys. The boys we talked about were not actually the boys who talked to us. We worshipped the ones who were older than us, or far above us in the intricate social atmosphere. The Jordan Burkes and Dan Houstons and Ryan Watkinses of our world.

Syl believed in destiny, and she would say things like, "Ryan and I will probably meet again when we're, like, twenty-eight. And he won't remember where he knows my face from, but he'll have this sense that we met before, like maybe he knew me in a past life or something. He'll feel like he's finally come home."

I was less trusting of fate, so sometimes I'd say, "What if he's bald when he's twenty-eight? Or a crack addict? Or you're already in love with someone else who's really awesome?"

But usually I let her fantasies stand. I understood them. Syl and I were devoted to boys who didn't know our names, boys we'd practically invented. We wanted them to notice us and recognize our worth. And this was just part of the larger fantasy: that one day the whole world would see our worth. We dreamed—as all ordinary, despairing teenagers do—of distinction.

THAT YEAR, IN GRADE ELEVEN, I got a boyfriend. His name was Jay, and he was nice and almost cute. He had knotty, pubescent muscles along his arms, and brown hair that he kept short. He worked part-time at Dairy Queen and he knew how to skateboard. We didn't have much to talk about, but that was okay. All we wanted to do was make out.

Our parents always seemed to be home, so we had to be inventive to find privacy. The gym equipment room at school was pretty good. So was the parking lot behind the Dairy Queen. Movie theatres. Empty parks. The best place was the Planetarium. We'd been there for a field trip, and had discovered its manifold advantages. It was only a bus ride away and it cost less than the five-buck admission if you were under eighteen. And there was the Sky Theatre, a dark room where images of the night sky were projected on a domed screen above us. We went there on Friday afternoons, when school got out early and the Planetarium was nearly empty. On Fridays, I chose my outfits strategically. I wore shirts with buttons, the only bra I owned, and sometimes—when feeling brave—a skirt.

Jay and I always pretended to the man at admissions, and to each other, that we were at the Planetarium for proper educational reasons. We'd waste precious minutes wandering through the exhibit rooms, reading about dark matter and supernovas, and neither of us dared make suggestive jokes about the Little Dipper or the Big Bang.

This was before a telecommunications company sponsored the Planetarium, so its exhibits had not yet lost their charm to technological innovation. The place smelled of cleaning products and plastics, and the walls were covered in graphs and posters and telescopic photographs. After a few visits, the informative panels became like well-loved poems. *The sun and planets were formed approximately five billion years ago, from a cloud of gas and dust left by dying stars.*

My favourite part was the model of the solar system. The planets looked rickety and seemed to be made of papier mâché. One of Saturn's rings—which I'd always imagined as a brilliant halo—had cracked. Some of Jupiter's gassy surface had been chipped away. The solar system, in this incarnation, was small and flawed. Maybe that's why I liked it.

Jay and I held hands and made our pilgrimage from one planet to the next. We started at Pluto, as this was before it was demoted.

"If you were a planet," said Jay one afternoon, "which planet would you be?"

This was the kind of shy conversation we made while we waited for the appropriate amount of time to elapse before we could go into the Sky Theatre.

"I'd want to be the sun. It's so bright and beautiful."

I wanted Jay to tell me that I was the sun. That I was bright and beautiful. But he replied in the sweet and patronizing way he must have thought guys were supposed to talk to their girlfriends. "The sun's not a planet, baby. It's a star."

"Yeah, I know that. Fine. Then I would be Mercury, since it's closest to the sun."

"I think you're the Earth." He put his arms around me. "You're familiar and comfortable."

I nudged him away. "What about you, then? What would you be?"

"I'd want to be Jupiter." Jay took my hand and led me toward the Sky Theatre, toward its darkness and mystery. "It'd be nice to have all those moons around. That way you'd never be lonely."

So there was that too, that held us together. A fear of being alone.

WE THE STUDENT BODY—that reluctant community, that dysfunctional family—got used to seeing Mary Louise in her wheelchair. After a while we didn't stare at her, though we did talk about the fact that she and Jordan had broken up. We assumed he'd dumped her because she could no longer use her legs, and he was unanimously viewed as selfish, superficial, a total dick. How else could we explain that when Mary Louise could walk, he had proudly paraded through the halls with her? And that now, she wheeled herself to her classes alone?

But—said some of us, daring to rise to Jordan's defence—Mary Louise was perhaps not handling her situation well. Months passed, and she did not live out the narrative we hoped she would. We had been raised on Oprah and adolescent self-esteem classes, and we expected her to prove her resilience. But she hardly smiled. She lost too much weight, maybe from stress, and her features became sharp and hard. And the worst was that she wasn't any friendlier to us ordinary people. In fact, where she had been aloof before, she was now anti-social. Some of her friends still talked to her, but she acted like she was in exile, and spent most lunch hours alone. She sat in a corner on the third floor, doing her homework, slowly eating a sandwich, and drinking from a juice box. Perhaps this was the difficult thing for Jordan: she was simply and always sad.

❦

MAYBE BECAUSE THE SKY THEATRE and everywhere else that Jay and I went was semi-public, I never felt alone with him. As we kissed, I could hear Syl's voice. It was like she was sitting next to me, dissecting the pros and cons, the shoulds and shouldn'ts, of sleeping with Jay. "Maybe you shouldn't because you don't even like him."

"Sometimes I think I do like him."

"Really?"

"No. I don't know. I can't tell. What do you think? Do you think he's cute?"

"I think you should be able to tell. I think that every time you see him, it should feel like you've died and gone to some way better place."

"I never feel like I'm dead."

"Maybe that's the problem."

I wondered, constantly, what other people saw when they saw us together. And what it said about me if I made out with a boy who was not particularly smart or handsome. I wondered, too, what it said about me if I liked it. And, of course, I wondered how I compared to the other girls that Jay had made out with, or had thought about making out with. I didn't know any techniques, so I asked Syl for practical advice. But she'd never been practical about anything, and had very little. So I fumbled with him and wished that I were as competent in those matters as Mary Louise must have been. I imagined that her hand jobs were legendary among the boys, mythic in their reputation.

As these kinds of thoughts whirled around in my brain, Jay and I pressed our lips together, opened our mouths, touched tongues, sometimes accidentally banged teeth. We kissed until our lips became swollen and raw. We kissed until we physically couldn't kiss anymore. Then we straightened our clothes, breathed, leaned back in our seats, and looked at the stars. We held hands, our palms sweating against each other, as Andromeda sparkled or aster-oids flew toward us. The Sky Theatre had a different show each week, but each was accompanied by a voice-over done by the same man. He had an accent that I couldn't place but that I adored. *The pattern of our days occurs because we live on a constantly spinning Earth. Because of this motion, day turns into night, the sun rises in the east and sets in the west, and summer turns into fall.*

In my mind, the man who owned this gruff but gentle voice was named something foreign, like Pavel or Armand. I settled on Armand, and once I'd named him, I fell in love with him. I imagined that he was dashing and elegant and better-looking than Jay. I imagined that he was romantic and confident. I watched the complex movement of the heavens—there was a swirling nebula, there Orion's belt—and everything Armand said seemed to be intended only for me.

From our earthbound view, stars appear to make a connected shape. But in fact the stars are not so connected, except in mythology and human imagination.

Once, I forgot myself and said, "I love his voice. I would marry someone who talks like that."

"That guy?" said Jay, with his Western Canadian accent—a form of speech so neutral that telemarketers in Delhi are encour-aged to adopt it. "I think he sounds like an asshole."

◆

THE PLANET CONTINUED TO SPIN on its axis, and fall turned into winter. By then I had been to the Planetarium so many times that two things had happened. One: I'd decided that I might as well have sex with Jay. And two: I was quite knowledgeable when it came to astronomy. For instance, I knew that the Earth was tilted at a 23.5-degree angle, and it was this happy accident that allowed us to experience seasons.

Another happy accident was that one of the girls on my field-hockey team threw a party when her parents were out of town, and I was invited. I'm not sure what transpired in the universe for this to come about, but someone, somewhere, had decided that I was cool. The party was held in a seven-bedroom house that was just outside the city limits. Syl and I had never even thought of riding our bikes that far, so I'd never seen houses so big. The roads weren't plowed and there were no street lights. It had taken me days to convince my parents that the winter roads were safe and that the party wouldn't be too wild. I got a ride with a girl on my team, and when I arrived I had to sneak into one of the bedrooms to call and assure my parents that I was okay.

Neither Syl nor Jay had been invited, so I was left to mingle with people who frightened me. I was an explorer among aliens, and I wished I had a notebook to record their habits and report back to Syl. Ryan Watkins and Dan Houston played video games and drank a heroic amount of beer. The girls—people like Nicole McPhee and Julia Vincent—drank a purple mixture that they'd made in a bucket and scooped out with their cups. Nicole actually talked to me. "Do you want some? It tastes like Kool-Aid, but it'll get you totally hammered."

"Sure." I watched her dip a Styrofoam cup as well as her entire hand into the bucket. "Thanks."

"Do you play field hockey?"

It was finally happening. I was finally being recognized. "Yeah." I nodded my head vigorously. "I am. I mean, I do."

"That's so great." Nicole took my hand and laced her fingers through mine, the way Jay sometimes did. "You know those skirts you guys wear? Could I borrow yours sometime?"

"I guess. I don't know. I sort of need it for practice."

"I think it would look cute with one of my sweaters."

After about an hour, most people were so drunk that they seemed to be handicapped. Ryan Watkins was unable to stand up from the couch. He kept calling people over to help him, and any girl who tried ended up on his lap.

Two other girls—Ashley and Bronwyn—sat beside him on the couch and made out with each other. Ryan and some of the other guys cheered them on, and every few minutes the girls stopped kissing and shrieked, "We're not lesbians! We're not!" I doubt anyone thought they were. They just wanted attention, and weren't pretty or interesting enough to get it in any other manner. They kissed in a way that I'd never seen before, with their tongues outside of their mouths. Watching it made me sad, and for the first time, I missed Jay. I was at a party with Ryan Watkins and other demigods, and yet I missed my unremarkable boyfriend and his ordinary way of kissing.

❧

IT WASN'T A BIG PARTY—I counted only twenty-four people—which I suppose meant that each person who'd been invited had been carefully chosen. But still, through some unlucky accident or cruel purposefulness, Jordan and Mary Louise were both present. They didn't speak to each other all night. Jordan mostly hung out with other guys, and didn't drink much. He wore jeans and a blue shirt that made his eyes sparkle. He reminded me of a doll with rhinestones glued to its face. Mary Louise spent most of her time on the periphery of the room. She drank beer, not the purple stuff.

I stuck to the Kool-Aid. I drank as much of it as I could, but it didn't help. Back then, alcohol didn't affect me until it was too late to do any good. I had first noticed this when Syl and I were on the phone one night and she said, "We should get drunk."

"Okay. When?"

"Right now. Over the phone."

"My parents are home, you freak. They're upstairs watching TV."

"My parents are home too. That's why it'll be funny."

So Syl and I each grabbed what we could find in our parents' cupboards and—counting to three into the phone—shot back whiskey and vodka respectively. We went shot for shot for about half an hour, about as long as the news program my mom and dad were watching. Syl's voice started slurring through the phone line and she dropped the receiver twice, but I didn't feel anything.

After we hung up, I topped the vodka bottle up with water, washed my face, brushed my teeth, and took the dog out for a walk. It wasn't until I went to bed that I became drunk. Then the room and everything in it—my desk and books and poster of Brad Pitt with long hair—spun above my head. When I closed my eyes, the whole universe seemed to swirl around me. I crawled from my room to the bathroom and threw up quietly, so my parents wouldn't hear.

A similar thing happened at that party. No matter how much I drank of that purple shit-mix, I didn't feel anything. I knew I'd feel it later—probably once I got home and saw that my parents had waited up for me. But right then I was as sober as a stone. I was so sober that I even came up with a theory. I figured it was my Superego, which was more muscled than vodka could ever be. It had such a tight grip on me that I couldn't get drunk. In fact, alcohol seemed to increase my inhibitions.

And that's probably why I ended up outside and alone. It was December and it was cold, but I put on my coat and went out onto the porch. I don't think anyone noticed that I was gone. I could hear music coming from inside—some band that everyone was supposed to like but that I always got confused with about three other bands. People's conversations sounded distant and sorrowful.

The house was far enough from the city that I could see the stars almost as clearly as in the Sky Theatre. I tried to pick out some of the constellations that I'd learned about, but in real life the night looked jumbled and chaotic. All I could recognize was Venus, the brightest thing up there. At the Planetarium, the model of Venus was accompanied by a panel that called it Earth's sister, and said that the planet might once have been covered in salty oceans. It was the most hopeful panel of all: *Someday, Venus might again be hospitable to life. Hundreds of millions of years from now, it may become Earth's true twin.* I watched it shine as bright as Jordan Burke's eyes. I wished I had my bike so I could ride home.

Then I did what I always did—what I still sometimes do— when I felt lonely: I fantasized about Armand. I imagined him showing up at this party on a motorcycle and declaring his love for me in front of everybody. Actually, I didn't care what he said, as long as he said it in that beautiful voice. He could lecture about black holes for all I cared. *Imagine a place where time stands still.*

Where the universal order breaks down. Where the unimaginable becomes reality.

I was so deep in thoughts of Armand—I pictured him with a craggy, dark face and a beat-up leather jacket—that I almost didn't notice when Mary Louise opened the door. She didn't notice me, and I watched as she tried to hold the door, keep her bottle of Molson from spilling, and manoeuvre herself outside. When I moved to help, she was startled by me. "It's okay," she said. "I got it."

I saw that she'd taken one of the blankets that had been thrown over the leather couch and draped it over her shoulders. She adjusted it to cover herself, and took a sip of beer. Without looking at me, she said, "It smells bad in there."

"It does? I didn't notice."

"I thought that's why you were out here too."

"I'm out here because I can't get drunk. It's this problem I have. There's something wrong with my body."

"It's probably your liver." Her eyes looked glazed over, so I could tell she didn't have the same trouble I did. "You're Christin, right?"

"Caitlin."

Mary Louise tipped the last of her beer into her mouth, then put the empty bottle on the porch's wooden rail. I could hear the snow crunch under her wheels as she rolled forward. Then she stopped moving and we were both quiet. We looked up at the Milky Way, that shimmering backbone of the night.

"There's supposed to be a meteor shower in Gemini this time of year," I said.

"What do you mean? Like falling stars?" Mary Louise

shrugged, the gesture so subtle that it was hardly perceptible under the blanket. Since she'd lost movement in her legs, it seemed the rest of her body had become less expressive too. "I've never seen one. I have bad luck with that kind of thing."

If I had been an astrologer, I could have told Mary Louise her future. I could have cheered her up. I could have told her that in a few months she would join a wheelchair-basketball team and she would start smiling again. And that a couple of years after graduation she'd marry Jordan, and eventually she'd become a successful radio broadcaster. I could have told her that years from now, long after she'd forgotten meeting me at this party, her voice would wake me up in the mornings.

But I couldn't predict the future, so I said, "If you were a planet, which planet would you be?"

"What? Which *planet*?"

"Yeah, you know, like, which one suits your personality? I can see you as Venus."

"No. Not Venus. I'd be Pluto." She looked at me. "Caitlin, what do people say about me?"

"About you? Nothing. I don't know." I was a terrible liar. I shrugged dramatically. "I'm only in grade eleven."

"Everyone thinks he dumped me, don't they?"

"You mean Jordan?"

"People just assume things." She closed her eyes and swayed in her chair. It must have felt like every star, planet, and moon was whirling around her, like she was the centre of everything's orbit. "You know, we still do it sometimes. When I feel like it."

"What?"

"Me and Jordan. We still do it."

"Oh."

"Everyone wonders about that, don't they? Whether it's still possible. Everyone's curious."

"I guess so."

"Sometimes he lays me out on the bed. Or sometimes we do it like this." Using her arms, she scooted herself to the edge of the chair and leaned her torso back. "Like this." Her head rested against the back of her chair and she closed her eyes. She kept them closed for so long that I thought she'd passed out. Then she said, "Do you think I'm still pretty?"

She sounded drunk. She sounded needy. She sounded the way Nicole had when she wanted to borrow my skirt.

I looked at her clear skin and closed, heavy-lashed eyes. Maybe it was the light from the stars, but she looked prettier than I'd ever seen her. Maybe her broken body made her face more endearing, more shocking. Death had brushed against her, and she'd been touched by a greater sorrow than most of us had seen so far. Loss lived inside her now, and this made her even more lovely.

I said, "You're beautiful."

She shivered, maybe from the cold. Then she pressed her palms against the arms of her chair and tried to straighten herself. But she couldn't do it. I guess she'd lost a lot of strength over the past months, or the alcohol had weakened her arms. She squeezed her eyes shut, shifted her weight, and struggled to make her body do what she wanted it to do.

"Let me help," I said.

"It's fine." She was out of breath. "I'm fine."

But still, I leaned down and put my arms around her. I lifted her body, which was heavier than expected, and sat her up straight. After, I didn't let go. I held her the way Jay sometimes embraced me. And she hugged me too, her arms around my neck.

We held each other for so long that the porch's motion-sensor light flicked off and it became dark. I could smell her hair and hear her breathing. It was like we were sisters, reunited after a long separation. Or like gravity locked us together: the Earth and its moon. All the rules, those social boundaries, seemed to waver and break, and I would never believe in them again. *Welcome*, I could hear Armand say, *to the world of Black Holes*.

When we finally separated, I straightened her blanket so she wouldn't feel a draft, and she said, "Thanks."

"No problem."

We never spoke to each other again. It had started to snow, so we stayed outside for only a few minutes longer. I watched the snow melt into her hair and she looked as betrayed as Christ. As heartbroken as Him too. She was Demeter, aged by her loss. She was Eve, cast out and cold. Or she was just an ordinary girl. An angry, heartbroken girl. In any case, I had told the truth: she was beautiful. And that's probably why she'd hugged me. She was probably just drunk and grateful for the compliment.

Or maybe it was more than that. Maybe she wanted me, in a way that Jay never could. Maybe she'd held on to my body because she craved it for herself. Maybe she wanted to switch skins, switch lives, switch fates. I was so ordinary in my jeans and coat that she wanted to inhabit me, to live in the temple of my normalcy.

I know why I held her. Mostly because I missed Jay and Syl and I didn't want to be alone. But it was also that I wanted to touch the divinity in Mary Louise; I wanted to see the sublime. I wanted to know what it was like to climb up on that rock and look out over a glittering lake. I wanted to still believe that the stars held a pattern. I wanted to feel the air on my face, just for a second, no matter the consequences. I wanted that moment, before the fall. Then I wanted to dive.

and the living
is easy

SHE CAME INTO OUR LIVES SUDDENLY, like a radio song—the type you can't stop humming no matter how hard you try. It was the summer after I'd finished high school, during the hottest months this city has ever seen. I had no prospects and no interests other than an impractical one in history, so it was decided I would apprentice in my father's tailoring shop. Each morning, my father and I walked from our house on Borden to the shop on Spadina. Once at work, I started looking forward to lunch. That's when we walked to the hot-dog stand and ordered beef smokies piled with relish and fried onions. We ate them on a bench outside the shop as the sun beat onto the tops of our heads.

Every day, my father would comment, "Not a bad life for us guys, eh?" I would chew and nod in agreement. When we finished our dogs, he'd say, "How about a cone?"

Then we'd walk to the ice-cream shop on Kensington, one of the first places to cater to the new market of tourists and students. That's where she worked. She wore an outdated uniform and a tag that said *Simone*.

When we met her, my father ordered rum-raisin—his favourite—and said, "This your first day?" He was one of those. The kind of man who instinctively flirts with waitresses and sales clerks. She was at least twenty years younger than him.

"Yeah." She bent to scoop the ice cream, and I'm sure we both noticed her greying bra strap.

"It's a terrible uniform they make you wear, isn't it?" My father leaned against the freezer. "What is that? Polycotton?"

She looked up at him. "I don't know."

"You should talk to them about ordering new ones. I've got some fabric that'd be perfect. A soft yellow. It'd look nice with your hair."

She handed him his cone.

"I could even whip up a blouse or something for you. No charge, I mean. Those old bolts of fabric, I'll never use—"

"I don't need a blouse."

"Good point. No blouse, then." My father dropped coins on the counter. "Simone has spoken. Miss Simone, the high priestess of soul."

"Can I get rocky road?" I wanted to kick my father in the balls. "One scoop?"

"You mean Nina Simone?" She leaned against the freezer. "I was named after her."

I figured she was lying. I figured she was angling for a tip.

"No kidding?" My father waved the change away. "You're a bit like her."

"No, I'm not." And she wasn't. This Simone was pale, freckled, and skinny.

"You've got the same regal air."

She laughed, and it reminded me of the small bell that rang each time the ice-cream parlour's door was opened. "No," she said. "I don't."

In all the years that have passed since that afternoon, I haven't had the courage to ask Simone what crossed her mind as we walked toward the door. Maybe she noticed my father's dark hair or his confident posture. Or maybe it was his suit: the elegant fabric, starched collar, and the way his trousers hung over his shoes in a perfectly effortless way. I'm sure she didn't notice me.

"A dress," she called out. The bell had just bestowed its charming ring, and we were nearly out the door. "You can make me a dress."

—

A WEEK LATER, she appeared at our house to pick up the dress. It was a simple sleeveless design, with a boat neck and a hem just above the knee. She put it on, then stayed for dinner. She didn't talk much, but she ate a lot. My father had made one of his famous lasagnas, and she took three helpings. For dessert, she'd brought a bowl of something made of canned fruit and gelatin that her mother had taught her to make. When she said the word *mother*, we all got quiet and looked at our plates.

After dinner, my brother, Sam, gave her a tour of the house. He said things like, "This was our rosemary plant, but it died," and, "Alex and the TV live in the basement." While he showed her around, Simone found Mom's records. She slipped one out of its jacket then set it spinning on our dusty record player. "It's Too Hot for Words" started up, and my father stepped out of the kitchen, that vein in his temple tensing, because no one since Mom had touched those records.

"Billie Holiday was my age when she recorded this." Simone moved her hips to the beat, and that yellow dress fit her perfectly. "It was before all the shit that happened later."

My father handed her a gin and tonic, the same as he drank, and offered Cokes to me and Sam. "I'll take something stronger," I said, hoping I sounded like Jimmy Stewart in the movies Mom used to watch. But my father ignored me, so I went to my room. I lay in bed but couldn't sleep because of the music. When they tired of Lady Day, they put on Ella Fitzgerald and played *Live from Carnegie Hall* all the way through, as loud as it would go.

<hr />

THE NEXT MORNING, I found Simone in our kitchen. She was drinking a glass of orange juice and looking through one of my mother's cookbooks. Sam was already at the table, reading what my dad called the funnies. My father was frying eggs in a buttered pan.

Simone looked up from a recipe for roast chicken and smiled. "Morning," she said, and flipped a page.

"Hello," I answered, and the hot pan spit at me.

The next day, I found her on the couch with a cup of coffee. The morning after that, I heard her in the shower. This went on for about a week, until it was clear she had moved in.

—

DURING OUR MORNING WALKS TO WORK, my father either whistled or told me his life story. If he whistled, it was a tuneless sound that had all the improvisation of jazz and none of the melody. If he talked, he told me about when he had learned to sew from his father, in the same shop where we now worked.

"And I hated it," he said. "I hated the shmattes. I hated the smell. I hated all the men who were just like my father." He had a quick, elegant stride, and he kept his hands casually in his pockets. "There was no way I was going to spend my life in that dank little shop, hunched over a machine. I decided that, when my father died, I'd sell the place and never walk down Spadina again."

I could have asked questions—"Why?" or "What changed?"—but my father told his story the way he might tell a joke, in the practised tone of someone who doesn't want interruptions. So I trampled people's lawns and listened to his history. After his initial reluctance to learn, he discovered he was good at tailoring. He was precise and calm and developed a love for the perfect fit, the timeless cut. He altered his young man's pride and recklessness and turned those qualities into a charming, understated masculinity. Around this time, he met my mother. He seemed to consider her something that had happened to him. He spoke of marriage and fatherhood as things that had taken him by surprise, the way a change in the weather might. "You wake up one morning," he said, "and you don't recognize your own life."

But despite this boyish astonishment at the way things turned out, I think he became what he always wanted to be: a family man, a flirt, a nine-to-five gent. For most of his life, he fit seamlessly into Spadina's noise and neighbourly business.

Now was a different story. The men and women he knew when he'd started—my grandfather's friends, people who most often did business in Yiddish—had left Spadina. They'd moved uptown, or to the suburbs, and were replaced by people from China, Portugal, and the Caribbean. People who opened restaurants, imported clothes instead of making them, and played music my father hated out their shop windows. Neon signs in Asian script were put up, along with paper lanterns, sculpted monkeys, and carved dragons. There were other newcomers too, Americans who sat in cafés and talked politics.

Jack Holtzman, my father, was the last stubborn Jew, the only person on Spadina who still wore a suit and polished shoes to work. He never discussed this, but he seemed split between the present world and some idealized past he reinvented and relived each day. Even with Simone, he was divided. He never took her to work with him, or anywhere else someone might see them together. No one would have really cared—by then we'd all heard the rumours of *free love*—but he wanted to maintain some kind of image, a style his father would have approved of.

❧

SIMONE GAVE THE HOUSE a feeling of ease, of languidness. She opened all the windows and left her magazines, her clothes, her empty packs of Juicy Fruit lying around. Suddenly our place was nothing like the tidy, airtight home Mom had kept. The house had been her idea—my father would have been happy to live above the shop—and Mom had been obsessive about its upkeep. When she was still well enough, she dusted, vacuumed, scrubbed and waxed the floors nearly every day.

But that summer, no one vacuumed or wiped water stains from the bathroom tiles. Simone spent most of her time on the kitchen floor with the phone to her ear, telling her sisters about the ice-cream parlour, or whispering things she and my father did. Sam built complex forts in the living room. He used pillows and chairs for walls, and draped my father's clothes for roofs. My father was so happy, so distracted, that he didn't get angry when he found his pressed shirts strewn around the living room. He spent his time cooking festive, complicated things: lamb shanks, brisket, squash stuffed with rice and hazelnuts. As though every day were a holiday. The house got even hotter with the oven on, but he didn't seem to notice.

After dinner, no one asked me to help with the dishes. Those sat in the sink while Simone and my father drank gin and danced to the blues in the kitchen. I'd go to my room, get into bed with the lights out, and use a flashlight to read a series of books I'd been given as a child. They were hardcovers about ancient civilizations. Pompeii, Babylon, Troy, Petra.

The text was simple, the maps and pictures faded, but I reread these books all summer. I had nothing else. I hadn't gone to the library in months, because it would have reminded me too much of Mom. When she was alive, we went every week. I picked out historical mysteries and she took home books about musicians, artists, politicians. In another life, I think she would have made a great biographer. Sam has a lot of my father in him: the wild hair, the vintage sparkle in his eye, and a tendency to view history as a series of styles that can be imitated. Mom saw the world as a tangle of stories, mostly painful ones. I've always been my mother's son.

⁓

EACH MORNING, I'd wake to the smell of the coffee my father had on the stove. "Eggs and toast, boys," he'd say. There was even something cheerful about the way he flipped pancakes or seasoned hash browns.

Eventually, Simone wandered in, her blond hair greasy and tangled. She wore my father's plaid pyjamas, and had to roll the waist of the pants to keep them from sliding off her hips. She'd usually announce her presence by executing a long, sleepy stretch. Then we'd all sit on the porch for the hour before the city was too hot to bear, and watch the neighbourhood wake up. My father served boiled eggs in glass egg cups and we ate them slowly, dipping our toast in the bright yolks. Even Sam sat still while he slurped his juice.

Then Simone went upstairs to change into the uniform she wore to work. She liked to do her makeup in front of the hall mirror, and we—my father, Sam, and I—would sit on the couch and watch her comb her hair or choose a colour of eyeshadow. She'd talk, her eyes catching ours in the mirror.

"If I have to work the late shift again, I'm going to shit," she'd say. Or, "Don't you think? My own sister? I can't believe—"

I doubt any of us listened. We just sat there—male and ignorant and entranced—and watched what she did with eye pencils.

DURING THE FIRST WEEKS of my internship, my father was proud and patient. "This is my son," he'd tell customers, and they'd smile at me like I was a newborn. But as July wore on, it became clear that I had no talent as a tailor. I was inaccurate and sloppy. After two weeks of bad measurements and crooked cuts, I was put in charge of filling out order cards and counting change.

"I'll deal with scissors," my father said. "You deal with people."

I wasn't very good at that either. Since Mom, I'd become even quieter. I'd taken to crawling into the very back of my brain and staying there. It probably gave me a strange, blank look. I think it frightened the customers.

After a month of this kind of failure, working with my father began to scare me. Some mornings I couldn't get any food down. Once at the shop I was exhausted, and sometimes fell asleep in my chair instead of observing his quick, talented fingers. He blamed it on the heat, and bought another fan for the shop. It buzzed like an insect and hardly moved the store's soupy air. I watched it all day, counted time by the spooky rotation of its head.

"Alex, wake up." My father waved an order card in front of my face. "This is a big one. Five wool suits."

"Wool?" I scratched my arms.

"Yes, sir." His voice and the movement of his lips made me dizzy. "In this weather. Must be a funeral."

Maybe it was the fan's noise or the heat or the word *funeral*, or all of it at once, but I fainted. Swooned like a girl and fell to the floor.

WHAT I REMEMBER MOST about my mother is the way she sat at the kitchen table, listening to a record or to the radio. Also her deep-set eyes and her silence. She could be quiet in a threatening way, and this could last for days. When it got really bad, she wouldn't read or listen to music or help us with our school work. She'd just sit in the kitchen and hold a smouldering cigarette in her hand. The table would be littered with long curls of ash.

During these times, my father would joke with her, tease her, kiss her roughly on the cheek, and say things like, "Hiya, sunshine." Even as a child I couldn't understand his strategy. It seemed obvious that it was best to leave her alone, wait her out. Eventually, she'd burst from this darkness on her own. At some unexpected, illogical moment she might turn on her record player or announce, "Who's up for a game of rummy?" But still my father persisted. He cooked her favourite food—chicken soup with *kneidlach*—and brought her bright, smelly freesias from the florist down the street.

Even when she was sick, my father maintained this cheery demeanour. He took her hand and squeezed too hard. He brought chocolates to the hospital even though she couldn't keep them down. He told jokes.

"How many doctors does it take to change a light bulb?"

She smiled faintly. "You've already told me this one, Jacky."

WHEN I CAME TO, my father knelt over me. "Alex?" he said, as though I was an acquaintance he hadn't seen in years.

Then he took my arm, helped me to my feet, and walked me home. When he left me at the porch, he mumbled something like, "See you later." He was going back to work—he never closed before five—and when he got to the end of our yard he turned and said, "Get some sleep, okay?"

I walked into the house and Simone was on the couch, chewing that gum the colour of wall plaster and reading an old, water-stained copy of *A Certain Smile*. She raised her eyes and looked at me over the edge of the book. "You look weird," she said.

I wanted to answer her with: "You don't even live here," or, "Why are you always reading such shit?" Instead, suddenly feeling the urge to punch someone, I said, "Where's Sam?"

"At a friend's place. Some kid with a swimming pool invited him over."

I could hear her chew as she talked, and I hated her more than I've ever hated another person since. I hated the way she sprawled on the couch as though this was her house. I hated that she was wearing the dress my father had made, and that she wore it every day, as though it were a ring. I hated the way she washed it each night in the sink and hung it, wet and dripping, in the shower. I hated most of all the fact that she was here, now, and nothing like my mother.

"Are you okay? Do you want something?" She raised an eyebrow at me—an eyebrow I'd watched her pluck during her morning routine. "Some gum or something?"

"No. Thank you."

"Are you sure? I mean, do you want to talk about it?"

"I'm not one of your sisters. I don't need to gossip about everything that happens around here."

"Okay. Good point."

She went back to her book and I looked at the wall. After five minutes, she uncurled her legs, leaned toward the coffee table, and grabbed her purse—a faded leather clutch that must have belonged to her mother. She pulled out rolling papers and a small bag of marijuana.

I'd seen people rolling joints before, but I'd never seen anyone use so many implements for the job. She had a pair of tiny scissors and tweezers, and she performed the whole operation on the surface of a pocket mirror. It was as mesmerizing as watching her put on makeup.

"My sister taught me," she said. "Kat's an expert in this kind of thing."

When we smoked it, I kept myself from coughing.

"This'll be good for you," she said, and flicked ash onto an empty gum wrapper.

She was right. It did ease me, and we spent the rest of the afternoon lying like coma victims on the couch.

After a long time, she said, "Do you think we're using up all the oxygen in the room?"

"No." My throat still hurt from the smoke. "The window's open."

"I wonder if you can die from sweating too much."

"Probably. You can die from anything. You can die from drinking too much water, even. And my mom died for no reason at all—they couldn't figure out why she got the cancer she got."

Simone didn't say anything to this, and I was glad. She had a talent for dancing to swing and big band, but she was good at being quiet, too.

After a while, she said, "Sometimes it's so hot at work that when I scoop ice cream I lower my whole face into the freezer."

"I'd trade my brother for some ice cream right now."

"And sometimes I go right into the storage fridge." She spoke sleepily. "It's cold and I don't have to talk or smile at anyone. I just stand there for a while, next to the tubs."

"That'd be nice." I watched the hypnotic hinge of her wrist as she fanned herself with her hand. "I'd like that."

AFTER MY FAINTING SPELL, my father went to work by himself and left me at home, with no specific instructions other than "Don't kill your brother." Regardless, I started most days by punching Sam in the arm, just hard enough to send him running to his room. Simone ignored this completely. She and I were sort of friends. I didn't hate her too much and I could even distinguish her moods. After her early shifts she came home cranky and tired, and went straight to the bedroom for a nap. On her days off she'd run errands—mail a letter to her family, or go to Kresge's to buy the ankle socks she wore to work.

While she did this, I sat on the living room couch. Sometimes I fantasized about a different kind of summer, the kind my friends were having. Swimming, canoeing, and living in cottages. They were with their mothers, who were alive, and their fathers, who took holidays. But most of the time, I wasn't unhappy. The house was messy but bright, and I liked to watch dust float in the sunlight.

Simone would find me in the living room and shake my shoulders. "Hey, Al. I have an idea."

I liked her ideas. Maybe she'd coaxed a five from my father before he'd left for work, so we'd see a movie. Or we'd walk down Kensington to see the crates of fruit and vegetables or to watch the poultry guy slaughter birds he kept in wooden cages. Sometimes we'd take what Simone called "family trips" to United Bakery to buy heart-shaped cookies. Sam ate most of them, which didn't seem to annoy her. Neither did the way he circled madly on his bicycle, or played tag and other games that allowed him to touch her body.

Once, we went to the deserted park on Howland. I slid down the staticky plastic slide and Sam stood on the middle of the teeter-totter. He'd grown tall, while my own body had stalled at an unremarkable height.

"Watch me! Simone, watch me!" he yelled constantly.

I joined Simone on the swings, and we floated lazily, careful not to sway out of the shade of the park's one tree. I suddenly remembered being on one of those swings when I was very young. It wasn't a clear memory—just a feeling of air on my skin.

"I think Mom used to take us here," I said.

Simone leaned back and lifted her face to the sky. She wore plastic sunglasses she'd bought at Kresge's, and they sat crookedly on her nose. "What was her name? Your mom?"

"Elise." I leaned back too, and let the sun blind me. "Dad never told you that?"

"I don't ask him about that stuff. He always wants me to be bright and cheerful."

"He's pretty nuts about you. I can tell."

"He did tell me one thing, though." She began to swing higher, her hands tight on the chain. "He said he's worried about you. He wants you to get a job."

"He said that?"

She dragged her heels in the sand under her swing. "Working's not so bad, you know. You get to talk to people."

"I'm not very good at talking to people."

"You would learn."

I swung higher to catch up. "Why doesn't he tell me this himself? If he's so worried?"

"I don't know. You're so quiet it makes him nervous. He's not sure how to talk to you, I guess." She kicked sand in Sam's direction. "Hey, Sam, you're dead! I just shot you."

"Did not!" He turned to her, furious. "Did not, and we weren't even playing."

"Nervous?" The motion of the swing made me feel exhilarated and sick.

"Did so. I shot you right in the chest." She turned to me. "What?"

"Nothing."

"I told him I thought you'd be okay." Her swing fell level with mine. "I told him I thought one day you'd wake up and have it all figured out."

⁓

AFTER THE PARK, we went to my room because the basement was the coolest place in the house. Simone brought a tub of pistachio ice cream and three spoons and we left the light off to keep cool. Sam and I sat on the floor while Simone sprawled on my bed. She closed her eyes and I noticed that the tips of her eyelashes were blond.

She sang in a sweet and shaky voice. *"Oh, your daddy's rich—"*

"That would be nice," I said.

She hummed the rest of the bar while bending her knees and kicking her feet in the air, admiring her own legs. Then she started to scat in a poor imitation of Ella Fitzgerald.

"Hey, Simone," I said. "You're off-key."

"Yeah, Simone, you're off-key." Sam was upside down, trying to stand on his head. In a mocking, singsong voice he added, "Simone is off-key-ey. And Al-ex is in love with her."

"Sam." I kicked his exposed belly. "I'm not in love with anyone."

"Ow." He slumped out of his headstand and held his stomach. "Are so."

Simone didn't seem to hear any of this. She'd gotten out her marijuana and was fishing in her purse for the tweezers.

Sam slid over to her. "What's that?"

She held up the bag so he could smell the green, earthy contents. "It'll make you happier."

"Yeah," I said. "It'll calm you down."

The joint was damp from the humidity, and we had to relight it four times. Sam coughed until I thought a blood vessel might burst in his face. Then he got sleepy and lay on the floor. We all closed our eyes and listened to a mosquito that had found its way into my room. It was the most peaceful moment my brother and I have ever shared.

"Sam?" I said, after what seemed like hours. "Are you awake?"

His eyes were open and he didn't blink.

"Hey, Sam." I poked his ribs. "Sam?"

Simone rolled from the bed and leaned over him. Her hair hung in his face. "He looks pale."

"Sam." I shook his shoulders. "Don't joke around."

Then his face turned red and his mouth twitched. "Tricked you!"

I punched him in the stomach, hard this time, but he was still hysterical. "I don't feel anything," he said. "I don't feel any of the things you said I'd feel."

"Damn it, Sam." Simone climbed back onto the bed. "That wasn't funny."

"I'm telling Dad!" He ran from the room. "I'm telling Dad what we did."

"Shit." Simone covered her face with her hands. "For a second I actually thought he was dead."

For the first time in months, I started to laugh. Simone propped herself up on her elbows and watched me. Then she laughed too. We laughed until we were out of breath and our faces hurt.

"Are you in love with me, Al?" she said, and that made us laugh even more. We laughed as Simone slid off the bed and crouched in front of me. We laughed as she touched my face and I saw a streak of green ice cream that had hardened on her wrist. We laughed as she tilted forward and kissed me.

There was something showy about that kiss, like the pranks my father played, the jokes he told. I didn't like the way her thin lips felt. Afterward, she touched my hair and began to hum again.

"Quit it." I pushed her hand away.

"What?" Her face was so close that I smelled her sugary, smoky breath.

"You don't even know what that song's about."

"So?" She shrugged. "Neither do you."

Then she climbed back onto the bed, put her feet on the pillow, and closed her eyes. I watched her breathe until my father came home.

—

WHEN I WAS SIXTEEN, I took the bus to the hospital after school and visited Mom by myself. I felt I had something to say to her, but once there—confronted with her thinned face, her bruised and ropy arms, the tubes and smells—I couldn't remember what that something was. She was asleep, and I was relieved. I studied her face, how the painkillers had slackened its muscles. I left after only ten minutes, because I knew my father would want me home for dinner.

Two days later, she died. This wasn't a disaster; it didn't destroy me. I didn't cry or shout. In fact, I didn't feel anything but a constant grogginess.

The funeral was traditional, with a reception at our house. After everyone left, my father sat us at the table, which was piled with bagels, lox, devilled eggs, and salad. He said, "We all knew it was coming. At least it wasn't a surprise."

Sam nodded. I stared at the wood tabletop.

Then my father stood and said, "I think we all need some sleep." There was a weariness about him I'd never seen before. He kissed us on the cheek, and his five o'clock shadow scratched my skin.

We spent the next week sitting shiva, which was the perfect way to remember my mother. We covered the mirrors, including the one Simone would later use for her makeup ritual, and observed a week of near silence.

—

IN AUGUST, Simone started to act differently. She was always tired, and slept until noon on her days off. Some days she'd lock herself in the master bedroom and refuse to come out, even when Sam begged her to go with him to buy Sour Chews.

He was always over-sugared and hyperactive, so as a favour to her I got him out of the house. I took him on delirious searches for the perfect shade. The two of us walked along the city's streets, smelling the fermenting garbage, until Sam would say, "Can we go home now? Please?"

One afternoon, we came back to find Simone at the kitchen table, crying into her hands. It was a wet, ugly weeping. We watched this for a while. Then I passed her a napkin, the cloth kind my mother used to save for special occasions.

"Shouldn't you be at work?" By then I'd memorized her schedule.

She gave me a look. There was annoyance in it, hatred even. "I called in sick."

Sam sat at her feet. "Do you want some ice cream, Simone?"

She shook her head, then blew her nose into the napkin.

I pulled up a chair beside her. "We could go somewhere. Like the park."

"Sorry, Al." She gave me a weak smile. "Maybe tomorrow?"

That night, she didn't eat any of the peppercorn steak my father served, and he used the same jokey tone he'd taken with my mother. "What's this? Miss Summertime isn't hungry?"

"She's sick," I said.

My father kept his eyes on Simone. He spoke with the impatient voice he sometimes used on Sam and me. "She's upset, that's all."

Simone stood and left the table. We heard her steps on the stairs, then the click of the bedroom door. My father didn't follow her. In my darker moments, I wonder how things would have changed if he had.

—

ONCE, YEARS LATER, I asked Simone how she felt about him. This was long after that summer. I was working construction, ten-hour days to save up to start my degree in history. I worked at a site on Spadina, converting an old textile factory into lofts and studio apartments. At the time the style seemed original and edgy, though I'm sure the tenants later found it regrettable: the walls were cinder blocks and the piping was left uncovered.

From the scaffolding, I could see my father's shop. He still worked there, I knew, and somehow that fact made the hours seem longer and my job more humiliating. It was after one of these days, spent sweating under a hard hat, that I asked Simone what she thought of my father.

"Then or now?" She was in our kitchen, flossing her teeth. I remember thinking it was odd that she would floss her teeth in the kitchen. I remember thinking that I didn't know her at all.

"Whichever."

"Oh, I don't know, Al." She had the same pale, freckled skin as when we'd met, but her body had changed: her shoulders were rounded and her stomach soft. I wanted to stand behind her and place my hands on her waist, where the seam of her skirt met her skin. "It's hard to explain."

"Try."

She squinted thoughtfully, floss looped around her index fingers. "He was funny, I guess." Then she smiled, perhaps remembering a private joke. "He always made me laugh."

For a second, I hated my father. Because, for all I'd done for Simone, all I still did, I rarely made her laugh.

But then she went back to flossing her teeth, and I put thoughts of my wife's past out of my mind, which was a skill I'd perfected over the years. And that was it. The only time I ever felt raging, heart-burning jealousy. Which is different from the guilt and loss I always carry with me.

———

THE NEXT MORNING, there was no coffee, no eggs, no buttered toast. In the kitchen the linoleum was cool under my feet, and Sam poured himself a bowl of stale cereal. My father sat at the empty table, his hands pressed flat to the surface.

"Where's Simone?" I asked, but nobody answered.

After a week of cereal, it was clear she had moved out. She'd taken all her clothes, including the yellow dress, and my mother's Billie Holiday record. For his part, my father settled into the respectable life of a widower. He packed the records back into their boxes and drank far less gin.

"I just don't know," my father said weeks later, over grilled cheese sandwiches. He leaned back in his chair and seemed tired.

For once, he looked his age. "I don't know what I'm supposed to do."

I didn't know what to do either. I checked the park, half expecting to find her on one of the swings. But I didn't think we should chase her. I remembered the way my mother would suddenly emerge from her days of silence, on her own time and never because of my father's coaxings.

"It's best to just leave her alone," I said, and my father listened to me as though he were my apprentice. He was as anxious and lost as a child, and I touched his arm. The sleeve of his shirt was newly ironed, but I didn't think he'd mind if I wrinkled it. I said, "It's best to just stay in one place and wait."

———

SINCE THEN, Simone and I have lived all over the city, mostly in basement suites. We learned to cook meals on one hot plate. We learned to pay rent on minimum wages and my meagre scholarships. We learned to look around a cramped, dirty apartment and say, "This isn't a bad life."

More recently, we've had good luck with real estate. When I got my first teaching job—at the same high school I'd attended and despised—we bought a half-duplex on Robert Street. It's only a block from where my father's shop used to be, where Sam now runs a clothing store that stocks three-hundred-dollar jeans.

We've been in this place over ten years now, and we've had an ordinary life, which doesn't imply a simple one. Simone works as an administrative assistant—my father would still call her a secretary, which would be more truthful. She manages to grow an impressive garden on our porch. We vacuum when we think of it. The girls have grown up, and our existence now revolves around mutual funds and keeping our cluttered house from falling to ruin.

Sometimes, I reimagine history. I see myself as a tailor, a bachelor who lives above the shop and works beside his father. I imagine years of listening to that off-kilter whistling and those same stories. I would have been annoyed with my father every day of my life. But I wouldn't have been unhappy, just as I'm not unhappy now.

Earlier this year, my father died in his sleep, a direct consequence of those extraordinary meals he loved. Until his death, he never missed a day of work. And he refused to visit our home. Though sometimes, from our upper-floor window, I thought I could see him on his morning walk to the shop—his pace slower, but proud and steady.

❧

BY SEPTEMBER, the temperature had begun to drop. Old people weren't dying of dehydration anymore, and I could look out at the street without seeing it waver in front of me. That's when Simone came back.

I was in bed, under my sheet and using a flashlight to read about the tombs of Petra, which were built to imitate the front of a typical house. I didn't hear Simone until she opened my window.

"Al?" She stuck her head into the room, and her face looked ghostly in the dark. "Are you awake?"

I shone the flashlight on her. "What are you doing here?"

"Get that thing out of my face."

"Did you and my dad break up?"

"I don't want to talk about your dad." She swung her legs through the open window. I kept the flashlight beam on her as she shimmied into my room. Her yellow dress rode up and it showed how her body had changed. She was less bony and girlish. Maybe it was all the ice cream, or my father's rich cooking.

"I said stop it." She grabbed the flashlight from me and flicked it off. When the room went dark, neither of us said anything. Then, "Hey, Al." I felt her weight on the bed. "I have an idea."

She rolled a joint and we had a smoke, lying side by side. The only light came from the smoulder that we passed back and forth.

"I'm so tired," she said. "You wouldn't believe how tired I am."

"Dad wants me to go to work with him this week," I said. "He wants me to give it another shot."

"Doesn't that make you suicidal?"

"That's one way of putting it."

She exhaled a long, sleepy breath. "I'm going to leave Toronto, go somewhere better."

"Yeah."

We gave up on conversation for a few minutes, until she said, "I'm going to have a baby."

I turned to her but could only see the outline of her face.

"He doesn't want me to keep it. He thinks I'm too young." She pressed her palms to her eyelids. "He thinks I'm a joke."

I remembered my father in the kitchen, his hands pressed to the table. The way he'd said, *I don't know what I'm supposed to do.* And maybe I should have told her this. Maybe I should have explained that, when she'd left, he hadn't laughed it off. But her chilled skin was touching mine. And since she'd gone, I'd thought about her constantly. I'd missed her, and it felt something like lust and something like mourning. I said, "I don't think you're a joke."

She turned and kissed me the way she had weeks earlier, except this time it was a wetter, sleepier kiss. She tasted like gum and Coke-bottle candies, and I didn't mind the way her lips felt.

"It'll be okay," I said, though I didn't know what I meant.

She turned on her side and buried her face into my neck, and I could picture her sleeping next to her sisters that way. I knew I'd get up the next morning and I wouldn't recognize my own life. I wouldn't sit on the couch, or smoke anything, or punch Sam even once. I would get a job—serving fries or pumping gas. I'd work hard every day of my life. I knew very little about Simone, but I knew we'd stay together.

I told myself that my father didn't understand her, and that he'd hardly miss her. That to him she was a bright plaything, a bit of sunshine, nothing more. I imagined him asleep in his room. He always slept soundly, on top of the covers and in his underwear. I had to squeeze my eyes shut and push this picture of him from my mind. I told myself—I believed—that eventually he'd forgive me. I was eighteen years old, and I had no idea how difficult my life was about to become.

"We'll be okay," I said, but Simone didn't hear me. She had already fallen into her kind of deep, breathy sleep.

r o m a n c e   l a n g u a g e s

YOU WILL HARDLY GROW, but your hair will darken, along with your nipples, and people will stop calling you Jilly. As you drift through classes on French vocabulary and hairstyling, you will wear skirts from department stores and knit hats that slant over your eyes. You will trip at your graduation ceremony, then redeem yourself by attending foreign universities with names no one at home can pronounce. You will live on two continents and speak four languages with the same ease as your mother reads palms or embroiders daisies on dishcloths. You will marry one of your students, and then an Italian you meet on an airplane. These two will be the only men, besides your doctor, to see you naked.

Your mother will visit once in these twenty-three years, when you fly her out to meet your Italian and his two sons. She will sit in your cold dining room and tell her kind of stories. About a woman who birthed a baby with half a heart, and children who lit their own heads on fire. Sleepy and honest from wine, she will even tell of the time she met—spoke with, slept with—a man who ate his own dog. And you will look into her face the way you would stare into a funhouse mirror. Your sense of irony tuned enough to know that she will speak of you—your stone house, tanned skin, elegant husband—in the same way she speaks of her dog man. The same sly, gossipy tone you might use, if you knew your own story, if you could tell it now.

NOW: IT IS AUGUST, it is raining, and you are twelve. Heavy drops slide down your forehead and fall into the neck of your jacket. You stand in a flooded cornfield, and your bony knees stick out of your mother's rubber boots. You hold your breath because a cricket has leapt into your palm. It folded its stick-and-hinge body into the cup of your hand, so you keep your arm steady, will your heart to still. You want to examine this miracle: the curving antennae, the wings, the strong black legs. If you had a jar, you'd trap it under glass. You know Marie is now looking into her scuffed mirror, clipping on earrings and frosting her lips. If you thought she would care, you'd scream, *Mom, come see what I got.* Because you want something to show, something to keep. Want it so bad that, before you can tell yourself not to, you shut your fist.

YOU LIVE IN A PLACE that's not exactly a port town, not a suburb, but a cropping of houses and fields along drenched coastline. In twenty years the farmers and fishermen will sell art to ferry tourists and the auto parts factory will move production overseas. This flat, foggy cut of coast will become part of the nearby city that stretches farther and farther down the highway. As an adult it will be easy for you to romanticize this place: fields of cabbage and pumpkin. Horses that graze under power lines.

It must have been easy for your mother too, who came here when you were still a bad idea in her belly. It was in fashion to leave the city and to stop shaving underarms, so she had no trouble finding the baby-blue trailer she rents from a farmer you call Mr. B. But she didn't come for retreat. She came to wash hair in the local salon, sell fresh eggs, serve pancakes in the highway truck stop, give women permanents in her kitchen, and tell people their fortunes. She keeps her money in envelopes marked *Food, Cigarettes, Jilly*, as though you are merely an expense. Every day, she sits at the table and shuffles twenties from one envelope to another.

"You've outgrown your sneakers already, haven't you?"

You nod, ashamed.

"Your feet are like boats." Ash drops from her cigarette to the floor. "I don't know where you get that from."

So most days you stay outside. You save worms from the highway after rain, or stand on the pebbly beach to imitate a heron's stance. This place is flat, wet, bare. The only things you like about it are the escape routes: water, road. And how, on sunny days, they melt into each other.

AS A TEENAGER, you will hate your mother the way all your friends hate theirs: she will be unbending, hard, and she will have frizzy henna-died hair. In the grocery store she will buy dried chickpeas and magazines that include articles on weight-loss creams and new Biblical scrolls discovered in Maine. She will run a maid service for working women who don't have time to dust. Some of your friends' parents will hire her, and some of your friends' parents will work for her, so this will be a constant source of embarrassment. She will never be in when you get home from school, so you'll steal and smoke her cigarettes. Then the two of you will spend hours in front of evening soap operas, you hemming your skirts, she crocheting scrap wool into scarves you will hate to wear.

⁓

FROM WHERE YOU STAND in the cornfield, through strips of rain, you see where the circus has begun to sprawl its tarps and tents. You knew it was coming because of the paper arrows taped to highway signs and the posters advertising *Four days! Four shows!* Still, when you watch it appear from nothing, the warped little town seems unbelievable. The Zavarra: it sounds exotic, but later—when you've lived where the Romans held chariot races and fights to the death—you'll know it's a nonsense word. And it's nothing like the European circuses you'll see, glamour shows of elastic women painted like ice queens. The Zavarra has a clown who stamps your wrist as Marie pulls you past the gate. It has a band, heavy on the brass. No ice queens, but men on stilts or unicycles, and pubescent boys pushing popcorn, candy floss, caramel-covered apples. There are no lions, but two bears—Kyla and Bill—wrap their stubby arms around each other and dance. An elephant raises her trunk for pictures. The ringmaster has a stagy whisper—*We need complete silence for this, folks*—and the grandstand seats creak. And off to the side are smaller tents. One with a woman who uses her mind to bend spoons, one with a 56-year-old man who has 56 tattoos. And one with a table, two fold-up chairs, and your mother.

You'll never know what she did to get this gig. But it seems natural that Marie is briefly and fully accepted by people who hold an undying belief that accidents happen in threes and that it's bad luck to look back during a parade. Later, when you tell this to your first husband, he'll shake his head and look at you with young, humourless eyes. He'll think you make this stuff up, so you'll say: You've never met my mother. You'll borrow her deep, dramatic voice: She was just like them—crazy, a cutthroat capitalist. And you'll describe the tent she improvised: a blue tarp to keep out the rain, with a maroon velour lining and a sign that read, *$5 for a palm reading, or three questions for $3.*

But now, you don't imagine how this will become one of your stories, how it will change in your hands. You sit on an empty tub of Pineapple Whip as people ask Marie their questions. Will there be a wedding? Will he love our baby? She answers in a husky voice and sometimes talks to people's dead relatives; she can do this too, as well as give hand massages. Tragedy, romance, ghosts—Marie takes these for granted.

"This mark shows you've touched God," she says to an elderly woman who wears a plastic bonnet to keep rain off her hair.

"See this semicircular line? It indicates family battles." This to a man of forty, a banker who wants to discuss his prospects of promotion. "Look at the way it swoops down. Do you have estranged children? No? You may have children you don't know about."

And to a graduate student in braids and a wool skirt: "Your heart line begins right under your middle finger, so my guess is you have a disregard for the responsibilities of love. A very sexual nature." Marie lowers her voice. "By sexual, I mean dangerous."

When customers leave the tent, she tucks their money into her back pocket. She is a businesswoman who understands a changing world. Women are working, couples are swinging, parents are splitting, and everyone wants to know what will happen next. You sit outside the tent, your face hidden in your hood, and suck on peanut brittle. Next to the circles of blush on your mother's cheeks, the varnished nails glued to her fingers, no one notices you anyway.

———

WHEN YOU LEAVE FOR UNIVERSITY, your mother will give you a stiff hug at the international airport. You will have taken everything you own from the apartment she bought two years before. Your records, your books, your off-the-shoulder sweaters will be tucked into a trunk held shut by two leather straps. Your mother will find a man—wearing a grey trench coat, and about to step on a plane— to lift the trunk onto the conveyor belt.

"Work hard, Jilly," she'll say. "And don't eat the cheese—I heard about a woman who got a stomach full of worms. They're centuries behind us when it comes to pasteurization."

Then she'll pull you to her and press your face to her wine-coloured hair. She'll pat your shoulder, then your head. You'll want something from her, some sort of guarantee. But she'll push you away and ask if you have your passport, your traveller's cheques.

———

"ARE YOU THE NICE LADY I should talk to about my future?"

You look up from your peanut brittle and see a man with a mouth that takes up half his face. He is smiling.

"Are you the lady with the magic eye?" He's not in costume, but you can tell from his accent that he works for the circus because Marie told you these people come from the other side of Canada, where they speak French. This man was obviously not prepared for rain. He wears jeans with reinforced knees and a button-up shirt with the cuffs rolled. He is soaked through. You don't answer his teasing, just look at him and grip your knees.

"Here, you want something?" He pulls a box of cinnamon hearts from his shirt pocket, and you shake your head. This is how you remember much of the past few years: as a swirl of men. When they acknowledged you, it was to shut you up with a bag of penny candy. You don't remember faces, only the muscle of denimed thighs that passed you in the trailer's kitchen as you coloured in a book or spread margarine on toast. You remember the way they messed the curls on top of your head. *Cute kid*, they'd say, or nothing at all. Your mother has jobs, but these men are her career. She goes months without one, then finds someone—someone older, lonely, well-off enough that he can help a girl out. Buy her wine, pay her rent. You have questions about your father—what was his name? what did he do? was he good at crosswords?—but you think of these men and never ask.

This man, still almost a boy, crouches beside you and taps your knee. "You sure? You don't want any?"

"Are you in the circus?"

"In a way." He picks at his mud-spattered boots.

"Can you fly?"

"I can climb things. Ropes, buildings."

"A cricket flew into my hand this morning. Just like that." You fail to snap your fingers.

"There are different kinds of crickets, you know. Some live underground, some on trees."

"What kind is this one?" You pull the crushed body from your pocket.

"Ah." He touches one of the snapped legs. "A nearly flawless specimen. This is a scaly cricket. If it jumped to you, it must have been in love with you. That's what crickets do. They fall in love every night and they sing about it."

"Put that thing away, Jilly." Your mother's shadow and her voice loom over you, and you shove the bug into your pocket. "People at the circus don't want to see dead things."

"Is that true?" You look up at her legs. "Do crickets fall in love?"

"Who is this?" Marie stands under the tent and looks at the man. A curtain of water separates her from you and him.

"Of course it's true. It's scientific," he says. "The females have eardrums on their elbows and that's how they hear the song." He stands and faces your mother. "Imagine that. Hearing with your elbow."

You watch him as he looks at Marie's blousy shirt and tight, flared pants. His eyes crinkle, his head tilts, and he steps an inch closer to her. All through your adolescence you will watch men do this in her presence.

The boy runs his hand through his hair and keeps talking. "In French we call them *grillons*. There's a song. About a couple who make love in a field and the crickets start to sing."

"Do you need something?" Your mother uses the same tone with him as she does with you, and you feel sudden ownership of him.

"He wants you to tell his future."

"I was told to visit you. I was told you can see things." He steps closer to your mother, and stands under the water that falls from the lip of the tarp.

"I'm supposed to be here for the customers. The people who pay to get in." Marie crosses her arms.

"It's actually a funny song. Eventually the crickets get so loud that the couple has to cover their ears. They have to hide under a blanket." He leans toward her and pretends to pull a cinnamon heart from her hair. "Candy?"

"I'm very busy." She steps back from him into the tent. On the inside wall, she has hung a poster of a gypsy woman. A mockery that doesn't resemble her at all, except for the hard glint in the eyes.

꩜

ON YOUR WEDDING DAY, you will send your mother a Polaroid: you and your student outside the Registro Civil. Him in sandals, a buttoned shirt, a tie. You in the blue skirt and jacket you sewed for the occasion. Out of practice with a needle, you struggled with the material—stitch, rip, restitch—and in the photo the skirt will ride up higher than expected.

Your student—no, your husband—will look at something beyond the camera: a pigeon maybe, or a woman sipping coffee. His posture will be perfect, and your head will tilt toward him, a curl of your hair blowing in your face. One of your hands will be raised to block the sun from your eyes. The other clasps his arm.

He's too cute, your mother will reply in a "Congratz" card. *Hold on tight.*

—

THE MAN'S NAME IS PAUL, and though his skin is becoming leathery, he is only twenty-three. He works as a roustabout, fixing guy lines, painting and repainting the purple barrels that the bears roll around on. You break off a chunk of peanut brittle for him and he brings you to the circus's muddy backyard. You see the clowns up close and notice their smiles are only painted on. A family of five rehearses jumps on their unicycles, and quilts cover the cage where the elephant sleeps. Two women and one man wear turquoise and groom horses. They shout something at Paul.

"Arrêtez, là." He puts his light, callused hand on your head. *"Elle est avec moi."*

He brings you to the wall that shields the grandstand from backstage, and points to a hole in the canvas. Inside, the show is on, and someone—hard to say if it is a woman or a man—swings high above the ground on a loop of rope. The crowd is quiet.

"That's the cloud swing." Paul kneels beside you. "I help set that up. It can hold anyone's weight."

You watch the performer hang upside down from one leg, then swing and shimmer in the spotlight.

"I have to be just as brave as him. I climb just as high. And if anything snaps, it's on my head." Paul laughs. "It's on all our heads, I guess, but you know what I mean. Took me a week to get the courage to climb that pole."

More interesting even than the slim figure flying through the air is the way Paul's mouth moves. You get lost in his slanted words and added syllables.

"Were you born in the circus? My mom says people are born here." You imagined weddings in the centre ring, births there too.

"Not me." He watches through the hole the size of a thumbprint. "You're mom's tough. *Chiante*. Tell me, does she like flowers?"

He stares through the hole in the canvas and you see sequins reflected in the curve of his eye.

"She probably wants me back now," you say. "She's probably wondering where I am."

❧

YOU WILL CALL YOUR MOTHER once a year, every New Year's Day. But it's the time you phone to tell her of your first marriage—its devastation—that you remember. The cost of the call will make both of you more concise, more honest, than in any of your letters.

"You fall too hard." The connection will be bad and her voice will fade in and out. "Always have. You're too sensitive."

"Is that bad? Sensitivity?"

"You scare people. You're like a tightrope act gone wrong."

This is her type of mothering and you'll appreciate its familiarity.

"People want grace, Jilly. They want magic."

You twist the phone cord around your wrist. "I'd say they want distraction."

"Either way, they're not looking for disaster."

WHEN THE SHOW FINISHES, Paul walks you and Marie out of the gate. He holds your hand and jumps with you over puddles, then offers a ride home in the spool truck. The road is dark, but in the light of passing cars you see wood shavings dusted through his hair and glittery paint stuck under his nails. He lets you rest your head against him, and you feel the movement of his forearm as he changes gears. You pretend to sleep, but still, he and your mother don't talk. You smell Marie's perfume and her Revlon lipstick. You hear her breathing and sometimes Paul's whistling.

At the turnoff that leads to your trailer and garden, she says, "Here," and he answers, *"D'ac."* In front of your place, he leaves the truck running. Your mother opens the door while he carries you inside, lays you on your bed, and covers you to your chin with a quilt.

HE ARRIVES THE NEXT AFTERNOON to pick you and Marie up for the second show. When you open the door, your mother comes out of the bathroom in a satin robe—a gift from a past boyfriend—and you step behind her. She doesn't wear makeup and her long hair is wet from the shower.

If he had brought roses, she would have laughed in his face. So he stands on the flimsy porch steps with an armful of sunflowers. Sunflowers, in this rain. The stalks are nearly as tall as he is, and their heavy heads tilt ridiculously from his arms.

"Madame." He bows, his body imitating the stems. "A token."

Your mother stares at him. "You're a child."

"Tell me my fortune."

"I'm not interested in your fortune." Meaning, of course, that anyone can see from the wear in his pants and his shirt's mismatched buttons that he doesn't have money.

He extends a flower to her. "So talk to me about now."

She leans against the door frame and nods to the sunflowers. "What am I supposed to do with those?" From where you stand behind her, you hear a smile, however slight, in her voice.

———

AROUND THE TIME you get a sessional position in Florence, your mother will meet Wallace, an engineer who works for a modest firm. She will call him Wally. One month of every winter they'll drive to Arizona. In her letters she'll include pictures of her and Wally and their terrier, Della. The three of them cuddling on a green couch, or sitting on their deck with an Arizona golf course in the background. In these photographs you'll see that Marie's hair has greyed and her arms got fat. Her eyes will look heavy but eased, and every year the skin of her face will drop a little—as though she has let it go, released her fist. On the back of these photographs she will write things: *This is us on the Grouse Mountain gondola* or *Della in her Christmas scarf!* A language you never heard her use.

—

FOR THREE DAYS, your mother is softer, kinder. She doesn't count the money in the envelopes, and she doesn't glare when you leave your jacket somewhere near the hot-dog stand. On the drives home, you sit between her body and Paul's, and you feel warmth on either side.

"I saw Mr. B. today. He was buying a stuffed animal." You chatter to the rhythm of the windshield wipers' slap on glass. "He says the corn in his field is mouldy from the rain. People could die from eating that." You put your hands to your throat and make a choking sound. "Couldn't they, Mom? They could die."

Your mother lets you stay up past eleven, and when she thinks you're asleep, she sits with Paul at the square kitchen table. From your tiny room, you hear her laugh.

"Long love line, short life line," she says. "That's always the way."

On the third night, they go outside despite the spitting rain. You watch from your open, half-curtained window as Paul tries to teach her to dance. She is clumsy and the dance is stilted. But you see his hand on her hip and can imagine the feel of his skin against the wet cotton. You hear his voice, faint through the rain, as he counts into her ear.

—

THE NEXT MORNING, you sit at the kitchen table and draw pictures of moths and grasshoppers. He comes out of her bedroom and puts a finger to his lips. While she sleeps, you show him how to feed the chickens, how to candle the eggs, where to empty the buckets from under the eaves so water won't rot out the garden. He repairs a loose porch step and offers to paint the mildewed windowsills. You wonder how his English got so good but then realize it's because he's all talk. He explains that crickets don't actually sing, just knock their wings together, and he pencils bird-migration patterns on the tabletop. He promises to teach you to do cartwheels, shoot a rifle, ride a bike. He makes a hummingbird feeder out of a scrap of plastic tubing. When Marie comes into the kitchen in her thinning robe, he is showing you how to mix the sugar water, and she doesn't say anything when you drink half of it.

THE FOURTH NIGHT, Paul can't give you and your mother a ride home. They need him to unhook the rigging, and in a few hours the big top will be folded into the spool truck. You help your mother roll up the poster, fold her table and chairs, and pull down the velour tent. Then the two of you walk to the grandstand and watch as Paul climbs the centre pole, going up the metal spikes like a ladder.

Marie watches his graceful, practical movement without saying a word. You take her hand and she lets you hold it, lets you feel what it will be like to be adult.

"That's not real rope," you say. "It's just firehose stuffed with cotton. Paul told me so."

At the mention of his name, she looks at you. There's something in her face, a flicker, and you wonder if she's just seen your future. She pulls her hand away. "Come on, Jilly. If we're walking, we'd better go."

She leaves the big top without looking behind her, but you stay and watch as Paul shimmies up the pole. He doesn't wear a harness, and there's no net. He seems to trust the pole, the rigging, his own balance. If he fell, it would be bad luck, not bad form. The elegant person you had seen on the swing has wiped the white off his face and now wears overalls. He stands on the ground, laughs, and calls out to Paul. You can't understand the words, but you can tell it's a friendly tease. Paul looks down, waves, and pretends to lose his balance. It's funny—the exaggerated arc of his arm and his comic, frightened look. And then, in the middle of this gesture, he sees you and his face changes. The second before his legs slip from the pole, his smile is wiped away. His arms reach, grasp air. You watch him fall the way you watched that cricket—you hold your breath. Until you see him grab a dangling end of rope. Until you see that this is rehearsed, maybe something the swing man taught him. Until he glides to the ground, his arms and legs wrapped around the rope, and lands lightly in front of you.

"Why are you still here, Jilly? Where's your mom?"

"How did you do that?"

"It's the tear-down now. We can't have anyone around." He taps you on the nose. "This is the secret part. No one's allowed to see the magician after the show."

"My mom left already. But she probably hasn't gone far."

"You run." He messes your hair. "Go catch up."

"Are you leaving?"

"We hit Prince George tomorrow. There's supposed to be even more rain up there."

"You should take us." This is obvious, the way it should go. You can't imagine another ending.

"You don't want to come with us. You'd have to learn French." He crinkles his nose, twists his big mouth into a grin. "And you'd always smell like an elephant."

"My mom likes you. She hasn't counted her envelopes in days."

He pulls the box of candy from his shirt pocket. "Here. You take this with you, okay?"

"Or you could stay here. With us. We could get a bigger place."

"I'm going to miss you." He kneels to your height. "*Pour de vrai*. But you have to leave."

"No." You cross your arms the way you've seen your mother do it. You look into his eyes and you hold yourself there.

"Jilly. You're a special girl." His smile is gone. "I mean that. You remind me of my daughter. She's younger than you, but she's bright too."

He looks into your face as though assessing damages, what can and cannot be fixed.

"You and your mom—it caught me by surprise. Do you understand, Jilly? Do you understand what I'm saying?"

You suck in your breath, stare at the blue of his eyes, the lines already pressed into his skin. Then you turn and run as fast as your legs can take you.

YOU ARE AFRAID OF YOUR MOTHER, GILLIAN, your Italian will say as he holds you in the dark. This will be after you showed Marie the drafty guest room and gave her towels for the morning. She leaves in a week, and seems glad of it. Earlier, over dinner, she said she doesn't trust Wally to water the plants, and you know this means she misses him. You will face away from your Italian and feel his hand on your stomach, his sticky breath on the back of your neck. I *was* afraid of my mother, you correct, irritated already with his habit of making statements.

And it's true, you used to be afraid of Marie's harsh, smoky voice and the way she slapped your face if you broke a dish. But you will not tell your husband that you're still afraid. What scares you now are your mother's strange, tragic stories. She has become more talkative, happy to share anecdotes. And in her stories, anything can happen. Maybe she exaggerates. Maybe no one really eats their own dog, and maybe no child is born missing a piece of his heart. But then again, maybe to you, no child will be born at all. And maybe Marie will find and keep a comfortable love, while both your marriages will be makeshift, stopgap. You never believed in her ability to know with accuracy. What will scare you as you lie in the dark is her willingness—later you might call it courage—to imagine the unexpected, the far-flung.

the separation

THE YEAR MY PARENTS SEPARATED coincided with the year I adored my sister. Claudia was fourteen, and was at the beginning of the long rebellion that would define her life. I was eleven and still looked like a boy: hair that my mom cut too short, legs that I hadn't started to shave. I wore the same outfit almost every day: jeans with embossed flowers and a green sweater. No wonder I was obsessed with Claudia. She listened to the Dead Kennedys and the Dayglo Abortions. She had purple hair and a fake ID that claimed she was nineteen and from Oshawa. She'd gotten her period, and boys had started to call our house asking for her. Sometimes I answered the phone in the evenings, and there would be a nervous male voice on the line, pleading, "Can I talk to Claudia?"

"Who's calling, please?" I desperately needed to know.

But Claudia was a slave to the telephone and always aware of its ringing. She'd smack the back of my head before I could get any information. "Give it, June. Now."

She was cruel and lovely and totally awesome. I snuck into her room to riffle through her shoebox of tapes any chance I got.

———

OUR PARENTS WERE AWED by the latest catastrophe they'd created. First, two daughters. And now this: The Separation. They talked about it as though it had capital letters, and they both seemed to want to make it as crazy as the parties they liked to throw.

They didn't seem to notice that, separated, they were more married than ever. Each obsessed over what the other was doing, or might be doing. They sent messages to each other through Claudia and me: *Tell your father/Please inform your mother*. These messages were angry or heartbroken or flirtatious. They were articulate, defiant, or funny. Usually, Claudia and I forgot them entirely, or forgot the most important part of them.

The Separation happened this way: first my mom left, and stayed with one of her sisters for a week. Then she came back and my dad stayed in a hotel for two days. Then he came back because the hotel was expensive—separation was expensive!—so for a few days the house was exactly like before: messy, crowded, loud.

But one evening, there must have been an argument. Claudia and I didn't hear it because we were in her bedroom listening to music. It was one of the few times my sister let me hang out in her room, and sometimes I wonder if she was protecting me, if she knew there was a fight going on downstairs. The point is, I never knew what caused The Separation because I was with Claudia, and Mickey DeSadist was singing us a lullaby.

———

WE WERE RAISED ON LENTILS, brown rice, Neil Young, and solstice celebrations. Our mother ran a local grocery co-op and wore skirts made of hemp before hemp was chic. Our dad was a ceramics artist who sold cups and bowls at the local farmers' market, had lost most of his short-term memory, and never got any of the big commissions that the tourist board gave out.

As young children, Claudia and I were encouraged to be wild. We were always outside, and often naked. The neighbours complained because our parents never mowed the lawn, believing that children should have high grass to play in and dandelion seeds to blow. There was a picture of us on the fridge: Claudia with ripped overalls and hair that looked like it had never been washed, and me, naked except for a T-shirt that read, *I Hate TV*. We took vitamins, ate vegetables, and recycled. We'd been humiliated countless times when our parents dragged us to marches against apartheid and solidarity dances for Cuba. One summer, when I was eight, we'd been forced to stand outside the local supermarket and protest the importing of grapes from Chile.

No wonder Claudia found it difficult to be a teenager. She wanted to rebel, but our parents didn't make it easy. Her first attempt, the one she undertook the year of The Separation, centred on music. Instead of Crosby, Stills and Nash, she listened to Minor Threat and Bad Brains. She went to concerts in people's basements and all-ages shows at Little Fernwood. She moshed and stage-dived, and spent so much time thrashing around with other dirty, sweating kids that once she got scabies.

And one evening, while Mom and I were in the kitchen, she cut herself thick bangs, bleached them, and dyed them purple. I was doing homework, and Mom was drinking tea and reading a book about the Buddhist practice of non-attachment. Then Claudia stomped into the room, with her purple hair and her boots that left marks on the lino. She heaved the fridge door open then slammed it shut.

Mom looked up from her book. "Hey," she said. "Great hair."

Claudia froze. She stood in front of the fridge for about three seconds. Then she stomped out of the kitchen.

Mom sipped her camomile. "Did I say something wrong?"

"I think she hoped her hair would annoy you."

"But I think it's cute. I think it suits her."

I twirled my pencil through my own hair, which had almost reached my chin, and wondered if Claudia had any of that purple dye left.

"It's oppressive," I said, trying out a word I'd heard Claudia use.

"What is?"

"How much you love us."

Mom set down her clay cup, one that Dad had made. "Do you have any idea what motherhood is like? It's like taking an endless multiple-choice exam, and none of the available answers are correct." She added, "Your father never understood that."

I'd never taken a multiple-choice exam. My homework still consisted of memorizing how to spell difficult words, like *friend* and *people*. Mom was always forgetting how young I was.

"Claudia Sky!" she yelled toward the other room. "Get back here, young lady! We need to talk about that stuff in your hair!" Then, quietly, to me, "How was that?"

"Great." My pencil was completely tangled in my hair and I wondered if I'd have to cut it out. "Very convincing."

———

DAD WENT AS FAR AWAY as he could on fifty dollars. He took the Greyhound up-island, as far north as it would go. Then, from a payphone, he called us. Had my mom answered the phone, he probably would have spoken triumphantly: "I'm in Port Hardy. I bet you don't even know where that is."

Instead, because I thought it might be a boy calling for Claudia, I ran to the phone, almost tripped over the cord, and grabbed it before anyone else could. The sound of my young voice over the line really did him in. "I'm in Port Hardy," he said. "I bet you don't even know where that is." Then he burst into tears.

"Hold on, okay?" I put my hand over the mouthpiece and screamed, "Mom! It's Dad! He's crying again!"

She took the phone from me. "Where are you? Port what? I don't even know where that is."

When she got off the phone with Dad, she called her sisters, her friends at the veggie co-op, and her Amnesty letter-writing group. That was one thing Claudia hated about The Separation: she'd lost her tyranny of the telephone. Mom was always talking to her sisters, women friends, and anyone else who was up for a little *schadenfreude*. Even her friend who lived in a tree stump in Beacon Hill Park found a way to call.

"Breaking news," Mom said each time someone phoned that night. "He's now sleeping in a bus depot in Port Hardy. I bet you don't even know where that is."

———

CLAUDIA'S TEENAGE REBELLION was awkward, an adolescent flail. In her twenties, she came to understand how to really get to our parents, and her techniques became much more sophisticated. But when I was eleven, I didn't understand how young and stupid she was, so I copied everything she did. I ripped my jeans the way she ripped hers. I coloured my hair with markers from school, so that my head looked and smelled like blueberries. I made mixtapes and listened to them until they unravelled. I took the music seriously—more seriously, it turned out, than Claudia ever did. It started as imitation, but in the end, it stuck.

———

"ON A SCALE OF ONE TO TEN, how much do you think your father and I have messed you girls up?" This was the kind of question Mom started asking over dinner. "A moderate amount? Or more than average?"

"You're so weird, Mom." Claudia brushed her fork over the quinoa on her plate.

"Yeah." I tried to copy Claudia's nonchalance, her way of averting her eyes from our mother's. "You're weird."

"We always tried to make sure you were happy." Mom covered her face with her hands. "We tried so hard."

It was sweet of Mom to worry, but I knew that, for Claudia, The Separation had its advantages. She had been the only one of her friends who lived in a two-parent home, and that had embarrassed her. And, bonus: she'd been able to fake tears—*my parents are getting divorced*, etc., etc.—to get out of gym class.

There was one thing I liked about it too. It meant that, every month, Claudia and I got to visit our dad in Port Hardy. This was farther from home than I'd ever been, and I loved the bus trip. On the first Friday of each month we caught the Greyhound at 5:45 in the morning. Claudia liked it because it meant we got to miss a day of school. I liked it because it meant a whole day—ten hours, including stops—with Claudia.

—

THE BUS HAD GREY SEATS with little footrests that flipped down, and wide windows that didn't open. Claudia and I always took a seat close to the back, because we knew from riding the school bus that this was where the cool kids sat. My sister always took the window seat and put the armrest down between us.

I can't speak for Claudia—she's still mysterious to me—but I can be almost sure that what we both loved most about those trips was the freedom. It's true that we were limited. Really, how much cool stuff can you do on a bus? When all you had was the ten bucks that your mom had given you to buy lunch? But still, when the door was sealed shut, we were fully separated from our parents—and this hardly ever happened, since school was full of parental replacements. That bus was our territory. Who cares that its seats made me lose all feeling in my ass? Or that the air that shot from the vents above our heads smelled like old carpets? Or that the sun poured in the windows and made us sweat? Our only responsibility was to call our parents from Campbell River, because they both insisted, separately, that we check in. Other than that, we could do or eat or say whatever we wanted. For ten hours, between Victoria and Port Hardy, we travelled fast, suspended above the road and outside supervision.

Of course, it turned out that when we were left on our own, we didn't usually feel like doing anything wild. I'd read adventure novels—Mom's old Trixie Beldens, or a Famous Five. Claudia would arrange herself so her sneakers were against the seat in front of her. She always brought a pillow, which she propped against the window. She listened to her Walkman and either slept or pretended to sleep. And I sat beside her, which was my favourite part. For once, she couldn't kick me out of her room, slam the door, or tell me to go somewhere and die.

THERE WAS ONE BUS TRIP that was different. It was September, and it would be our last trip up-island, but we didn't know that yet.

Things started out wrong: after Mom dropped us at the depot, Claudia waited until she had driven away—so I couldn't run and tell on her—then insisted that we sit in separate seats. As we dragged our backpacks through the parking lot toward our bus, Claudia said, "I'm not sitting beside you. I feel like being by myself."

"Yeah, right. Mom says some guy will sit beside us and fondle us if we don't stick together."

"Oh my God." Claudia stepped onto the bus and showed the driver her ticket. "You're such a crybaby."

Another thing that went wrong was that the last seats of the bus were already taken by people who were obviously cooler than us. So Claudia chose a seat in the middle. She sat near the window, and put her legs up so I couldn't sit down. "I'm not kidding," she said. "You're not sitting here."

I sat directly behind her. "You're such a bitch." I spoke through the space between the back of her seat and the window. "I hope you do get fondled."

———

IN PORT HARDY, our dad moved from place to place, and finally ended up renting a room in a house where people like him— people without luck or money—ended up. It was a big, crumbling house by the water. The wind coming off the ocean was so loud that when Claudia and I stayed there, I couldn't sleep at night. There was a smokehouse in the back, but Dad didn't know how to use it and had almost burned it down accidentally. After that, the other tenants teased him by calling him White Man, even though most of them were white too.

Living there for less than a year had aged our dad. Maybe it was all that wind battering his skin. His hair was always tangled, and he wore clothes I'd never seen before: fraying plaid shirts, jeans that were too big for him, rubber boots.

He spent a lot of time with one of his neighbours, a woman named Laura. She had a tattoo of an eagle on her back and a baby named Roger that she carried in a Snugli. She was pretty, with shiny dark hair and a round face. I liked her because she gave us jujubes and other petroleum products that we weren't allowed to eat at home. Claudia liked her because Laura shared her makeup. And she would let us take turns holding Roger, teaching us the right way to carry him. His soft baby breathing even calmed Claudia's hormonal rages.

Mom was convinced that Laura was Dad's girlfriend, but I was never sure. I think Laura just felt sorry for him, and for us. But when Mom found out about her, her hands and her voice got shaky. With a new urgency, she phoned everyone she knew.

"Breaking news," she said. "He's now dating Pocahontas." She paused. "Not that I don't respect the Salish people and their culture."

Then she inhaled and exhaled, deeply and calmly, the way she'd learned to do from a book.

—

ONE GOOD THING about being separated from Claudia was that I got a window seat. I was able to look out at deer munching broom on the side of the road. I saw birds in their flight. I had views of the vast and untamed ocean.

It turned out that I got bored of that pretty quick. By the time we hit Ladysmith, it was all I could do not to lean over Claudia's seat and start smacking her head with my book.

The only reason I didn't do that was because there was a stranger beside me—an overweight woman with a winter coat, despite the fact that it was hot in the bus. She sat next to me, purse on the floor, coat spread over her legs like a blanket. She turned on the little light above her seat and started to read a novel.

The book's cover had a picture of a dark man in a feather headdress, holding a pale woman in his muscular arms. The woman looked like she'd swooned or died or had low blood sugar. Her eighteenth-century dress was slipping off one shoulder. The man in the headdress looked like some of the guys my dad hung out with at the Legion, except a lot less hunched and exhausted. He had huge pecs and there was a forest behind him. I could tell from the cover and the tag line—*In the wilderness of New America, she found a wild stranger*—that this book was full of sex. From Victoria to Nanaimo, I kept trying to read over the fat woman's shoulder.

❦

EACH VISIT TO OUR DAD'S was pretty much the same. After we arrived on Friday night, he'd take us to the Legion. All the guys there recognized us and said, "Hey, little ladies. How are the princesses this evening?" They asked us about school and we told them stories. Usually Claudia and I invented some adventure about the bus trip, some fantastic thing that involved several near-death experiences.

Then, on Saturday, Dad always wanted us to do something in nature. We went hiking or fishing, and after, we'd usually hang out with Laura and Roger. And at least once over the weekend, Dad would cry.

Usually, it started like this: "Do you girls want me to come home? I mean, if you do, then I will. You know I love you like crazy. Just say the word."

Sure we wanted him to come home. But we'd been raised to let people go on their own journeys, to allow others to grow and change. So we just stood there with our hands dangling at our sides. Anyway, we figured that Dad would sort it out on his own, since he was our dad, since he was a grown-up.

"If you want to come home," I said, "why don't you just say so?"

"That's very sweet, June. But life is more complicated than that."

"No, it's not."

That's when the tears started. "I just need to know that you girls are okay." He knelt down so he was at our level. "I hate to think of you being harmed by The Separation. I hate to think that my children have been damaged."

"Hey!" I said, suddenly remembering a message I was supposed to pass on. "Mom says you should pay for therapy for us."

"She said what?"

"Dad, you're the one who's damaged if you think I'm still a child." Claudia was good at ending these sorts of conversations. She understood something that our parents didn't get: that they could never really damage us. That we transcended them, lived outside of them. They were *them* and we were *us*. We had our own concerns: Claudia had her period and boys who called her on the phone, and I was growing out my hair and memorizing the lyrics from *13 Flavours of Doom*. What our parents didn't understand was that we were busy.

WHEN WE STOPPED IN NANAIMO, a stranger got on and sat beside Claudia. He must have been a young guy, but he seemed old to me at the time. I could easily tell a ten-year-old from an eleven-year-old, but everyone over twenty seemed vague and dangerous. He carried a backpack and wore a toque. He said, "Is anyone sitting here?"

Claudia said, "Nope. Go for it," despite the fact that I should have been sitting there, that I was her sister, that I was stuck next to a woman who wouldn't share her sexy book.

Mark put his backpack on the shelf above the seat and sat down beside Claudia. I knew his name because, once he was seated, he turned to my sister and said, "How's it going? I'm Mark."

He asked my sister where she was headed and she said, "Port Hardy," which was the truth. Then she added, "To visit some friends," which was a lie.

Mark said that he was going to Port McNeill, the stop before hers. "I work in Nanaimo. But I go back to Port on weekends."

"Cool," said my sister, as though it really was. "What do you do? When you work?"

"Construction. I'm an industrial welder. You?"

"That's so cool." Claudia sounded fascinated, intrigued, amazed—I'd never heard her exhibit so much interest in anything in my life. "I don't really work. I'm a student."

"Oh, yeah? At the college?"

I could feel Claudia's elation in the air. I could almost inhale it. She might have told the truth: that she was only fourteen and attended Vic High. But the purple bangs and the makeup had paid off, and she was going to cash in. "Kind of," she said. "At the university."

"Sweet."

"Yeah. It's all right."

Then they didn't talk for about twenty minutes. Mark didn't get out a book or anything, and I imagined that he was sitting there with his legs spread wide, staring at the seat in front of him.

When we'd passed Wellington, my sister took out her Walkman and Mark said, "What are you listening to?"

"D.O.A. They're this band from Vancouver." Mark didn't say anything, so my sister, her voice full of hope, asked, "What kind of music do you like?"

"I like tons of stuff. I listen to pretty much everything."

And it became official: I hated him. I was only eleven, and my musical snobbery was in its embryo stage, but still I knew a fraud when I heard one. *Everything*. The only people who claim to listen to everything are the ones who know nothing, who are happy to swallow whatever the radio feeds them.

"Totally," said my Judas of a sister. "Me too."

———

CLAUDIA AND MARK talked for the next three hours. She let him listen to her tapes and gave him the kind of musical education some people pay money for. He told her how his girlfriend had cheated on him when she went on a three-week tour of Europe, and Claudia seemed to feel real sympathy for him. "That totally sucks."

He said that, since the breakup, he'd just focused on work. "You're pretty much the first girl I've talked to since then."

He showed her pictures of his two dogs, and at one point they both held up their hands to compare them. Next to his workman's hands, Claudia's looked like they belonged to a child. Which they did.

Between Bowser and Courtenay, I couldn't hear what they were saying because they started talking more quietly. I couldn't make out words, but I could hear their soft voices and Claudia's laughter. They leaned close to each other, and in the space between their seats, I could see that their heads almost touched.

WHEN WE HIT CAMPBELL RIVER, where we had a forty-minute stop, they acted like best friends. They got off the bus together and my sister didn't wait for me, didn't even turn around to look at me.

I followed her into the depot's bathroom, which had only two stalls, an empty soap dispenser, and an overflowing garbage. Names and life stories had been penned onto the walls, and usually Claudia and I hung out in there and made fun of people who wrote things like *Linds B. wuz here* and *I wanna do Kris 4ever*.

"Thanks for waiting." I kicked the door of the stall Claudia was in, but she didn't say anything back. I heard her peeing, and I said, "That guy you were talking to was such a loser."

Claudia flushed the toilet and came out of the stall. She didn't answer me or look at me. She turned on the faucet and ran water over her hands.

"And the woman beside me is so fat. And she's reading this sickening book."

"Shut up!" Claudia slammed her wet hand against the mirror, against the image of her own face. "Who cares? Who cares if she's fat? Who cares what she's reading?"

"What's your problem?"

"You are. I don't want you to talk to me anymore."

"I have to talk to you. Mom gave you the money, and I'm hungry."

"Here." Claudia took a five-dollar bill from her pocket and threw it at me. "Take this and leave me alone. Don't look at me. Don't breathe on me. And every time you want to talk to me, just remind yourself that you don't even know me."

—

USUALLY, IN CAMPBELL RIVER, we bought chips and pop from the vending machine and ate them while sitting on the depot's row of plastic seats. We weren't used to carbonated beverages, so they made us hyperactive and strange. We jumped from seat to seat, and competed to see who could jump the farthest. Claudia always won because she could leap over four seats at a time. I'd been hoping to break her record.

But instead, I sat in one of those seats alone. The hard plastic dug into my neck. I bought a bag of chips and ate them by myself. Actually, I didn't eat them. I licked the dill pickle flavour off them and left them in a wet pile on the seat beside me. But even that was no fun without my sister to tell me I was disgusting.

I used some of the change to phone our parents, since Claudia seemed to have forgotten that we were supposed to do that.

When Mom picked up, she said, "Is that you, Juney-looney?"

"Yeah."

"That's great—you're ahead of schedule."

"Yeah."

"Is everything okay?"

"Yeah."

"Did you have lunch?"

"Yeah."

"What did you have?"

"Sandwiches."

When I called our dad, he said, "Hey, June-bug!" He spoke in his ultra-happy voice, the one he used when he was trying to convince us that he was ultra-happy in his new life. "You in C.R.?"

"Yeah."

"You're ahead of schedule!"

"I know."

"Is your sister behaving?"

Through the bus depot's dirty window, I could see Claudia and Mark. They sat in a sunny part of the parking lot. She'd taken off her hoodie and wore just her Converse, jeans, and a black tank top. One of the straps had slipped off her shoulder, and Mark kept looking at it. And she kept looking up at him, through her purple bangs.

"No," I said.

Dad laughed. "You keep her in line, then. You lay down the law."

For the rest of the stop, I leaned against the payphone and watched my sister and Mark. They talked and laughed as they shared fries and a cigarette. If our parents had found out, Claudia would have been so dead. It was one thing to smoke weed that the neighbours grew. But to support the big tobacco companies was out of the question.

WHEN THEY GOT BACK ON THE BUS, they acted awkward, like strangers. All the way to Sayward they didn't talk. Mark slept with his face turned toward my sister. If I had leaned forward, I would have smelled his cigarette breath coming at me from between their seats. He'd taken off his toque and exposed his blond hair. I don't know what my sister liked about him. Maybe it was that he looked as vulnerable as a baby: pale skin, wet lips, fly-away hair.

She listened to her Walkman, and I could hear the tape rewind, play, rewind again. I wanted to ask her which song she was listening to, but I didn't dare. I tried to read my book, but it seemed boring and childish now that I'd seen the kind of book I could be reading.

As we passed Woss, Mark woke up from what I imagined to be dreams about fondling my sister. He jerked awake, and his twitch made him and my sister laugh. Just like that, they were friends again. They started swapping party stories.

I'd had no idea that Claudia had ever been drunk. Our parents had always said that they didn't mind if we experimented with alcohol as long as we did it in their house. They'd rather we tried that kind of thing at home, where they knew we were safe. Every time they said this, Claudia crossed her arms. "I don't drink anyway," she'd say. "I'm pretty much straight-edge."

But she had some good stories. About throwing up off a balcony. About passing out then waking up beside her friend's hamster cage with the hamster kicking wood chips into her face. About eating mushrooms and walking down Government Street to watch the tourists' faces melt. After a while, I realized that her stories sounded familiar. They belonged to our parents.

"That's fucked." Mark laughed. "That's awesome."

He told about the times he dropped acid, went skinny-dipping in Duncan, and lost a pair of shoes in Vancouver. Then he said, "We should hang out sometime. How long are you in Hardy for?"

"Just the weekend."

"Maybe you and your friends could come down and party with us."

"Yeah. Maybe."

"Or you could just get off with me at the McNeill stop today and the two of us could hang out tonight."

"Really?"

He said this after we'd passed Nimpkish. This far north, it was visibly colder. Some muddy snow was scattered along the side of the highway. It looked like it had been left behind, forgotten, though it must have been the first snowfall of the year. We were ten minutes away from Mark's stop, from the town on the edge of the ocean where he lived, from the place where I was going to be separated from my sister forever.

"You could stay at my place for the night. It looks out over the water. You'd like it."

"I don't know. My friend's sort of expecting me."

"You can call her. And I'll give you a ride up to Port Hardy tomorrow."

Claudia must have understood how easy it would be to go with him. She knew she'd get away with it because I'd never betray her. I'd tell Dad that she'd stayed in Victoria for an extra day, for volleyball practice or something, and that she'd arrive tomorrow. Dad was so disoriented and absent lately that he'd believe anything.

"You have a car?" she said. "That's really cool."

I didn't say a word. I didn't even kick the back of her seat to remind her of me, of *us*, of the secret and unspoken pact we'd had since we were too young to speak. A pact to stick together, to be sisters, no matter how much we hated each other. I didn't say anything because part of me wanted her to do it. I wanted to see that it could be done. I wanted to watch my sister grab her backpack and strut away. I wanted to watch her hop off the bus and into the arms of a wild stranger, or anyone else she chose. I wanted to know that separation was possible. That we could cut ties, break free.

"I can't," she said. "My friend would shit. We've had these plans for practically forever."

I didn't understand why she said that, just like I didn't understand why our dad came home a couple of months later. Maybe Laura got sick of him, or he was tired of being so poor, or he missed us, or he missed the way Mom swayed heavily through the house in her hemp skirts. He would leave again over the years, and Mom would leave him too—whenever they craved some entertainment—but they always came home.

I didn't understand, but I was relieved.

"Okay. That's cool. That makes sense." Mark sounded genuinely disappointed, as though he actually liked my sister. "But maybe I could give you my number? In case you change your mind?"

"Sure. Yeah. I could call you."

Mark wrote on a scrap of paper and handed it to her. "It was awesome meeting you."

"You too." Claudia put the paper in the back pocket of her jeans, and I felt her movement in my knees, which were propped against her seat. "Thanks."

What I did understand, later but still way before Claudia did, was that it was impossible. That we could never break free. No matter what we did, we could never separate *them* from *us*. Our bodies were built by the lentils and flax they'd fed us. Their bone structure lingered in our faces. Their humour and neuroses were planted deep in our brains, and we'd inherited their voices, their sayings, their stories. They were our parents. Even when Claudia's rebellion was complete—when she ditched the punk scene and left that territory to me, when she started wearing brand names and married a stockbroker—even then, they forgave her and loved her and got really high at her wedding.

A COUPLE OF NIGHTS before we left for Port Hardy, Claudia listened to Nomeansno in her room and I sat at the kitchen table, using my pastels to draw a picture of Sid Vicious. Mom was in the kitchen too, rolling her evening joint. And I knew that, twelve hours away, Dad was doing the exact same thing.

"Juniper?" said Mom. "Why don't you come sit on my lap?"

I looked up from Sid's pretty snarl. "Because I don't want to."

"Why not?"

"Mom, it's gross. I'm not a baby anymore."

"I know that." Mom lit the joint and I heard the paper crackle as it burned. "I'm just sad tonight, I guess."

The truth was that I did want to sit on her lap. I still liked the way she smelled, of tea and smoke and lemongrass shampoo. And I liked the way she ran her fingers through my hair. It felt soft and ticklish and usually put me into a trance.

"I'll sit on your lap for ten seconds," I said. "As long as you promise not to tell Claudia."

Mom smiled in this way that made me think that maybe, in secret, my sister still liked to sit on her lap. Maybe Claudia liked the hair thing too.

"Okay," said Mom. "Promise."

———

WHEN MARK GOT OFF THE BUS, I tossed my backpack over onto his seat and said "'Scuse me" to the woman beside me, who had almost finished her novel.

I sat where Mark had been, and the seat was still warm from his body. For a second I almost understood my sister—why she might want to be close to him, or someone like him. Then I said, "He was so ugly."

"Fuck you."

Claudia put on her earphones, adjusted her pillow, and closed her eyes. I sat beside her, and I was hugely, oppressively happy. She was my sister and I loved her. I stole one of the buds from her ear, stuck it in my own, and Joey "Shithead" Keithley yelled at us as the afternoon sun poured through the window. I leaned against Claudia as though she was a pillow. "Get off me," she said, out of habit, without meaning it. I rested my face against her bare arm, and the moisture of our skin stuck us together.

ACKNOWLEDGMENTS

THANK YOU TO THE EDITORS OF *The 2006 Bridport Prize Anthology*, *Event Magazine*, and *PRISM International*, where stories from this collection have appeared.

I'm indebted to the faculty and my peers in the University of Victoria's English and Writing departments. I'm also grateful to the staff at Munro's Books, who are more like family than coworkers. I especially want to thank Jim Munro, whose enthusiasm for and encouragement of my work have been extraordinary. Thank you to those at Penguin (Canada), especially my editors, Jennifer Notman and Nicole Winstanley, for their belief in these stories and their help in making them as polished as possible. Many thanks to Julia Novitch and everyone at Harper Perennial for their exceptional commitment to short stories and to this book.

I also want to thank my family for their encouragement, and I need to specially mention Pauline Willis, Gary Willis, Graham

Hunter, and Charis Wahl for their invaluable help with this manuscript. Many thanks to my friends, especially those fellow writers who generously read earlier drafts of these stories: Marjorie Celona, Amanda Leduc, Garth Martens, Aaron Shepard, Jeanne Shoemaker, and Sarah Taggart. Thank you also to Trevor Williams and to the lovely Pichu Kalyniuk for their help along the way. Many thanks to my roommates, Manusha Janakiram, Tamiko McLean, and David McLean, for being such good company during the time I wrote many of these stories, and for not minding when I spread my manuscripts all over the living room floor. Lastly, I want to thank my buddy, Ben Schwartzentruber, for his support, humor, and kindness.

Insights,
Interviews
& More . . .

Meet Deborah Willis

DEBORAH WILLIS was born and raised in Calgary, Alberta. Her fiction has appeared in *Grain*, *Event*, and the UK's *Bridport Prize Anthology*, and she was the winner of the 2005 Prism International Fiction Prize. *Vanishing and Other Stories*, Willis's first book, has been named one of *Globe and Mail*'s Best Books of the Year and was nominated for a Governor General's Award. She has worked as a horseback riding instructor and a reporter and currently works as a bookseller in Victoria, British Columbia.

A Conversation with Deborah Willis

*Writer and blogger Evadne Macedo
interviewed Deborah Willis in
November 2009. Macedo's Web
address is books.macedo.ca.*

**Are there any experiences that you can
look back on as being defining moments in
your career as a writer of fiction? At what
point, did you seriously think of yourself
as being a "writer" and did this require
some sort of outside validation?**

It wasn't until very recently that I was
able to admit to people that I was a writer;
to say it out loud made me feel both
pretentious and vulnerable. And now that
I've published a book, people sometimes
refer to me as an "author," which sounds
even more strange to me. My writing has
always been something I took seriously
but that I kept fairly quiet, simply because
writing is inherently quiet and solitary.
But something certainly changed for me
when I published my first story ("Traces,"
in *Event* magazine). I felt much more
confident.

**Terry Fallis spends months creating
detailed outlines, John Irving writes his
last sentence first, and Miriam Toews jots
down notes until the story overtakes her.
How would you describe your personal
approach to writing? Would you say that
your current process has been refined over
time from less successful methods, or is
this how you have always written?** ▶

3

A Conversation with Deborah Willis
(continued)

Writing is often very laborious and time-consuming for me. Like Miriam Toews, I usually begin by jotting notes down in a notebook. Then I often write reams of pages which I eventually edit down to the finished story. It has happened a few times that I've been able to write a story from beginning to end, almost as if it dropped into my lap. But usually I begin somewhere in the middle, with no idea of where I'm going to find the beginning or the end.

When you set out to write a short story, what are your goals in terms of plot, character development, or the craft of writing itself? Are there any nonfiction guides or great works of literature that you have found helpful in improving your writing?

When I actually sit down to write, I rarely think of such well-defined goals. I begin very intuitively, and often am surprised by the structure or the voice or the plot of a story. I'm always pleased when I surprise myself, because I hope that means the reader will be similarly surprised.

I find that I rarely read writing guides, though some can be helpful when I'm feeling stuck. I think writers learn more about technique from reading literature. In fact, one of the things that I find disturbing about being a writer is that I've almost completely lost the ability to read innocently. I can never be wholly wrapped up in a book the way I was when I read as a child. I now always read with one eye on the story, and the other eye on how the story is put together. I'm always trying figure out how a writer does what she does, and to learn from it.

At every writing event I have gone to, there is always a question about the mechanics of an author's writing. Could you please comment on the practicalities behind your writing? For example, do you keep notes in a notebook? If so, at what point to you transfer them to a computer? Do you write on a laptop or a desktop? Do you hide yourself away in a quiet room or write at cafés? And the biggest question of all: Do you use a Mac or a PC?

First things first: I use Mac laptop. But I only use the computer after I've fleshed out some of the story in a notebook. If I move to the computer, it means I've made something of a commitment to that story. And when I'm writing, I usually need quiet though sometimes I'll decide that I want some noise around and I'll go to a public place like a café.

All writers are influenced by the work of other authors. My personal influences include Margaret Atwood and John Irving. Who has influenced your writing the most, and in what ways? Have you tried to distinguish your writing from these authors in any way? ▶

A Conversation with Deborah Willis
(continued)

The stories of Alice Munro have certainly been my biggest influence. Her use of time and the imaginative way she structures her stories thrilled me. I've also admired the fact that her stories are quiet, but not boring. Much happens in a Munro story. By that I mean, of course, that they have depth. But, to be totally obvious about it, they also have plots. As a kid, I grew up reading people like Stephen King and Elmore Leonard, and though I'll never be able to write books like theirs, they left me with a sense that stories should generally have a good plot. Though my stories are short, I want them to have movement and drama.

When Miriam Toews spoke at the Humber Writers' Circle on October 26, 2009, at Harbourfront, she indicated that it was very important to have someone in her life who felt that her writing was a legitimate use of time. Have you been mentored by someone? If so, in what ways was this helpful to you?

I was so lucky to be taught by some wonderful people in the English and writing departments at UVic. Lorna Crozier and Lorna Jackson were very important influences for me, because they are wonderful writers and because they are wonderful women. I also have friends who are at about the same stage in their writing careers as I am, and being able to talk to them about the whole process has been so helpful to me.

Some authors rely on friends, peers, or trusted advisors to review and provide feedback on early drafts whereas others write in seclusion and pass it only on to agents and editors once it is complete. Where do you fit on this spectrum and why?

I do like to show my stories to trusted friends before I send them off to an editor. For one thing, it forces me to put the story away and not look at it while my friend reads it. When I come back to it, I have a fresh perspective, and I also have comments from a reader who can see things that I've missed.

When I first spoke with you, I was surprised to find out that you did not have an agent, and yet had been able to get your book published and nominated for a Governor General's Literary Award. Could you please describe how you got to this point after completing your manuscript?

I was offered a book contract based on a partial manuscript (about eight stories of the eventual fourteen that made up *Vanishing*). The process began after I won a fiction contest in *Prism Magazine*. My stories found a passionate advocate, who is my boss at the bookstore where I work, Jim Munro. He's not an agent, and in Victoria, he's far from any center of literature. But he adores short stories, and was impressed by the story that ▶

A Conversation with Deborah Willis
(continued)

appeared in *Prism*. (That story was "Vanishing.") He gave out copies of the magazine to anyone he thought might be interested in reading it, and eventually, it found its way into the hands of Nicole Winstanley, one of my editors at Penguin. She asked to see more of my stories, and then offered me a publishing contract. I was lucky in the sense that my stories found their perfect readers, and I'm sure that's essential for any writer's success. (A note about the GG: as far as I know, those nominations have nothing to do with agents. Publishers submit books for each year's award, and the judges of the award choose the shortlist.)

You are rather lucky in that you have published your first book, and received literary accolades, at a relatively young age. Do you have any thoughts about where you would like your career as a writer to go next and how to get there? Has your life changed in any way as a result of having published this book? What about after having been nominated for the GG literary award?

Being published is wonderful and strange. I think it's disconcerting when what is mainly a private endeavor is suddenly thrust into the marketplace. I don't mean that I was totally unprepared for this transition; I was certainly aware of the business of bookselling though my job at a bookstore. And I always intended for my stories to be published. But it is an added pressure. It is frightening sometimes, but I'm also hugely grateful for it.

And no, my life hasn't really changed! I still work at my little job, and live my little boring life. And that's probably a good thing.

Do you have any final words of advice or encouragement for aspiring writers?

I think most aspiring writers who are serious about it already know what they need to do. I can remind them to read a lot and write a lot, but that's not too original. I think the secret is to keep going, even though writing is difficult in the sense that it doesn't pay and there's never enough time for it. To remain in love with it despite all that seems to me to be only way to continue, and to continue is part of the point. ❧

The Double Life

IN ONE OF MY LIVES, I'm a writer. This means, essentially, that I contemplate the human experience while wearing my pajamas. The writer in me constantly reads and writes and thinks about stories. This writer—let's call her Deborah Willis—has spent whole, pleasant days worrying over commas. She prefers to be alone. If the telephone rings while she's working, she stares at it, horrified, and refuses to answer. Her shoulders are hunched from bending over a notebook, her eyes strained from the computer screen, and she recently developed carpal tunnel in her wrists. Who says the writing life isn't strenuous? It can lead to, among other disorders, self-obsession and a vitamin D deficiency.

Fortunately, there's another me, and she gets out more. She works in a bookstore, which means that she's always on her feet, carrying books up and down stairs, putting them on and taking them off shelves. She can recommend children's books, Canadian fiction, and foreign-language titles. She makes change, deals with till-tape, runs debit cards though machines, sends special orders, and receives magazines. For her, books are to be displayed, alphabetized, and sold. This is an exaggeration, of course—books are not only products. In fact, her work has made her love them more. But she has been a bookseller for almost five years, which is long enough for the job to become an identity. She wears it like a second skin. Her name is Debbie, and she would be happy to help you.

The bookstore where I work, Munro's Books in Victoria, British Columbia, used to be a bank. It is grand, spooky, beautiful, and almost as untidy as my apartment. It's an old building with character, part of what guidebooks accurately call Victoria's "historic and picturesque" downtown. It has marble countertops, art on the walls, dark wood shelves, creaky floorboards, and a reputation for being haunted. My favorite part of the store is the part customers never see: the basement, which is made up of a series of steel-and-concrete vaults.

When Munro's was a Royal Bank—during that era before banks were housed in huge, anonymous buildings—these vaults must have held receipts, checks, and safety deposit boxes. Now, they're where we keep the overstock. It's like something Lewis Carroll might have imagined, if Alice had fallen down a rabbit hole and into a booklover's fantasy. Vaults with heavy metal doors open onto to other vaults, and each one is filled with books. There is something romantic and wonderful and completely backwards about this: finance replaced with literature, scurrying bankers replaced with scurrying booksellers, the sterility of numbers replaced with the unruliness of words.

I fell into this job in the same way I've always fallen in love—by accident. I needed some income to pay the rent during my last year of university, so I dropped off a resume and spoke to the owner, Mr. Munro. I believe he hired me partly because he found my resume ▶

11

amusing (my list of accomplishments included scooping ice cream at a shop called Wonderlicks and getting fired from a barista job because I didn't take the "coffee art" seriously enough).

On my first day, I was given the keys to the store, taught the combination to the safe, and told to call Mr. Munro by his first name. It turns out that Jim is an exceptionally kind, trusting, and generous man. To be hired by him is to be immediately welcomed into his family. He runs an independent, old-fashioned business, the kind of place that big-box stores and the Internet can never replace, but often do. It's the kind of place where employees stay for decades. One clerk even identifies himself as "Steve from Munro's," as though the store were his hometown.

I don't mean to make it sound like a museum piece, since Munro's is a profitable business. I also don't mean to romanticize the work. A job is a job, after all, and anyone who has worked in retail during the Christmas season knows that customer service can be its own particular hell. And though it's one of the best jobs I can imagine, a bookstore can terrify a writer. The sheer number of books makes me feel nervous and unnecessary. Classics, mysteries, romances, essays, histories, poetry—they arrive in box after box of hardbacks, trade papers, and mass markets. Then, a year or so later, many are returned unsold to publishers, to be remaindered or pulped. This is the stuff of writers' nightmares. When faced with it in reality, it's hard for me to convince myself that the world needs another book, especially mine. *Why bother?* I often think as I put labels on the newest page-turner about a vampire shopaholic, or the latest novel hailed as "a triumph, full of wry wisdom." These are the moments when the bookseller in me is in conflict with the writer. *Why do you get up in the morning?* she asks. *What's the point?*

If the bookstore forces me to ask these questions, it then conveniently answers them. Most obviously, the books I've borrowed or bought from Munro's have inspired my admiration and my writing. While working amid the stacks, I've discovered Alexandar Hemon, Miriam Toews, David Sedaris, Jack Gilbert, Miranda July, David Grossman, Lewis Hyde, Shalom Auslander, and Anaïs Nin. I've discovered *Before Night Falls* and *Our Man in Havana*, *Revolutionary Road* and *Death in Venice*. The beauty of a bookstore—a real physical store, with real physical books inside it—is that it allows people to browse, pick up a book, hold it in their hands, read a few sentences, and say to themselves, *Yes*.

But Munro's has done more than introduce me to books. It has also introduced me to those who read them. I mean, of course, my coworkers, that delightful and eccentric family. They have dedicated years of their lives to the book trade, and not because the money's good. Many of them buy their body-weight in books each year. They read everything: chick lit, travel accounts, fantasy, philosophy, graphic novels. ▶

But it's not just the employees who hang around Munro's for decades; many customers become part of the family too. There's the gallery owner who buys so many art books that we've given him his own account at the store. There's Mrs. Gupta, who has perhaps ordered every book on Hinduism ever printed, and who—as though we were her grandchildren—gives us Werther's Originals from her purse. There's Jamie, who orders biographies of Charlie Chaplin and Margaret Thatcher and Grace Kelly, but can only pick them up once a month, when he receives his disability check. As if they were kittens in a pet store, he comes in almost every day to visit his books. He holds them, flips through them, says, "This looks fantastic." And there's Mr. Anderson, a man in his seventies who orders romance novels. He buys them by the dozen. Nora Roberts, Cynthia Harrod-Eagles, Lisa Kleypas, Maeve Binchy, Julia London. He wants love stories, not erotica, but doesn't mind some titillation. "I like a little slap-and-tickle," he says.

My favorite customer is Michael. He has long hair, wears a black leather jacket, and one of his boots has a spur. When he walks into the store, you can hear his spiked heel click and spin with every other step. He is polite and soft-spoken, and he looks exactly like Keith Richards. He lives in a motel off the highway, but once I passed him on the street with his hat out, asking for change. If I didn't work at Munro's, I would never guess that he spends much of his money on books. I would never guess that he listens to literature programs on public radio, or that he reads everything from Proust to *Gravity's Rainbow* to *The Irish Country Doctor*.

These people—the employees, and the customers who make their jobs possible—are unlike the people I met at university, where books are sometimes called "texts" and read because they are feminist, or Marxist, or feminist-Marxist. They are unlike the writers I know—myself included—who can't read without keeping one eye on the *how*, the craft, the way the author achieves a purpose. The people I've met at Munro's are readers, and it occurs to me that most writers don't get many chances to meet them, except on book tours. I've had the good luck to encounter readers almost every day, and I've learned that they are intelligent and demanding. They are rarely snobbish but always discriminating. They read in a deep, engaged, and straightforward way. They read for knowledge or for escape or for both. And to that question—*What's the point?*—they are an essential part of the answer.

It would be impossible to keep my two selves separate even if I wanted to. And it would be inaccurate to suggest that "writer" and "bookseller" are the only roles I play, the only sides to my personality. But day to day, they are my main identities. And they had, up until recently, remained fairly distinct—one staying home and behaving like an incompetent housewife, the other ▶

going to work and paying the bills. Then, last year, they collided.

Vanishing was published in Canada last May. I would like to say that its release date was the best day of my life, but it was fairly ordinary. I went to work at my job at the bookstore. My book was put out on the shelves alongside all the other books— *The Great Gatsby, Barney's Version, The G.I. Diet, What Your Poo Is Telling You.* Seeing it there, with its beautiful cover and its solid 288 pages, made me happy and queasy. It was like watching something being born, while also realizing that it had died.

In keeping with his tireless generosity, my boss at the bookstore threw me a launch party so big and elaborate that it felt like my wedding day. My coworkers got drunk on champagne. I swanned around in a dress, emotional and tipsy, a regular Mrs. Dalloway. My friends and family bought copies of the book and I signed them, just like a real author. One of my coworkers—a woman whose areas of expertise include French *Vogue*, the Anglican church, and the mystical properties of gemstones—read me the numerology of my book's ISBN.

"This is a good number." She gave me a long and significant look. "It has a positive energy."

But it wasn't until later that week that I understood that my bookseller self and writer self would have to become friends. It wasn't until I stood at the till, behind that marble counter, and sold a copy of my own book.

I believe it was a Thursday, because

I was working the late shift. A woman brought my book up to the counter and started fishing in her purse. I didn't recognize her, but assumed I must know her from somewhere. I had a hard time believing that anyone who didn't know me and feel sorry for me would buy my book. I stared at the woman's face, trying to guess where I might have met her. At a dance class? The grocery store? The dentist? Maybe that was it. Maybe she was my dental hygienist.

"Hi there!" I spoke in my cheeriest customer-service voice. "How are you today?"

"Fine." She handed me her Visa card without looking at me, and I rang her purchase through.

If writing and publishing books puts me in danger of becoming wildly self-absorbed, selling anything—books or donuts or furniture—must be the cure. It is an exercise in humility and self-effacement to ask, over and over, with that mix of attentiveness and blandness, "Would you like a bag for your purchase today?"

"Yes, thanks." This woman was not particularly friendly, and I was beginning to doubt that she was my dental hygienist.

I handed her the receipt and said, "Thank you," to which she replied, "Thank you," to which—typical Canadian—I answered with, "Thank you."

Then she picked up the book, which she had now paid for, and which therefore did not belong to me anymore. Out of a ▶

desire to hold onto it, to keep my baby close, I said, "Do you want me to sign it?"

"What?"

"Do you want me to sign your book?"

For the first time, she looked at me. She smiled without using her eyes. "And why would I want your name in my book?"

I could have hugged her. I could have kissed her on the mouth. Because this woman was definitely not my dental hygienist. This woman was a stranger. Unlike my friends, and my parents, and my parents' friends, and my boyfriend, and my ex-boyfriends, and my coworkers, and my aunts and uncles—such loyal fans!—this woman didn't *have* to buy my book. Perhaps she had seen the book on the shelf and simply thought it looked interesting.

I blushed like a happy, stupid child. "I'm the author," I said.

She raised one eyebrow. She looked so skeptical that even I doubted it. I looked down at myself as if to check, to make sure I was the person I claimed to be. "When I'm not here," I said, my two identities fusing for a moment, "I write stories." ❧

Favorite Books on My Shelf Now

Riffs and Reciprocities, by Stephen Dunn (Norton)

I recently reread this collection of essays that are as short as poems, and was again awed by them. Dunn writes in pairs, matching up two tangentially related words (like "Anger" and "Generosity," "Passion" and "Paradox"), and creates a series of tiny, perfect essays. Dunn is mischievous and intelligent, and to spend a day in the company of these pieces is a delight.

A Journey to the End of the Russian Empire, by Anton Chekhov (Penguin Great Journeys)

This gorgeous book chronicles the trip Chekhov took through Siberia, by carriage and boat, to the island of Sakhalin. I love how casual, funny and warm Chekhov is in his letters home. I love his sense of adventure, the pleasure he takes in travel, and the details of his journey. Mostly, I love the insight into how Chekhov, as a doctor and as a writer, was affected by the hardships he witnessed in a Russian penal colony.

Our Man in Havana, by Graham Greene (Penguin Classics)

I read this on a recent stay in Havana, and even in the midst of such chaotic and beautiful streets, I couldn't put this novel down. The story of a vacuum-salesman-turned-spy is satirical and charming. And in its details about Havana life, the book demonstrates that ▶

there is much that hasn't changed in that port city.

The Gift: Creativity and the Artist in the Modern World, by Lewis Hyde (Vintage)

I would recommend this book to every artist on earth. Nothing that I've read deals so thoroughly with the dilemmas, problems, and joys that writers and other artists encounter when they try to make it in the economic world. This book has been essential to me.

Flirt: The Interviews, by Lorna Jackson (Biblioasis)

One of the funniest and most original books I've read. These short stories can only be described as fictional nonfiction, a series of bogus interviews with athletes, musicians and writers. The interviewer is a woman who is dealing with her own demons by "flirting" with the likes of Alice Munro and Ian Tyson. She is dark and hilarious, and in each "interview," she reveals more of herself. ◞

Don't miss the next book by your favorite author. Sign up now for AuthorTracker by visiting www.AuthorTracker.com.